Dr. J's Year

Jerry Hammet & Harold Guerry

Library of Congress Control Number:		2011913283
ISBN:	Hardcover	978-1-4653-4319-2
	Softcover	978-1-4653-4318-5
	Ebook	978-1-4653-4320-8

To order additional copies of this book, contact:
Xlibris Corporation
1-888-795-4274
www.Xlibris.com
Orders@Xlibris.com
101078

CONTENTS

DECEMBER 2007

"I KNOW MY STUDENTS in classroom 315, Philosophy 306, are sitting in quiet anticipation, watching the door, wondering what sort of off-the-wall entry I'm going to entertain them with today. Well, I won't disappoint 'em. Half of 'em are sweating bullets now, and the other half are sorry that the semester is ending. Anyhow, they will be better people for having had this course. I'll miss 'em, that's for sure. Always do." No disappointment today. The bell rings, the door opens, and the expected figure enters—the professor they have learned to love and respect, the one with the unexpected introductions and equally unexpected conclusions. A loud note from a trumpet held by Dr. John Witherspoon Stewart—affectionately and respectfully called Dr. J by all who know him—precedes his appearance through the door. It is a depiction of Gabriel (without wings) because after this earsplitting entrance, Dr. J sits on the edge of his desk and begins his matter-of-fact announcement, which could go in one of several ways. (Archangel Gabriel and his trumpet are the official announcer of things to come, as described in several roles in the Hebrew Bible, the Christian Bible, and in the Koran of the Islamic faith. Gabriel announced things to Daniel in the Old Testament, announced the pending births of both John and Jesus, gave Mohammed instructions for the Koran, and is expected to sound his trumpet to mark the end of time and the final judgment.) It is soon evident that Dr. J has selected to announce the end by saying, "My friends, this is Judgment Day. But should you be afraid? What do you have to fear? Surely you have prepared for this day a long time, and it's finally arrived. You are here to take a final exam, and I trust you will all do exceedingly well." His steel blue eyes sweep the room and meet the wide-eyed looks of a variety of feelings. Some eyes are sparkling with confident amusement, some with intent attention, and some with stark terror at what Dr. J might announce.

"The exam will be in three parts. The first part will count one hundred points. Let us assume that Mrs. Moore from AC Flora High has invited you to speak to her tenth-grade class on the subject titled "What Is Philosophy?" You will have forty-five minutes to prepare your remarks. The second part of the exam is to list the names of ten other students in this class. This will allow you to have a bonus point for each name you list. Nicknames for the first name are acceptable, but you must correctly spell the last name. Now at this point, some of you are capable of making 110. The third part of the exam is to list the name of the lovely lady who cleans the hallways and keeps the restrooms sparkling. You probably don't know that she has worked for this university for twenty years, doing the same work. She has three sons, and all of them graduated from this campus. All three are professionals who make significant contributions to Columbia. She paid for their tuition through her wages from this job of hers. She speaks to each of you each and every time she sees you and knows all of you by name. If you can name her, it'll be worth fifteen points. So you have the possibility of making a score of 125, and that's an A+. Wouldn't that look good in your records? And maybe it would even be worthy to list the accomplishment of earning such a score in my class on your resume."

Dr. J continues, "I will not be able to stay with you while you take this final, but I have two very capable assistants here who will serve as proctors. When you finish, the proctors will receive your papers and place them where I'll pick them up later. Your grades will be available by the middle of the week. Now let me take a moment to say to you that it's been a pleasure to serve as your teacher, and I do trust that you have learned something that can be put to good use in the future. I don't know if I will be seeing some of you in the future, but I hope that from time to time, I'll pick up a newspaper or hear in a conversation about some good that you are doing in this world. You have been blessed with good minds, so don't hesitate to use them. With that, I'm off. Farewell, and I wish you well. May God bless you in all of your good works."

One of the students in the back of the room stands up and calls out, "Dr. J?"

J turns and looks at the young man wearing a navy-blue-and-red-striped bow tie, white shirt, navy blazer, and khaki pants, who said, "And blessings on you, and may your life be filled with good things. We have been privileged to take part in this class. I can say from my experiences that it has never been dull!"

When finished, the whole class stood and applauded. J, for once, is at a loss for words or a snappy comeback but uttered a simple "Thank you." He turns, waves, and exits, leaving the confident and the terrified to their final exam in Philosophy 306. With a lump in his throat, J walks briskly through the hallway, bypasses the elevator, leaves the building, and heads for his prized chariot that awaits him, his one-ton 1955 baby blue University of North Carolina Ford pickup. J slides in, inserts the key in the ignition, and with a slight touch, smiles as he hears the instant rumble of the mighty V-8 engine.

His pride and joy, his baby, his mechanical lover responds to the releasing clutch and heads for the parking lot exit automatically. Had he turned the steering wheel? The adage "A thing of beauty is a joy forever" flashes through his head.

Approaching the stoplight at the corner of Pickens and Greene, the adage remains in his head as he notices a young lady standing at the corner. J doesn't recognize this long-legged, dark-haired, well-proportioned female but thinks, *Hey, there are thirty thousand students here. I'm sure I haven't seen them all, but I hate that I missed seeing her before. Strange. She doesn't have any makeup on. Surely she's not Pentecostal. Got good posture too.* J recalls his first sergeant of the unit he served with in Korea, who was considered the old man of the outfit, telling the boys to be sure their girlfriends had good posture and teeth, and the rest would be okay. Never got around to asking Pop why he thought posture was so important. Never really knew if Pop, with his ninth-grade education, knew what posture meant or if he was using the right word. Wonder what happened to Pop Kozac. Just before the light turned green, a young man driving a red Mazda MX 5 convertible screeches up to the curb in front of the young lady and waves her to hurry up and get in the car. He must have said some unnecessary words that J couldn't hear because the young lady frowns and makes her way to the car with some obvious reluctance.

The light turns green, and J drives Blue Baby through the intersection and down the Pickens Street hill while Mr. Arrogant and Ms. Pretty ride straight ahead on Greene Street.

Although taking different routes, both J and the Mazda occupants arrive at the Richland Memorial Hospital physicians' building parking lot at the same time, but the red Mazda driver takes the advantage and enters first and parks in the first parking slot. J parks Blue Baby in the next available space, closes his door without locking it, and heads for the elevator. Ms. Pretty is already on her way and holds the elevator. "Good afternoon, Dr. J. What floor?"

"I'm flattered that you know who I am. Thanks. And the third floor please."

Ms. Pretty says, "Well, everybody at the university knows Dr. J." The third floor appears, the doors open, and they exchange pleasantries. Ms. Pretty continues upward to a higher floor.

J walks the familiar maze to suite 304, the offices of Dr. Stanley Woods, MD, oncologist, FACS. There are two receptionists behind the counter. The older of the two ladies looks up, sees J, stands up, begins to walk around the counter, and opens her arms, "Oh, Dr. J, it's so good to see you!" They hug, and he kisses her on the cheek. Before he can say anything, Mrs. Penny Culclasure, Ms. Penny to all who know her, told J, "Go on in to Dr. Woods's office. He's waiting for you." J nods and walks in the direction of the doctor's office.

When he's a few steps away, just out of earshot, the younger lady behind the counter looks at Ms. Penny as she returns to her station. "He must be an old and special friend."

Penny answers, "He is. I've known Dr. J. Stewart since he came to the university. We used to go to the same church, and he might still be a member, but I haven't seen him there lately. He's my Jimmy Stewart, and I've told him so." The younger woman smiles and chuckles. "Well, he might be your Jimmy Stewart, but he looks more like Dirty Harry to me. He's a Clint Eastwood look-alike if I ever saw one." And indeed, she is right; he does look somewhat like Dirty Harry. His almost-totally-gray hair is short but scruffy, indicating that in his daily battle with a comb, the comb loses. His ruddy face reflects his obvious love of the outdoors. His sinewy body is well developed. His genuine smile, the one he just gave to Ms. Penny, could melt an iceberg; but his ice blue eyes, unaided by spectacles, indicate that he might be able to create an iceberg on demand, if need be. He wears a blue oxford button-down shirt, no tie, cotton khakis, and a sweater with little tufts sticking out here and there, recording his walks through the woods and the inevitable snags by bushes and weeds. As a matter of fact, he smells faintly of newly fallen longleaf pine needles. His brown Rockport shoes could, and should be, introduced to shoe polish. He has a slight limp, which could have been eliminated had he taken the time to finish the physical therapy sessions once prescribed. His posture is erect, and his walk is precise, holdovers from his military days. His hands are rough and mildly calloused, with fingernails that are clean but uneven. If identified by someone as being a university professor, the new acquaintance would suspect he is a civil engineering professor, not a tenured philosophy professor.

Ms. Penny speaks up, saying, "I agree that he does look a little like Dirty Harry, but he's not as old as he looks. He's had some tough times, serving through two wars, earning a Purple Heart in the last one, and living through some terrible family tragedies. The limp is from his Vietnam injury. Lost his wife several years back but continues to live out in the country in a house full of memories. They were the model loving couple. They were always smiling, always touching, always happy to be with one another. Had a very active social life both here and in Winnsboro, near where the house is. He still goes to some functions, but most of them are things he is expected to attend and not necessarily enjoy. He might look a little rough around the edges, but he looks just as good in a tuxedo as he does in what he has on. Wish he would do something about that sweater, though. His wife, if she were living, would never let him out of the house with such a worn and picked thing. He's such a gentleman too. Always lets the ladies go first, opens car doors for them, and always has something sweet to say, like commenting on your perfume or your hair or your dress. He's a sweetie, I'll tell you. Knows the Bible well and taught Sunday school for years. He doesn't flaunt his religion, though. He just walks the walk and talks the talk. You always know where he stands, nothing wishy-washy about him. I know I've rattled on about him, and I didn't mean to. He's a good man and a favorite of mine."

J walks into Dr. Woods's open door and taps on the door facing to get his old friend Stanley's attention. Dr. Woods looks up and immediately stands up and sticks out his hand. "Come in, J. Good to see you. Let's sit over here where it's more comfortable, and I'll see if Penny can get us some coffee."

J frowned and countered, "That bad, I guess. Never had coffee with you before at your office."

Dr. Stanley Woods, MD, is about twenty years younger than J. His hair has receded to the point that he keeps most of it cut off. This lack of hair and his black-rimmed glasses with round lenses make his head look like a chubby round ball sitting on a white lab coat. Woods is stocky, a couple of inches shorter than J, and is immaculately dressed in a white shirt, tie from the Metropolitan Museum of Art collection, charcoal gray pants, and expensive black Johnston shoes. Woods is an adjunct professor in the university's medical school across town. His framed credentials line the walls of his office: BS in Chemistry from Duke University, MS in Inorganic Chemistry from Cornell, MD from Cincinnati School of Medicine, Fellow in the American College of Surgeons, additional credentials in nuclear medicine, oncology, and other subjects. Woods is a native South Carolinian and a longtime personal friend of J.

Woods began by saying, "You know something, J, I've about decided that I'm going to recommend to potential patients that I know to go to someone else. The news that I have to give you is not good, and it gives me great sadness to have to tell you. The tests results show that you have glioblastoma multiforme. It is a brain tumor that has a history of erratic growth, but the end result is the end of life without radical treatment. The other not-so-good news is that the radical treatments many times have poor track records. Sometimes they prolong life a little while, and sometimes they result in loss of quality of life. We have two choices. We can attempt surgery to remove the tumor, which, at present, has only a 30 percent chance of success. The other choice is to begin extensive chemo treatments. These treatments produce better odds of success in that most of the time, the tumor growth is arrested or slowed down. The side effects of chemo, of course, are not pleasant and may affect you in unpredictable ways. Of the two approaches, I recommend the chemo, but the choice is yours. I'm sorry, J. This is a part of my job that I hate, especially to have to tell this to somebody I have known for as long as I have known you."

J nods in understanding and, after a moment of silence, says, "Stanley, there's one more choice, isn't there? And that's to do nothing and let nature take her course. I've known a couple of people with this or a similar ailment. One, a fellow professor at Carolina, chose surgery. After almost a year of recovery from the surgery, the tumor was back, and he died two months later at home. The other person, an attorney—you remember him—chose chemo but died six months after the treatment started in a hospital room filled with plastic tubes that resembled vines in the Vietnam jungles. Thanks, but no thanks, Stan. I'll pass and ride it out as long as I can."

Dr. Stanley Woods replies, "I knew that was what you were going to say, and I can't say that isn't the best choice for this type of tumor. Like I said, growth is erratic and not predictable. But, J, I encourage you to leave here and register with Carolina Hospice for your last days. By registering now, you have a better chance of them being able to accommodate you. There are so many who need their services, and their funding depends entirely on donations. Carolina Hospice is the best group in my opinion, although I can't say that for publication. Please do that for you and me."

J replies, "As my lawyer always tells me when I suggest a brilliant tactic, I'll take that under advisement. But I have two questions. The first is the time frame I can expect and the symptoms I might have as time goes on."

Dr. Woods rises from his chair and looks out of the window, replying, "As to the time frame, it's really hard to predict. Sometimes the tumor hits a growth spurt for some currently unknown reason and grows quickly. In other cases I have had, it stays sort of dormant for months at the time. But the average time from this point of diagnosis to death is ten months to a year, maybe a few months longer, but not much. God, I'm sorry, J. As to things that you can expect, there will be days, or partial days, maybe for just a few hours at a time, that there will be headache on one side of your head. When that happens, the best thing to do is to stop what you're doing and lie down. Sometimes you'll be dizzy, and you could fall. Sometimes you fall without warning. As time goes on, you will probably have mood swings, sometimes significant variations in your behavior. You may have paranoia, you may become intolerant of almost anything anybody does, but you may become loving and ebullient. The loving personalities are probably okay. But when you feel yourself becoming intolerant, try to stay away from everybody, especially those you are close to. You only hurt the ones you love, you know. You may also have some amnesia in some form or other. For example, you may discover that you suddenly don't know where the hell you are or how you got there. If you're driving, pull over and sit there. If you're out in your woods, sit down. Keep your cell phone with you all the time, even though you may not know what to do with it. You may have tinnitus or ringing in the ears. You may have vision problems, such as losing part or all sight, or blurred vision or seeing double. You may have weakness, paralysis, including paralysis of the face. You may have difficulty talking, choosing words, thinking, and remembering. Your balance may be compromised. You may have changes in your sleep or interruptions of sleep, and you may have projectile vomiting. I say 'may' because not all people with this condition have all the symptoms.

You know this already, I suppose, but it's time to get done those things you need to do. Update your will. Travel while you can. See or talk to those people you have been putting off communicating with. Seek pleasure and satisfaction. The life you have is too short to bother with difficult situations. If you have suicidal thoughts, call me the instant they come to mind. You have my cell phone number, and call it. I'll answer immediately unless I'm probing around in somebody's brains. Call me often, J. Once a month now and in the spring once a week. There's another thing, J. Tell somebody. I know Elizabeth is gone, and even though she is, you can still talk to her—but I mean, someone you trust to tell you the truth and who sees you just about every day. Observant, caring people can tell subtle differences that you might not notice. They need to talk to you about those little things, real or imagined. Maybe we can do a little adjusting when changes happen to make your life a little easier. Would such a person be Pat? I know you trust her implicitly, and she does a lot for you around the place."

J nods in agreement and stares out of the window. Little Christmas trees adorn many of the office windows. Some have some lights strung. Some cars have big red bows on their hoods. *Wonder how they get them to stay there.* His thoughts shift to Elizabeth. *Yes, even though she's not here in person, I can talk to her. We'll set aside a time each day and a place to meet and talk. I'll tell her what's on my mind, how I feel, things I plan to do, what friend I ran across—all those things. And I know just the place! That rock, that boulder in our yard is sort of shaped like a love seat, but a little wider. We'll meet there often. She'll be there all the time, and all I have to do is show up. We'll laugh and joke together like we used to. But we won't be able to touch.* Tears welled up in his eyes—not tears of disappointment about the turn his life is taking, but tears of regret that he can't reach out and touch her hand and have that return squeeze.

J regains his wits and returns to the reality of now. "Stanley, I will talk to Pat and try to tell her all you've told me. There was so much to take in that I might have forgotten part of our conversation. You have my permission to talk to Pat, if you would like to. She's a good girl—lady now—and has a good level head. She's the best person for right now. I'll get around to talking to the kids, but they've got a lot going on, and there's no need to add to their few gray hairs. I expect I'd better go. You have things to do, and the afternoon's not nearly over. I think I would hate your job, Stanley, having to tell patients like you have just told me that the gates of eternity are opening and it's time to think about going in."

Stanley removes his little round glasses, revealing moist red eyes. "And it doesn't get any easier, J. Thanks for taking the news like you have. It helps." Out of character and out of his strict professionalism, Stanley offers a hug, unhesitatingly accepted by J.

J says nothing more and leaves the polished mahogany office with all the credentials and puts on a smile. "I swear, Penny, you look prettier every time I see you! You must take a bath in sunshine every morning! It's worth pretending to be sick so I can come over here and just take a peek at you!"

"Liar, liar, pants on fire! But I love it. Come more often."

"I might just do that," J shoots back. "Gotta go. Got places to go and people to talk to." *Yeah, a ghost,* he thinks as he mentally summons his last memory of Elizabeth as she drove off that day for the last time. Then he kisses Penny Culclasure on the cheek. An exchange of well wishes for the Christmas and New Year season follows, and J makes his exit.

The hallway to the elevator seems longer today. The summoned elevator is empty and glides without a bump and very little descending sensation to the parking level. *Where did I leave Blue Baby? Hello, what's this?* These mental questions pop up as he sees Ms. Pretty in the midst of an argument with big man on campus, second-year law student Frank Lee Howell Jr. J can't hear all of the conversation from that distance, but the gist of it is that Frank is saying, "You will!" and Ms. Pretty is saying, "I won't." As J walks closer, he sees that the couple is in the middle of the shortest distance to Blue Baby. Frank says very loudly, "You will! You can ruin your damn life, but you'll not ruin mine. I made you an appointment, and we're going to keep it!"

Ms. Pretty retorts, "There is no way I'm going to have an abortion. I will *not* do it!"

Undaunted, Frank says, "You will, and you'll do it today. Get in the car!" He opens the Mazda's door, grabs Ms. Pretty by the arm, and forces her into the car. He slams it, but before he is able to get to the driver's side, she's out. If the situation weren't so serious, it could look comical. He pushes her in and runs around to the other side just in time for her to pop out. After a couple of these exercises in futility, Frank grabs Ms. Pretty by the arms and shakes her violently, then says in a more conciliatory tone, "Listen. You are about to destroy both of our lives. Get in the car. Let's do it and do it now."

The answer was an emphatic "No way!"

As the pair attempted mutual stare-downs, J reaches the battle zone. "May I be of some assistance here?"

This offer is met by Frank spinning around, facing Dr. J almost toe-to-toe. Frank frowns, looks J in the eye, and says, "Dr. J, this is none of your business."

J replies, "That's right, Frank. It's not my business, but this shoving match has gone a little too far, and it has made it my concern for your mutual safeties. So I'll be here until one of two things happen. Either this young lady voluntarily gets in the car with you and both of you ride out of here, or she walks away or you drive off and leave her here. The next move is up to you."

The impasse is broken by Ms. Pretty walking away and toward the parking garage exit. Seeing the obvious conclusion, Frank gets in his Mazda, slams his door forcefully, starts the engine, and burns as much rubber as the little Mazda can muster. Taking the downward curves in the parking garage amplifies the tire squeals and the grinding gears but dramatically signals Frank's exit.

J slowly walked to Blue Baby, admires her, marvels at the smooth engine, and drives to the exit with no tire noise whatsoever. Upon reaching Beltline Boulevard, he sees Ms. Pretty walking along briskly with her head down and her arms trying to protect herself from the dropping December temperature. *What to do? Not my business. Probably happens several times a year in a university population of thirty thousand sets of raging hormones. Maybe it does happen, but I got in the middle of that. Besides, she's cold, and it's twenty blocks to town. Oh Lord! She doesn't even have a pocketbook or anything. Well, John Witherspoon Stewart, PhD, who stuck his nose in somebody else's business, do what you need to do.* With that self-lecture, he pulls Blue Baby to the curb next to Ms. Pretty. J pushed the retrofit button, allowing the passenger window to go down and said, "May I assist you in some way?" To his mild surprise, Ms. Pretty opens the door and gets in without saying a word in reply. "Where may I take you?"

The sniffled reply is, "I don't care. Anywhere I can be alone and think."

J, noting that he was parked in a traffic lane just around a curve and that he must move, drives two blocks to the CVS Pharmacy and parks where there were the most parking spaces. "I know you don't feel like talking, but there are a few things I must ask. First, do you have a place to stay?"

The muffled answer was, "No," followed by the explanation that she had moved into Frank Lee Howell Jr.'s apartment just across the river in Lexington County because he had hinted matrimony and in the process answered several of J's unasked questions. No, she does not want to go back there. No, she doesn't have a purse or pocketbook, she doesn't have her ID, she has no money with her (and very little elsewhere), she is a graduate student in journalism and has only one more test to go, her former dormitory roommate found another place, and she can't return there. Her home and her parents are in New Jersey, where her father works on an auto assembly line, and he's going to kill her when he finds out she's pregnant. She is Roman Catholic and has strong pro-life religious beliefs, she thought Frank loved her and respected her and that they could have a wonderful life together after graduation, and she has no solution to her dilemma and does not know what to do—all punctuated with tears and sniffling and squirming in her seat, delivered in machine-gun speed.

JERRY HAMMET & HAROLD GUERRY

J listens intently, asks no more questions, but nods in understanding. He reaches over and pats Ms. Pretty on the back of the hand and tells her, "Wait here while I do a little shopping in the drugstore and at the tobacco shop next to it. I'll leave the keys in the ignition in case it gets too cold so you can start the engine and turn the heater on. May I get you anything?" More tears and a head shake from side to side give him the answer.

J returns several minutes with a combination of things from the drugstore. The red-and-white CVS bag contains a box of tissues, a six-pack of Snickers candy bars, a package of licorice, pipe cleaners, and a cigarette lighter. The other bag, as Ms. Pretty later discovers, contains a new pipe and a package of pipe tobacco from the tobacco shop.

J opens the box of tissues and passes it to Ms. Pretty. "I don't think I've heard your name. What is it?"

Through sniffles and dabs with tissues, Ms. Pretty answers, "Yes, you do need to know that. My name is Marie Tradonio. And I have another problem. I have a final in journalism tomorrow, and I don't have my books or my notes. I can't afford to miss this test. It's the last one, and Dr. Strogens takes no excuses for final exam absences." Tears begin again.

J looks at his watch (the one with the black dial and the nylon wristband he had purchased at a yard sale for $5) and says, "Well, it seems to me we're not going to solve anything sitting in this parking lot. My housekeeper and friend is supposed to be in my house at this time. My house is away from everything and therefore quiet. I have to be back in Columbia in a couple of hours for a meeting, so let's ride out there. You think, and I'll drive." Glancing at the bag from CVS, he adds, "I'll need to make one brief stop to take something to a friend who lives close to my house, and the trip won't take long." Marie Tradonio, a.k.a. Ms. Pretty, nods in agreement between involuntary snuffs, while J guides Blue Baby back in the direction they came from and onto Highway I-277 that ends at Richland Memorial. In a few minutes, Blue Baby merges onto I-77 North with her engine steadily humming along. They ride in silence for another few minutes until they reach the Blythewood exit and shortly thereafter a two-lane county road. They soon see a very large black man sitting on a kitchen stool beside the road, who waves at every vehicle that passes. J signals and turns Blue Baby to the shoulder of the road, stopping in front of the man. Marie looks at him with amazement. He is dressed in a black suit, black shirt, black tie and is wearing a black bowler hat. Had he not opened his mouth to reveal twenty-eight sparkling teeth, he would have looked like a motorized plywood cutout. J instructed Marie to lower her window; and when the opening is wide enough, the giant sticks his great head, hat, and all, into the truck cab. Marie recoils as the two men greeted each other. The large lump exclaims through his pearlies, "Dr. J!" and sticks out his hand.

J grabs the ham-sized hand and heartily greets, "Dr. Bubba! Dr. Bubba, I'd like for you to meet Ms. Tradonio, who is visiting."

Dr. Bubba directs his wide grin to Marie and says without hesitation, "An' yu gonna hab baby, enny?" Marie gasps with obvious shock. Her eyes look like to be as big as saucers.

J comes to the rescue and says, "Well, we'll have to see about that. Brought you something for all the hard work you do, keeping everybody on this road happy," and passes Bubba the six-pack of Snickers.

Bubba takes the package, which is almost hidden in his large hand, and asks, "Thank yu, Dr. J. How yu kno I wuz gon' be hyuh?"

"Oh, a little bird told me, Bubba, a little bird told me." They shake hands again, and J says, "I wish you well, my friend. Brighten the day of everybody that passes by. Waving does that. Takes their minds off their worries for a little while, and we all need that."

"I duz wha' I kin, Dr. J. Das wha' I be bawn wit, tuh mek folks happy." J begins to move back onto the highway; and Marie, still wide-eyed, raises the window.

They ride in silence for another mile or so until Marie asks, "How did he know I was pregnant?"

J replies, "He has one of those inexplicable gifts that God gives to people that you least expect. It's sort of like Santa Claus and magic. You see and hear, but try not to believe. I wish I knew."

At that point, J guides Blue Baby into a dirt lane, bordered by fieldstone fences running off in both directions. Atop one of the stone columns is a concrete square with a weathered brass plaque bearing the word "Shalom." Marie, still wide-eyed, looks at J and asks, "Are you Jewish, Dr. J?"

J smiled and replied, "No, I just have a deep appreciation for the word. I'll tell you about that sometime." Blue Baby bounces down the road that needs some repair for about a half mile, and the house comes into view around a sharp curve. It is a curious mixture of Southern elegance and eclectic imbalance. The large house boasts two stories with brick on the outer wall, two stone chimneys (one on either end), and two unbalanced wings on the lower level. About a hundred yards from the house, on the right of the drive, is a cemetery. Tombstones indicate a lapse of a hundred years between burials. Most are old and ornate, but there are three stones that are much newer, side by side. On the left of the drive, closer to the house, is a large rock nestled under a large white oak tree. The rock has the strange shape of a large sofa, except the large "seats" are curved as if to encourage conversation. The large fallen white oak leaves are clustered around the base of the rock. A lamppost with a lantern-shaped top was located near the rock, giving the impression of it being a freestanding lamp next to a sofa. "That's my thinking rock," J says with pride. "When I need to think, to cogitate, to solve a problem, I come out here and sit in the sofa seat near the lamppost. I can stay out after dark that way and oftentimes do. Mosquitoes and other bugs make it a little uncomfortable on occasions. I need to hook up a bug killer for the bugs attracted by the light."

Marie notices two vehicles in the yard. One is an older Oldsmobile sedan, and the other is an aging pickup. She draws her attention to the pickup. *What brand is it? Not evident.* Looks like all the small pickups manufactured before her birth. *What color? Not sure.* Looks like a combination of brown, faded green, and mold. Paint is scratched beginning at the front and tapering off at the rear. *Does it run? Maybe.* It is adorned with a current South Carolina license plate, complete with month-and-year stickers. Her attention switches to the Oldsmobile. *Is that Dr. J's car also?*

J guides Blue Baby to a favored spot near the side of the house, gets out, and motions Marie to enter the kitchen door, located around the right wing as it is faced. J opens the door to allow Marie to enter. An oval drop leaf plantation table with all leaves open is located in full view. Sitting in a chair on the far side is an attractive tall, slim light-skinned black woman, patiently waiting. J makes no attempt at introductions but points down the hall as if to indicate the restroom was in that direction, with the unspoken word that women of all ages want to visit the restroom on arriving from anywhere. She senses tension between J and the woman and mentally agrees that she should explore the hall for the obvious restroom. She looks over her shoulder for a second to see the woman has rushed over to J, flings her arms around his neck, and then sort of slides down to her knees, still clutching him, crying with her face to one side, "Oh my god! Oh my god!" From there, Marie hears or sees nothing more but accelerates her pace down the hall.

A full minute passes with the woman and J frozen in place. J says, "I guess Stanley Woods called you."

"Yes, a long time ago. Where've you been? I've been worried about you. Yes, Dr. Woods told me all about your ailment and how it would affect you. I don't know what to say, Dr. J. And you kept this from me! How dare you! Have you told anybody? I knew you were having headaches and were dizzy sometimes, but . . . ." She rises to her feet, releases her grip on J, straightens her dress, and listens to the faint sound of a flushing toilet. "And who is that?"

J hangs his head and says, "I guess Stanley was right. You only hurt the ones you love. Sorry, Pat. I should have brought you into the first tentative diagnosis. I rationalized that maybe it would turn out to be something else, like a pinched nerve in the neck, or one of my old war wounds was working a bone loose or something. Hindsight is great, however. And I should have been up-front with you and not lied, telling you that Stanley still wasn't sure. Some truth in that too because it wasn't confirmed until Stanley got the results of the MRI. I didn't mean to hurt you or shut you out. I need you like I have for the last how many years, and I'll obviously need you more than ever now. You'll need to watch me closely for changes that I might want to forget—but we'll talk about that at the rock soon." Then he hears approaching steps in the hall. "As to who she is, she's just another one of God's children in trouble like so many we've taken under our wings. Let me introduce our visitor, Ms. Marie Tradonio. Did I pronounce it right?"

Pat offers her hand and says, "I'm Pat Brown. Dr. J needs a keeper, and that's what I do."

J added, "And does a good job of it too. Keeps me not only acting right, but thinking right." He turns to Pat and tells her, "Pat, on what we were talking about, we'll deal with this issue as time goes by. Like Franklin Roosevelt, there is nothing to fear but fear itself." With that, J dismisses his and Pat's conversation with a let's-talk-about-it-later-but-not-now look and turns to Marie. "Ms. Tradonio, let me introduce you to my thinking rock. This way please." He waves for her to precede him out of the kitchen door. "Pat, would you make us a little snack and make believe it's tea time? Thanks."

The afternoon is one of those South Carolina late fall ones, with the temperature bouncing between the upper sixty degrees and lower seventy degrees. Tomorrow? The comfort level might be anything from cold to brisk to pleasant. Coats are not necessary.

J makes a momentary stop at his truck, reaches in, retrieves the bag he brought from the Tobacconist, and begins to fill his new pipe with a walnut/cherry blend. By the time they reach the rock, he's lit it. He throws back his head, smiles, and says, "I have missed this," releasing a fruit-and-nut-flavored cloud into the air. They reach the rock, and he motions for Marie to sit on his left. A couple of silent smoke clouds later, J asks, "Now, young lady, how can I help you?"

Marie answers with sincere frankness, "I really don't know."

J lectures and questions, "Well, let's start with the immediate. Have you finished all of your exams?"

"No, I have one more to take. It's scheduled for this afternoon at four. I don't see how I can take it, and right now, I don't want to."

"I might be able to help you there," J offers. He pulls his cell phone from his pants pocket, looks up a stored number, and makes a call. Marie picks up from the conversation that he is being connected to the dean of the School of Journalism. J says after the usual pleasantries, "Al, I have a student of yours with me right now, and she is going through a very stressful time. She tells me she has an exam she is supposed to take this afternoon, and she really doesn't feel up to taking it—emotionally, that is. Her name is Marie Tradonio." The following minutes were taken up with a series of the following: "I see," "I remember now," "Okay," "Uh-huh," "No," "Good idea," "Might work out," "I hadn't thought of that," many times repeated. The long-listened-for "Thanks, Al. And it's been good talking to you. Probably see you over the holidays, maybe at the president's reception. Good-bye" is finally said.

Jay lights his pipe again. (Pipes are notorious for losing their fire and requiring relighting frequently, especially until "broken in," that is, until a layer of tar, carbon, and tobacco coats the bowl.) He turns to Marie and says, "Well, first of all, good news. The good dean agrees that you are one of the best students he has ever had, and he had thought about exempting you from this final and should have and has now done so. So you don't have to worry about that. The other thing he talked to me about was to remind me that he had recommended you to me for the part-time job I want to fill. I don't think he ever mentioned your name because I thought I was looking for a male student, one who could live out here and do the work I need done. The last thing he said was that he wasn't aware of your having a personal problem but trusts that it will soon pass favorably."

Marie's eyes well with tears. She struggles to part with a simple but sincere "Thank you, Dr. J."

Their afternoon on the rock sofa is interrupted by Pat walking up. She begins with a disapproving tone, "You're smoking. When did that come back?"

J answers with a casual yes-I-know-it's-a-bad-habit-but-please-mind-your-own-business reply, "I bought this pipe on the way home from school today, and I didn't realize how much I missed it. Don't you like the walnut/cherry blend? I think it smells like fall, Thanksgiving, and Christmas." Pat's only reply is the fanning of air away from her face with her hand and a look of disapproval and disgust on her face.

"Where are the girls?" asks J. "I haven't seen them since we arrived." With continued disdain, Pat suggests that the girls are probably asleep in the sun in back of the house, like the worthless hounds they are. J smiles and whistles loudly, directing the sound toward the house. In seconds, two large lady dogs bound around the corner of the house and run full tilt to the rock to respond to their master. Marie is frightened at the speed of their travel, as well as their size. Two golden retrievers, each weighing over eighty pounds, run full speed to their master, friend, protector and sit at his feet as if to say, "You whistled, boss?" J looks at them and lowers his head, a signal to lie down. They immediately obey and gaze lovingly at him with their front paws crossed. He begins a conversation with them, "Hello, girls. How are you? Did you rest well this afternoon? Marie, I want you to meet Victoria and Princess, our four-legged protectors out here in the wilderness. Don't have any fear of them. They're large, but the only danger is when they might try to force your hands out of your pockets to get you to pet them. They are playful and obedient, at least most of the time, and are wonderful friends and sometimes necessary protectors." Adding quickly, turning to Pat, "Almost as good a friend as I have in Pat."

Pat smiles and tells him in a motherly tone, "You know you're in trouble with that pipe. You're just trying to smooth it over and pat me on the head just like the dogs. I know you, Dr. J." She adds after a slight pause, "And I wouldn't want it any other way. You're a scoundrel, Mr. Dr. J, and I love you for it!"

"Guess I'm just bad to the bone and born that way," the faux-remorseful Dr. replies.

Pat responds with a resounding "Amen!" This friendly banter brings a much-needed smile to Marie, as she watches these two caregivers/care receivers as they swap roles.

"Come in to the kitchen and get some sandwiches and apple cider for your redneck 'tea,' as you call it. It's getting chilly out here, and none of us need to be sitting on that cold rock," Pat offers in her best mother role and begins walking to the house.

After "tea," while still sitting at the plantation table, J resumes his questions. "I think we've taken care of the exam problem, so let's tackle the rest. What else can we do to help?"

Marie took inventory and begins, "Well, there are a couple more problems that I don't know how to handle. The first are my clothes and possessions. I made up my mind late last night that I would have to end my relationship with Frank, so I packed everything up after he went to sleep. I need some way to retrieve them and a place to store them temporarily. I have a key to the apartment that, as pure luck has it, I put in the only pocket I have this morning. Remember that my purse is in Frank's car, or at least, that's where I saw it last. The second problem that comes to mind is that I need to contact a girlfriend whom I'm supposed to ride with to New Jersey with tomorrow. She and I have hometowns that are close to each other's. I plan to spend the holidays with my parents."

Pat speaks as she finished tidying up the kitchen, "I can help with the first one—that is, if Dr. J is willing to let me borrow a vehicle. I have to go to the university and pick up a cap and gown, and I'd be delighted to help you pick up your stuff and deliver it. Dr. J, may I borrow your truck?" J smiles a wicked little smirk and tells her the Toyota (the nondescript one with the scratches and the questionable paint color) is available, but not his Blue Baby. Pat makes jokes about his love for Blue Baby being greater than for her but reaches for the Toyota keys hanging on a key storage board located near the door.

J offers a space in the basement of his house as a place to store her belongings until her return to Columbia after the holidays, which is instantly accepted by Marie.

"When do you plan to return?" J asks.

Marie tells him that she plans to return with her transporting friend around January 2or 3. "There's one more problem I need help with very desperately, and I just thought of it. You've done so much for me already that I hate to ask, but may I have a place to spend the night? I won't spend another night with Frank, and my former roommates have no room, and I can't afford a motel."

J looks at Pat and nods, saying that he would be happy for her to stay at his house, in the Lincoln room, just down the hall on the first floor. Pat agrees and leaves the kitchen to check on the room. When Pat is halfway down the hall, J says, "Marie, I don't want to give you any advice that you don't want to hear, but I think I should. Let me strongly suggest that if you are ever going to tell your parents about your maternal condition, you should go ahead and do it up front when you get home. I suspect you don't plan to do that. But you'll be amazed, the same as I always am, that parents are resilient, loving, and compassionate regardless of the situation. Will you do that?"

Marie shakes her head and replies, "No, Dr. J, I can't do that. At this time, I don't plan to share this sort of problem with them. They have enough on their plates. My dad has been laid off from the assembly plant he's worked at for thirty-three years. It has closed, along with about a dozen other manufacturing plants in town and in the surrounding towns, and not likely to reopen. He has only a grade school education. And this job loss has thrown his alcohol restraint, if he ever had one, to the winds. I'm his little girl who can do no wrong, and I'm afraid this would put him over the edge. Mom told me the last time I was home that he makes suicidal comments when he's deep into his cups. Mom's no better. She has always taken issue with everything I have ever done—the typical mother-daughter relationship. She resisted my coming to Carolina, resisted my choice of journalism for a major, doesn't like the clothes I wear, and on and on."

Actually, Dr. J mused to himself, *I think I agree with Mom about clothing and the way you dress. An inch and a half of tantalizing cleavage in December is a little off the scale of everyday dress. Might even be an inch and three-quarters.*

"In addition to worrying about Dad, she has to work part-time at night, stocking goods at K-Mart, after she gets off work at school where she teaches history. I can't, Dr. J. I'll make some excuse for not being able to visit again for a long time, and maybe things will change or maybe—I just don't know. But I can't tell them I'm pregnant and homeless and not married to a good Catholic boy."

J nods and reaches for his pipe and a jacket. "Marie, I understand the circumstances with your parents. I know many parents of Carolina students who are going through the same thing. In this community, for example, the mills at Great Falls are silent now, after once employing three thousand people in a town that has two thousand citizens. Mack Trucks had a manufacturing plant in Winnsboro, but they moved away. The little community of Blaney changed the name of the town to Elgin because the Elgin Company came to town to save them, and now Elgin has moved on. The Haile Gold Mine just up the road near Kershaw has ceased operations, and the only people there now are the landscapers filling up the holes. But I will say that I have been around many decades more than you have, and my knowledge tells me that you should rethink your approach. Overriding all of that, however, is the overwhelming belief that each person must be responsible for their own destiny, and individual choices must be made. You've made a decision, at least for the time being, and I respect that. May

God bless you, my lovely lady." He adds, "I need to smoke and think, so I'm heading for my rock."

Marie sits where she is in her ladder-back chair that matched none of the others silently for several minutes and makes the sign of the cross. Her lips move in semisilent private prayer while tears appear in the corner of her brown eyes and run down her pretty cheeks.

Pat returns from freshening up the Lincoln room and silently provides a Kleenex. "Time to go!" Pat says with as much cheer as she can muster and offers Marie a sweater to ward off the increasing coolness of the afternoon.

A ride in the Toyota that was older than either of the ladies is an adventure. The towels on the seats must be rearranged prior to every use. The windows and the rearview mirrors have to be cleaned. Various pieces of small tools and machinery, boxes, and some lumber are simply thrown out of the truck bed to make room for Marie's worldly goods. When the ignition key is turned, a pleasant transformation occurs. It runs! Actually, it purrs. Dr. J, as Pat explains, is at odds with himself when it comes to the care of vehicles. Looks are secondary; and for the Toyota, it is eight times down the list, whatever that means. Mechanical operation is vastly different. Buddy Van Doren, the mechanic on Highway 21 in Great Falls, who takes meticulous care of the trucks running gear, pleads with Dr. J good-naturedly every time it is serviced to at least wash it—all to no avail. (Buddy can't read or write but can overhaul an engine with a magic touch.) Dr. J is attracted to people like Buddy and "Dr." Bubba. These people, along with many more J has cultivated friendships with over the years, possess unexplainable skills.

There's Jane, the clerk in the police department in the Flopeye Community, who has the interrogative skills that the CIA would lust after. Jane could have located the Beirut hostages in a day and a half had she been sent there. Elvira, who lives in the lowest valley between Winnsboro and Ridgeway, can soothe burns by "talking out the fire" and only rubs a hand to make warts disappear. "Dr." Bones will conjure up a mixture guaranteed to cure your headache or your ingrown toenail, whichever one you want to go away. People with unusual gifts are found in every race and in every community if sought, and J has a knack for finding them and making them his lifelong friends.

As Pat and Marie reach the end of the driveway to Shalom, Pat points to a neat arts-and-crafts-style cottage diagonally across the highway from the driveway's entrance and tells Marie that she lives there with her son,

Hab. She takes a few minutes to drive into that front yard and runs in to check on her son and give him a short verbal list of chores to complete before she returns.

Marie says, "That's an unusual name, Hab. Where did he get it?" Pat smiled and tells her that it's really an acronym. His name is Henry Aaron Brown, and Dr. J has called him Hab from birth, and now it has stuck.

After the two have gotten under way, Marie asks, "How long have you worked for Dr. J, Pat?"

Pat laughs and says, "I don't work for Dr. J. We look out for each other." Marie turns and looks at Pat in shock. "You mean . . . you mean . . . you . . . Dr. J . . . I had no idea. I'm sorry . . . I didn't mean . . . I mean, I don't know what to say." She blushes and looks the other way.

Pat bursts out laughing to the point of almost running off the road. "No no no! There's nothing going on between us! For God's sake, woman! This is the Midlands of South Carolina! Young black women don't shack up with old white men, especially one who happens to be a university professor whose family has lived here for two hundred years! Not in the daytime, anyhow! This is Fairfield County, South Carolina, and I don't care if it is the twenty-first century. Things like that might happen in New Jersey, but not here, girl. No no no. Let me explain when you get your color back. Do you need a Coke or something?" Marie's color had turned from a brilliant blush to a shade of sallow white.

Marie says, "Please. This whole day has been the most bizarre in my entire life! I would love to have a Coke or something, but I'll have to pay you back. I don't have a cent to my name with me."

After the emergency stop at BoBops Shell Station and a couple of sips from the twenty-ounce cola eighty-nine-cent specials, Pat begins to explain. She tells Marie that Dr. J knows everybody, especially everybody in upper Richland and Fairfield counties in the South Carolina Midlands, and everybody knows him. J was born in Columbia, where his father was a university professor. After high school and college, J entered the U.S. Army during the Korean conflict. He was sent to Korea as a brand-new lieutenant and was thrust into combat without a whole lot of preparation. Pat relates some of his stories of how his crusty old first sergeant saved his butt on several occasions. After returning home from Korea, the army sent him back to school where he earned a master's degree in military science. He resumed his army career and was sent to Vietnam as an intelligence officer. Pat tells Marie that J doesn't talk much about his service in Vietnam, but he returned home with gray hair at age thirty-eight and with a limp that he still has. When asked if he was awarded the Purple Heart, he just laughs, admits that he does have the award, and says it was because he was shot in the gluteus maximus by a nearsighted Vietcong. She has never heard the full story. Pat relates that she has seen some of his medals, tucked away in his underwear drawer. When J retired from the army, he returned to the university and earned his doctorate in philosophy and immediately began to teach there. J and his family bought a small place in Blythewood, north of Columbia, where their son, Jack Jr., and daughter, Rebecca, began school. Schools in South Carolina were integrated for the first time in 1970, and Jack Jr. and Pat began first grade together in 1981 and were in the same homeroom many of their school years. Pat was a guest at Jack Jr.'s parties all during school. JJ, as she refers to him, was a football quarterback on the Blythewood High Blue Rocks team; and Pat was a cheerleader.

Pat goes on to say that she was married shortly after graduation from high school and had her son Hab the next spring. Jack Jr. went to college, was an ROTC student, and entered the U.S. Air Force upon graduation. Rebecca also graduated from the University of South Carolina and became a college professor, like her father, and now lives on the West Coast. Pat confides that her marriage was a sham, that her husband was her same age but was a violent man, beating her and threatening her the entire time they lived together, that being only a few months. Pat continues, telling her that Mrs. Stewart was the midwife who delivered Hab and rescued her when her husband beat her minutes after the delivery, took her home with her where she remained for some time. She returned home to her parents after her husband left town. After a year of recovery from her wounds, both mental and physical, she talked to her parents about going to college. The money just wasn't there, she was told. Her three older brothers were in various stages of completing their educations, and there just wasn't enough to go around. Pat's Dad is also a Vietnam army veteran who works as the grounds maintenance coordinator at Fort Jackson. Pat continues, telling Marie that her mom was the janitor in the Philosophy building at the university (now known as Building Maintenance Technician III). Pat relates that one day, J noticed that her mom was eating her lunch in the maintenance closet and insisted that she take her breaks and lunch in the student lounge. She finally consented and began to sit in one of the corner tables, where she picked up on students' names and their backgrounds. Pat explained that J is a person who prefers the student lounge to the staff lounge, where he seeks out the person who sits alone in the corners, sits with them, and talks to them. In the same manner, he began talking to Pat's mom, who told him about her children and grandchild and how Pat wanted to go to college and the futility of such dream. J told her that he remembered Pat as one of the students who was always popping in and out of his house when JJ was in school. One day, during their lunch breaks in the student cafeteria, J sat down and removed some papers from his jacket pocket and told her mom to give them to Pat. It was an application for an educational grant with a strange name, the Shalom Society for the Advancement of Education. The grant was a very generous one that would provide for tuition and a living allowance, provided the recipient maintained superior grades. "She might just get it," J told Pat's mom as he left her that day.

Pat continues by saying that she has never been able to find this grant on the Internet and really doesn't know what group is responsible for it. She was awarded the grant and began college the next fall, taking the minimum number of courses. After seven years, she will finally graduate this year. In addition to the luck of receiving the grant, J approached Pat's parents after his wife died with another windfall. It seems as if J had purchased a small house near the entrance to Shalom and proposed that Pat and Hab live there and, instead of rent, maybe Pat could help him with housework and Hab could help with yard work and that sort of thing. She jumped at that chance, and her father found her a gently used 1993 Oldsmobile 88 which would allow her to come and go as needed.

"So," Pat concludes, "I do and I don't work for Dr. J. It's more than that because I really run the house. I arrange for the exterminator, remind him to pay taxes, make sure he pays the electric bill, arrange for repairs, meet the cable installer, and that sort of thing. Hab and I have most of our evening and weekend meals there. But I'm not paid."

"I also need to tell you about Dr. J's wife's death. J's wife and two of his younger children were killed in an auto accident several years ago. This had a life-changing effect on Dr. J. He used to dress immaculately with his little bow tie and blazer when he taught and everything had to be just right. His car had to be washed and waxed, his yard manicured, and such. It began slowly, the rough-cut look. He won't let me get rid of that ragged sweater he has on now. He used to be an avid hunter. Was a great dove shooter and went on deer hunts frequently, but I don't recall seeing him with a shotgun or a rifle in his hands in years. Says that he has no desire to kill God's children. But don't peg him as a sissy or one who is a pacifist. When those blue eyes look like sharp ice, something's going to happen. He can't stand any form of social injustice. In some cases, he's gone overboard in defense of and in his help to the black community.

Another thing, he's become less predictable. I hear his classes at Carolina are a hoot. He might come in wearing kilts one day, blowing a bagpipe, or he might dismiss and reassemble the class on the lawn outside, or bring in a statue of some philosopher or demonstrate a chemical reaction right there on his desk.

Also, there's no telling what he might bring home. He found that stupid concrete inscription that's on the entrance gate from a Jewish synagogue being demolished and had someone cement it in. "There hasn't been any Jews in his family since Abraham," Pat spouts.

This discussion consumes the entire trip to Columbia. Meanwhile, J is deep in tobacco smoke and in conversation with unseen friends gathered around his rock when he noticed that in the background there seemed to be occasional bird chirps echoing through his head and that his right hand was trembling for no apparent reason.

The collection of Marie's possessions goes smoothly. Her books and her computer are the heaviest objects to move. For a college student, her total possessions are few. The pickup is almost full, but not piled high. Pat's cap and gown only need to be picked up and hung in the narrow space behind the pickup's seats, and they are ready to return to Shalom.

Marie shares her story with Pat, comparing her upbringing with Pat's and finally confiding the news of her pregnancy and her pro-life decision.

Upon arriving back at Shalom, Pat's son Hab is dutifully engaged in raking the large white oak leaves and had created a large pile close to the driveway. Hab is a neatly dressed light-skinned black fellow of fourteen, several skin shades lighter than his mother's. After introductions, Hab goes to work transporting Marie's things into the basement of the Shalom house. J, Hab explained, has gone to his room for a nap.

By this time, the December evening shadows began to lengthen and the red-and-gold sunset fingers to the west started their color scheme for the day. Pat prepared supper, as dinner is referred to by true mid-Carolinians. Since Marie's visit had not allowed time for grocery shopping, Pat relied on the stock items found in most country kitchens. The result was grits, red-eye gravy, ham, hot biscuits with molasses on the side. The grits was an adventure for the New Jersey girl, with the rest being a delight.

Hab was the first to be excused—homework, you know. After assisting with the dishes, Marie is the second to go, explaining that this had been an extremely long and eventful day. No disagreement from J and Pat.

Pat follows shortly thereafter and drives off into the early December darkness, leaving J with the evening news.

The next morning, the sounds of kitchen activity awaken Marie. She finds Pat bustling about the kitchen, preparing breakfast from the kitchen basics.

Marie adapts well to helping with kitchen cleanup, drawing on her Italian-American upbringing and then anxiously waits for her friend to pick her up for the ten-hour-plus drive to New Jersey. *Probably take longer*, she muses. Al Roker, the TV weather guy, is showing blizzard conditions above Washington, District of Columbia. Marie leaves the kitchen to check the time on the clock located high in the two-story foyer. Complaining, half under her breath, Marie says, "This is gonna be a long day. I can't understand anybody being almost an hour late for a trip like this. We won't get to Washington before dark. This is December 21, the shortest day of the year anyhow. I thought Ann was always on time." Pat laughs, to Marie's surprise, seeing no amusement in Pat's laughter. Pat explains between fits of laughter, "I'm sorry! I'm sure you think I'm rude and have no feelings, but I need to tell you that Dr. J never gets around to changing the time on the foyer clock from daylight savings time because of where it's located, taking a lot of effort and ladders to change the hour. Dr. J says we can remember to mentally change one hour for six months because the clock's right the other six months. Your friend's not late. As a matter of fact, there's a car coming up the driveway now."

Marie begins laughing at her own frustration, thinking to herself that she'll never get used to the practical wisdom of old South Carolinian men.

After hurried good-byes and quick hugs, Marie departs. As soon as the car disappeared around the curve in the driveway, Pat turned to J. "When's she coming back, Dr. J?"

"She says she'll be back on January 2 or 3, I think she said." Pat lays down her dishcloth and stands in front of J with a black cast-iron frying pan in one hand as he sits at one of the mismatched kitchen chairs and gives J some unsolicited advice.

"Dr. J, you don't need to take on that stray. You know I haven't said a word about any other person you've taken under your wing in the last ten years. This one is trouble with a capital T. I know you well enough to see it coming. You've got stress enough to kill a saint, or you should have. She's one of those "Come here's" who thinks she knows the ways of the world and doesn't have enough Christianity to keep her pants on. What's she gonna do when she gets back? Lie around all day, get fat, and then let a rug rat run all over this house and you and me?"

J notes, as he should have, that Pat's emotions are escalating with every breath, and motions for her to sit down but, most importantly, to put the frying pan down.

"Pat, first of all, I don't know whether she'll return or not. There's close to fifty-fifty odds on how that'll work out. If she follows my advice to her, she'll tell her parents what her situation is, as she obviously has told you. If so, we'll never see her again. But she's got some strong thoughts and opinions. If she does return, I'll do everything I can to help her. Don't know exactly how, but I will. You know, Pat, Providence is wonderful. It drives our daily lives. All things happen for the best, and we never know where our next steps will carry us, and that's the beauty of life. Providence brought you and Hab into my life. Had you gone to the hospital to have Hab instead of my wife delivering him and had I not decided to get that extra cup of coffee and sat down with your mother in the break room, my life would not be nearly as complete as it is now. Your help to me is one of those things God saw me needing and providentially guided your being here right now, threatening me with that black frying pan. We'll see how it shakes out."

"Dr. J," Pat counters, "sometimes you need a good dose of cast iron frying pan applied to your head and shoulders, but I guess today's not a good day for such treatment. You know Hab and I and my parents love you and thank you for your providential actions. You're not laying some of that epistemology philosophical crap on me, are you? That's out of my understanding. I'm a chemistry major. And speaking of that, tomorrow is the day I've been looking for! Imagine me, about to walk down that aisle and have that sheepskin popped in my hand! It's about to be a Martin Luther King Jr. day! Free at last! Free at last! Thank God Almighty, I'll be free at last!" She adds, "At least from going to college."

J nods in agreement, slips on his heavy coat, and heads out of the door to the rock for a time of thinking and smoking, and conversations with unseen people. He hastens a bit so Pat wouldn't be able to see the sudden trembling of his right hand and the occasional twitch in his right eye or maybe hear the cacophony of bird sounds resounding from the back of his head. He hopes that she wouldn't notice that he was clutching the banister of the kitchen steps for support or notice his slightly erratic path to the

Rodin Rock. Halfway there, he returns to find a boat cushion in his shop to protect his gluteus maximus from the cold absorbed in the rock.

The morning of December 22 breaks clear and cold. Pat and Hab arrive full of excitement and jubilation. After Pat sends J back to his room for a more appropriate dress, the three head for Columbia in Pat's Oldsmobile (refusing to ride in Blue Baby for this occasion) for the graduation ceremonies scheduled for ten o'clock. Pat joins her classmates while Hab goes with J to his office to help with his robes and colors.

The graduation ceremony is on the better side of the usual. The speaker is mercifully brief and unusually insightful. He is a second-level academic from another university, as is usual for midterm graduations. The long-awaited reading of the list of graduates finally begins, and the line of penguins with square hats moves. Pat's parents, her brothers, their wives and children, and associates from church all join Hab and J in the audience. The announcer comes to the name Patricia Althea Brown and pauses to note that Pat is receiving a dual major in chemistry and math, with highest honors. After the ceremonies, Pat, Hab, J, and her parents joined the dean of the chemistry department, the dean of the School of Arts and Sciences and their spouses at the university faculty house for lunch, served by formally attired waiters. J and the deans and spouses are no strangers to the Faculty House, located on campus in one of the beautiful old buildings.

After the lunch and the accolades, J, Pat, and Hab head home. As they leave the campus, J suggests that they return by way of Two Notch Road. This is one of J's usual unusual actions. Pat swears he has never taken the same route twice to anywhere, an exaggeration of course, but with too much truth to ignore. Suddenly, J instructs Pat to turn her Oldsmobile into the Dick Smith Toyota dealership. They walk into the showroom where Pat and Hab ooh and ah at the various models while J asks for someone who is summoned, and they begin to talk.

Shortly, J summons Pat and Hab to the middle of the floor to the garnet-colored Camry sporting a large red ribbon wrapped both lengthwise and crosswise, topped with an oversized red bow. Pat and son climb in and point to different features and carry on an excited conversation when J sticks his head in and tells Pat to step out of the car and sign some papers.

Pat looks quizzically at J and asks, "What papers?" The salesman smiles and says, "The papers to transfer ownership of your new Camry. Do you like it?"

"What car? I haven't bought any car and won't be able to even think about one, especially a new one, until I've worked a while."

The salesman counters, "Well, that's not what these papers say. They say you not only have bought this car but it has been paid for. Just a couple of signatures, and I'll get the key and show you the unique features."

Pat turns to J and says, "Dr. J, what's going on here?"

J explains, "Well, you just graduated with honors from the university with a double major in two extremely complicated subjects. You are driving a nice heretofore dependable 1993 Oldsmobile, which is not fitting your new status, and you need a car. So I came in and started the paperwork, paid for it, and conned you into coming here. I think that's about it. Now if you don't like the color or the model, we'll do something about it. If you want to take a few minutes and consult with Hab, go ahead. I've got the rest of the day free."

Pat retorts, "I can't afford this car."

J parries, "You don't owe anything. The only thing is insurance and taxes when they come up next year. There's nothing to not afford."

"I won't accept this. I can't. It's not right."

"Okay, will it make you feel any better if we worked up a promissory note and you paid me back at some date in the future?"

"I think I'm being sandbagged."

"Yes, as a matter of fact, you are."

After the end of that conversation, papers are signed, ownership is transferred, and Pat and Hab begin their orientation of their new 2008 Toyota Camry. J requests the keys to the Oldsmobile and drives away, but not before sitting in the cool outdoors and enjoying a pipeful of walnut cherry blend.

Upon arriving at Shalom, Pat and Hab find J just where they thought they would, sitting on his boat cushion on the right side of the thinking rock, smoking. Pat shoos Hab home and joins J in the left rock sofa seat. "Dr. J, I need to talk to you. I can't afford that car, and you know that. A promissory note is worthless. It's going to be years before I can pay you back."

J confessed, "To be totally honest with you, Pat, I really don't expect you to ever pay me anything for that auto. It's a gift of appreciation for all you have done for me since Elizabeth and the kids died. You've led me through some difficult times and still do. You even sent me back to my room three times this morning to get the right clothes. You've cooked practically every meal I've had, kept the house clean, bought groceries, kept up with the mail, make sure I pay the taxes and insurance on time, and fed the dogs. You run things around here. I'm going to miss your care so badly that I really don't know what I'll do when you go to work, which I assume you'll do as soon as possible. With a major like yours, trying to find a job around here, other than teaching, will be next to impossible."

Pat says, "But I don't plan to go to work next month."

J raises his eyebrows and asks, "Really, why not?"

"I think I ought to stay here with you, you know, because of your illness, at least until—"

"You mean, until I die. Pat, I might be dying, but I'm not dead yet. I have an undetermined time to live—probably a year, maybe less and maybe more. I've got a pretty long list of things I want to do, to see, to experience. I add to the list every day. I am limited in what I can do. For example, Dr. Woods told me that international travel was out of the question. That cuts in to a list I already had. For example, I have always wanted to live one of Jack LeCarre's scenes, dressed in my trench coat, standing on the bridge between Buda and Pest. Another travel that I won't do is to meet somebody in Trieste. A third is to have a drink in Casablanca, like Humphrey Bogart did. But there are—"

Pat interrupted, "Dr. J, I'm freezing! It's beginning to snow, and I have to go in. Come in, and let me make us some coffee. I bought a new can of Yuban last week that's never been opened. I need to ask a lot of questions, so come on in."

J follows dutifully. Snow comes sparingly to the Midlands of South Carolina and only lasts a short time. No accumulation was forecast for tonight. The little frozen spits, which are perhaps sleet instead of snow, sting his cheeks as he puffs on his pipe and walks slowly.

Coffee is brewed and served. Pat calls Hab and tells him she will be late, to clean the house, lock the doors, and watch TV until she arrives. J situates himself in his favorite chair in the den, and Pat sits on the floor in front of him. She begins, "Dr. J, I have a lot of questions about your illness and what I should look for. I need to know what Dr. Woods told you and how he is treating you. My idea is that I should postpone looking for a job in a scientific setting for a while until . . . until things settle down. Maybe I can pick up some part-time work while things are going well. What do you think about my plan?'

J silently nods his head for almost a minute. He begins talking slowly, still thinking, saying, "Pat, this plan of yours is magnanimous on your part. You are telling me that you are willing to put your life on hold while mine winds down. You've worked for years to complete college and are now willing to wait some more. For my part, I would be very foolish if I turned you down. There is no doubt in mind that I'll need someone, and not just anyone, to escort me through the last mortal pathway. Being alone during these last months is something I don't have a plan for. Yes, your plan is much in my favor, but not for yours. I would consider it only if I could adequately compensate you for it. Let me ask, what sort of job offers have you had?"

Pat tells him about her interviews. She has tentative offers from a defense contractor in the North Carolina Triad, from a cosmetic manufacturer in New Jersey, and from a chemical manufacturer in the Chicago area. The entry salary ranges offered are higher than those offered to younger students. Of the three offers, the annual salary range has a low of $55,000 to a high of $72, 000. She had been approached by the local school district human resources department to teach math in high school, which amounted to about $40,000 a year. She admits that it would probably be best for her to accept the job with the most money, but she is afraid to move away. Her mental abilities are superior as far as understanding advanced math and most of the branches of chemistry endeavors, but she is not street-smart. She had been sheltered from a lot of meanness found in big cities. She had not traveled widely. She is uncomfortable with her foreign languages, those being French and Spanish. She confides that perhaps the best thing for her and Hab would be to take a teaching job nearby or at least in South Carolina and maybe see how that goes.

J makes an offer of $50,000 per year, paid in equal monthly payments or on a draw basis with a $50,000 annual cap. Her duties would be to keep on doing what she is doing now—running the house and keeping an eye on him. He urges Pat to not give him an answer for ten days or a due date of New Year's Eve.

Pat presses on. "Okay, I'll give you an answer by then, but you have to give me some answers tonight. I will not leave here until you tell me about your ailment and what you might do or what might be done to you. I need to know what your plans are for the Wop, and I need to have an idea of what happens after your death. Deal?"

Deal it is. More coffee is brewed, which gives Pat time to face the corner of the kitchen and pray. "Jesus, stand by me while I hear what Dr. J has to say. Help me to talk without crying and to hold back the tears when I want to cry. Give me strength, Lord, give me wisdom, and help me ask the right questions. Amen, Lord, Amen."

The explanation of the brain tumor comes first. J dutifully tells Pat everything Stanley told him. At one point, Pat asks, "Dr. J, why are you winking at me? What we're talking about is not funny." She then realizes that the intermittent eye flutters were not voluntary. "Dr. J, is this one of the things to look for?"

J, with his usual ability to find humor in every situation, answered, "Well, Pat, I've had such things all my life. Remember that I told you years ago that Mama dropped me on my head when I was six months old, and I ain't been right since?"

"Doctor, I know you've never been exactly right, but don't kid with me. When did that begin?"

J sips on the hot black Columbian blend and says, "Strange you should ask. I don't think I've told you this, but I've been talking to Elizabeth a lot lately. She comes to visit when I'm sitting on the rock. She loved those warm afternoons in November. She looks so good, Pat. She's well, and the children are well also. Anyhow, when I told her about my ailment, she told me that she knew it months ago. But that was one of the rules—she couldn't tell me. I had to find out from some other source. She then reminded me that the first symptom I had was when I thought I tripped over the rug in the kitchen, but I didn't. I simply didn't have control over my foot. I remember it well.

"This is a little out of order, maybe. But while I'm at it, let me tell you about the great visits I've had with Elizabeth. She tells me things I ought to do, things I ought to get done. From her advice, I asked for a sabbatical from teaching yesterday. I was given permission but was requested to write a book on one of the many subjects of philosophy. Got to get started on that. She told me to be in touch with Rebecca and Jack Jr. I'm still working on contact with Rebecca, but I'm happy to say that Jack is coming in tomorrow to stay until the first of the year. I'll need to pick him up in the morning. She gets cryptic about some things, though. She keeps telling me to do something about my grandchild, and I keep telling her that I don't have one. She keeps bringing that up. She tells me that I'll be in touch, providentially, with a lot of my old friends and tells me to get closure. 'Closure on what?' I ask. Then she tells me that closure will come. She tells me, the same as Stanley has, to make a list of those things I always wanted to do but didn't—even if it means stepping out of normal restraints. So, Pat, watch out for what I might do. Prevent me from hurting other people if you can. Keep me in line if I get too wild. I don't plan to talk about my pending demise with anybody except you and Stanley, at least for a while or until I see it's obvious my behavior can be seen by others. I'm going to smoke my pipe because I enjoy it, and tobacco isn't going to kill me before this thing in my head does. I might drink a little more too, although I never cared much for alcohol. Elizabeth tells me to make my feelings toward those who offend me known to them, and that ought to be fun. She says that I should recognize people for the good they do and reward them, so I began with you. I urge her to move back into the house, but she refuses. Says she has to live in her little place on the side of the driveway along with the children. And the children come sometimes too. They haven't grown, but they're just as pretty and playful as ever. It sure is nice to be able to see them again."

Pat excuses herself, citing too much coffee, and manages to stifle her sobbing until she reached the hall half bath. *O Jesus*, she prayed, *take this burden from me. I can't do it. I'm going to burst out crying right in front of him, and I don't—no, can't—do that.* And Jesus calmed her but didn't remove the yoke of responsibility. She dried her eyes and straightened herself up and returned to the den.

"I'm happy to hear Jack is coming tomorrow. I'll have to pull out the recipe for pecan pie that he likes so well. Christmas will be so much better with him here."

J agrees and then continues, "I'm not sure what to do if the Wop, as you call her, does come back. If she does, providence is telling me something. Maybe she fits in somehow into completing the things I want to do. Pat, I use the term providence a lot, and you may think I use it loosely. I mean, Providence, with a capital P, to mean divine guidance. Providence, or God's guiding hand, causes things to happen for the fulfillment of his wishes. People cross paths providentially and good things happen. God guided Elizabeth into my path, and I will be forever grateful. God made me happy that day I met your mother, with the end result of your being here now. That's Providence. Providence is the road map of our lives. Providence leads us home. The word comes from Latin *providentia*, which means "foresight, prudence," from *pro*, "ahead," and *videre*, "to see." The current meaning of the word "divine providence" derives from the sense "knowledge of the future" or "omniscience," which is the privilege of God. The initial meaning of *provider* remains in "to provide," which means "to take precautionary measures."

December 22 began with rosy rays bursting over the leafless trees and into the warm kitchen of the Shalom house. This was going to be a wonderful day. Jack was arriving at the Columbia Airport (which is actually in West Columbia, if one wanted to be picky) after a series of flights beginning in Colorado Springs and the US Air Force Academy. Jack entered the Air Force upon graduation from the university and has been riding a fast track since. But why not? Jack had the looks of a Steve Canyon, tall (just over 6 feet 2 inches, slim, athletic build, classic features, impeccable manners, fluent in four languages, master's degree, and the ultimate in Officer Efficiency Reports [OER]). He somewhat followed his father's military specialties, but with less hand-to-hand training. Jack was finishing his assignment at the Air Force Academy and would be returning to the real world of Middle Eastern conflict, murder, and mayhem. Just where and in what capacity J was not privy to.

J finishes the morning TV news and the print news from the State and carefully checks his pockets for the absence of his pocket knife or other metal objects that might ring chimes tuned by airport security. He lights the slightly moist walnut/cherry blend and smiles when Blue Baby responded with a purr/growl when the ignition key was turned.

The traffic around the Metropolitan Columbia Airport is heavy, as might be expected on the eve of Christmas. Families are scurrying to meet relatives, and road warriors are returning home for the rest of the holiday season. J and Blue Baby drive through aisles of short-term parking spaces without success and begins the second round when J recognized a familiar figure walking out of one of the aisles on his way to the terminal. J stops and speaks to his longtime friend, Tom McLeish, another resident of the Blythewood Community. Tom explains that he is meeting his wife, Meg, who had been visiting children and grandchildren in Colorado. Tom told J that there is a vacant space right next to his SUV on the aisle he just walked out of. After a series of promises to get together during the season, J turns Blue Baby down the aisle, spots the space, and turns his left-turn signal on. As he begins his left turn into the space, a little red sports car zips into the vacant space. J rolls his window down and speaks to the young man, who is none other than Frank Lee Howell Jr. as he emerged from his car. "Young man, didn't you see my turn signal and see that I was turning into that space?" Young man answered curtly,

"Yes, I saw your signal but I'm in a hurry to meet my girlfriend and it pays to be swift and nimble, old man." J's mouth drops hearing this incredulous, rude, biting remark. He can't believe his ears! This is the Christmas season! This is the season when people should respect their elders and the courtesy of turn signals. Several flashbacks race through J's brain. The first is the snowy scene near the DMZ in Korea when he was a young lieutenant. His unit was ordered to move on short notice from their campsite shared with South Korean soldiers. The unit had been there for several months and had adopted a pregnant female mongrel dog and nursed her through her delivery of six pups. It was impossible to take the animal family with them so they were turned over to the South Korean troops to provide food and shelter for them, which they promised to do. As orders from higher military headquarters often go through the fog of war, the unit was ordered to return after a half day's march. When they returned to their camp, they were shocked and angered to see the Korean troops roasting the pups over the campfire. That was the first time the young lieutenant took command and ordered First Sergeant Hansen to put down his gun.

The second flashback is another military scene, this one coming from the jungles of Vietnam. The village of Quon Now was one of the pro-American ones then Major Stewart gathered intelligence from. He and his small group of sweat-stained "advisors" were quietly entering the village when it was suddenly taken over by the Vietcong. Women and children were bayoneted, and the grass-roofed houses were torched. There were no men in the village, and there were no firearms or means of defense whatsoever. Major Stewart and his men watched helplessly from their distance, unable to do anything, being seriously outnumbered. The cruelty of war left its indelible stamp in J's brain.

The third flashback is dated much earlier. As a boy of ten, J and his father were waiting in the local barber shop. One of the town leaders, maybe mayor, maybe just a prominent person, was dressed in his suit and tie and was having his shoes shined by the black shoeshine who had been crippled since birth. When the final tap on the bottom of the shoe came, indicating that the shine was complete, the Big Man in Town took two dimes and a nickel and threw them on the floor and laughed as the crablike shoeshine scurried to pick up the coins.

The final flashback is a replay of the scene of Frank forcing Marie into that same red Mazda, insisting that she go for the abortion he had arranged.

J also remembers the messages from Dr. Woods and from Elizabeth: Do those things you want to do and feel that should be done. Life is short, particularly yours, they told him.

The young man has now disappeared, after smiling and displaying a digit.

J places Blue Baby's transmission drive in park, leaving it where it was in the middle to the parking aisle, and marches over to the offensive sports car, pulls out a wooden match from his shirt pocket, and proceeds to deflate the tires of the vivid little red car. Impatient drivers are backed up, unable to drive around Blue Baby, and begin honking their car horns. J ignores them and continues his delightful revenge. Airport security arrives just as J is finishing deflating the last tire. "Sir, what are you doing? You can't just leave your truck in the middle of the aisle. This is one of the busiest days of the year. Please get in and move it." J is moving in the direction of compliance when the security guard notices the four flat tires and J calmly replacing the wooden match in his shirt pocket.

The security guard is shocked. He thought he's seen everything during his career as a law enforcement officer and as an airport security guard, but he is wrong. With flushed face and bulging eyes and swelling neck veins, the security guard yells, "What in the hell do you think you're doing? You let the air out of all four tires! What's going on?"

J calmly approaches the security guard and stretches his hands out, smiles, and says, "I let the air out of all four tires on that car, just as you said. I have committed a crime. I think it is probably vandalism. I'm guilty. Put the cuffs on me and arrest me."

The guard stares at J with his mouth open for a second and then takes action in the order of priority, just as his training dictated. *Got to take care of the traffic first,* his mind tells him. He orders J to move Blue Baby to the side to allow for traffic to flow again, receives the keys to Blue Baby when he requests them, and begins to direct traffic, at the same time requesting backup via his radio secured to his lapel. After many minutes of ironing out the mass confusion of traffic control, backup arrives from both directions, complete with flashing lights and revolving beacons. By this time, the planes bearing Colorado passengers have arrived; and among those walking up to the crime scene are Tom McLeish, his wife Meg, and J's son Jack, still in uniform. They arrive just in time to hear J tell the security guard supervisor while standing in front of him with his arms outstretched, "Sir, like I told your officer, I have committed a crime. I have let the air out of an arrogant young man's car tires, therefore committing at least vandalism.

JERRY HAMMET & HAROLD GUERRY

I am guilty and as visible as a red-ass snake. I did it. I was caught in the act, and I would do it again. Handcuff me and arrest me."

The supervisor complies but explains, "Okay, sir. You seem to insist that I do something, but we do not handcuff in that way. To leave you handcuffed with your hands in front of you will give you the advantage of one large fist instead of two and will allow you to possibly beat the crap out of me. Turn around, and I'll oblige you by cuffing you with your hands behind your back. I'm not, even though you might insist, going to chain your legs. It appears to me that you might have trouble walking from here to the terminal with no chains on. Get in the security truck, and we'll haul you off somewhere."

Tom enters the verbal fray by asking what the problem was. The security supervisor declines to answer, but J quickly tells Tom and Meg and Jack the whole story. Tom is the former editor of the *State Newspaper*. He tells J that he'll make sure to keep the story out of the news, but J quickly disagrees. "No, Tom. This is news. Let it be known."

At this moment, Frank Howell Jr., with a long-legged honey blonde on his arm, arrives. He identifies himself as the owner of the Mazda and receives the news of the incident. When asked if he wanted to press charges, Frank quickly agrees. "Throw the book at the old son of a bitch. He's already stuck his nose in my business and needs some toning down. My dad'll see he gets some jail time for this."

Ms. Blonde Long Legs asks Frank who J is, to which Frank answers loudly, "Oh, he's just a disgruntled old fart who pickled his brains in Vietnam and does something at the university. Pushes race relations and considers his self to be a friend to the black janitors and generally butts in where he's not needed. Don't worry about him. My dad runs Columbia, and he'll put old fartface away in the looney bin where he belongs. Let's go get a taxi and get out of here."

Tom yells to J, "J, if you want publicity, you've got it! I'll take care of it!"

Jack identifies himself as J's son and is successful in retrieving the keys to Blue Baby and promises to move it. When asked about his father's behavior, Jack has nothing to offer but follows the entourage to the airport security office. The security supervisor catches up with Frank Howell Jr. and tells him it is necessary to file paperwork in the security office if he intends to press charges.

Meanwhile, the airport security director is in a state of great distress. He is talking on the phone to the airport operations director. "Dan, I need your help. Please come over to the security office as soon as you can. I know you know Dr. J from the university. Well, it seems as if some young punk pulled in to a parking space, cutting him off, and then laughed at him. Dr. J then proceeds to let the air out of his tires. He was seen doing this by the security officer, and he admits and wants to be cuffed and arrested. On top of that, Tom McLeish is one of J's friends, as many of us are, and he's going to put the story in the newspaper. The kid with the flat tires is Frank Howell's boy, and they're all going to end up in this office in just a minute or two. This could be real messy, and I need you here from the get-go." The only sound the security director hears is the sound of scurrying and a click.

The security director's premonition proved to be quite correct. Just as the airport operations director pulled up to the security building, the WIS TV News camera crew was parking. Before he could enter the building, two Lexington county deputies with blue lights flashing turned in (much to the delight of the camera crew), followed by an unmarked black Mercury sedan, with its lights beaconing through the front and rear windows, obviously the car belonging to Sheriff Jimmy Spears, the high sheriff of Lexington County. The last of the entourage was a car belonging to Steve Montgomery, crime reporter for the State. Already inside are Dr. J, his son, the security officer who saw the crime in progress, the security shift supervisor, the airport security director, Frank Howell Jr. and Ms. Blonde Long Legs. All were serious as pallbearers except for Frank Howell Jr., who has a smirk on his face and Ms. Blonde Long Legs, who is shivering and has tears forming in the edges of her large blue eyes.

A long and sometimes heated discussion follows. J is asked again what happened, after having had his Miranda rights read to him, and he declined counsel. J maintains his guilt and is ready to face the proper punishment. Frank is asked if he really wants to press charges and he answers, "Hell yes!" and is about to pontificate about the prisoner and what he deserves, which brought a curt reminder from the security director that he didn't allow such profanity in his presence. After a short semiprivate conversation between the deputies, the sheriff, the security director and the airport operations, Sheriff Spears declared that the Lexington County sheriff's office had jurisdiction and would take care of the prisoner. Frank Howell Jr. protests, expounds on "good ole boy politics," how his father will have their asses and profanes some more. This time Sheriff Spears approaches Frank and in a calm, low, authoritative, advisory voice that would have frozen equator water and tells young Frank where the county line begins and ends, that there are two separate and distinct counties and political systems, that he will not allow profane words and precisely whose ass will be had when and where and under what circumstances. Frank's smirk disappears and his face turned an ashy gray color. Ms. Blonde Long Legs begins to cry. J turned around to see if Elizabeth was there because he distinctly heard her say, "Yes!"

Sheriff Spears turned to J and told him that a hearing before a magistrate could be arranged and he would more than likely be allowed to go home after posting bond. J shook his head. "Is this usual, Jimmy? Are magistrate's courts usually called into session on occasions like this?"

Sheriff Spears said it was not, but J says, "When is it usual to go before the magistrate?" Sheriff Spears told him that magistrate's court usually convened about nine the next morning, and J said, "Then that's what we should do. I shouldn't expect any special treatment and I don't. Take me to jail." Steve Montgomery, the newspaper reporter, almost broke his ballpoint pen. After glances to each other all around the room, Sheriff Spears tells one of the deputies to take the prisoner to Lexington. The other deputy whispers in the sheriff's ear that there has been a wreck on I-26, and he needed to assist. The sheriff nodded and the second deputy leaves, followed by the WIS TV News Crew. They are about to leave when Frank speaks. "Sheriff Spears, this is obviously a hostile environment. I am requesting that one of your deputies escort me to the county line because I think I might be harassed."

The deputy assigned to transport J was instructed to escort Mr. Howell and his party to the county line and return for Dr. J. Airport security officers report that they have arranged for Frank's tires to be inflated; and since there was no sign of other tire damage, he was ready to go.

The deputy politely escorts Frank and Ms. Blonde Long Legs out. Ms. Long Legs seems hesitant, but Frank pulls her by the arm, almost enough to cause her to fall.

The remaining group sits and coffee is served and they chat about better times.

An hour passes and the deputy has not returned. Sheriff Spears calls and receives this explanation. It seems as if Frank and his friend get in his car, after an inspection to verify there was no damage, Frank backed out, squealed his tires, turned out of the parking aisle, and almost hit an elderly couple walking to their car. The deputy stopped Frank and gave him a ticket for speeding in the parking lot and reckless driving. Frank rolled up the car window after receiving the ticket and mouthed several obscenities and drove off. He drove to the exit, paid for his parking time, and squealed tires again, reaching sixty-three miles per hour in a twenty-five-mile-an-hour zone, and the deputy stopped him again and gave him a speeding ticket. Frank repeats his thinly veiled disrespect and drove off again, only to run a stop sign. The deputy explained that he stopped Mr. Howell Jr. once more and was writing the ticket when Ms. Blonde Long Legs opened the door and attempted to leave but was forcibly pulled back by Frank. This was repeated twice more until the deputy intervened. Ms. Long Legs was screaming that Frank had hurt her and she wanted out of the car and out of his sight. The deputy asked if she wished to press charges for assault. She said she does and would if she could do it soon because she really wanted to get back to the terminal and go home. The deputy called for backup and a tow truck, arrested Frank for assault, and had the other deputy transport Frank to the Lexington County Jail. He said he was advising Ms. Blonde Long Legs that she would have to return to testify when Frank's court date came up and was transporting her back to the terminal so she could receive medical attention and book a flight back to wherever she came from. The deputy apologized for the delay but would be there shortly to transport Dr. J. Professionalism ruled supreme as Sheriff only said, "I see. Thanks," but could not stifle a smile and did not share that information with any present.

The events that follow are pretty routine for booking, turning over valuables, suicide prevention, issuance of orange suits, and obtaining instructions. J is escorted to a cell shared by twelve other men, and the door is locked.

Frank's situation was a little different. When given the opportunity to have his phone call, he called home, hoping to get his father and update him on the Lexington County injustices he has just endured. However, his mother answered and refused to talk to him but insisted on talking to the attending officer. Mrs. Howell was obviously intoxicated and obviously unhappy. It seems as if she found out that her husband, who was allegedly hunting with friends and could not be reached, was in fact spending these few pre-Christmas days with a lady friend in a luxury suite in Greenville. Mrs. Howell was preparing to travel there for a holiday surprise, if she could find the door and the gun. And as to Frank Jr., he could rot in the same place that Frank Sr. was going; and besides, he wasn't Frank's son at all. Mrs. Howell requested that the clerk tell, "The cocky little son of a bitch, this is a good time to cool his heels." The clerk smiled at the irony of Mrs. Howell's description of her son, thanked her for providing much more information than was necessary, and then took steps to dispatch a Richland County deputy or a Columbia city police person to Mrs. Howell's house to be sure she didn't attempt to drive. Frank was also suited in orange but placed in another holding "tank."

J and his new found associates eyed each other. Five were young black men, approximate ages twenty-two to thirty. Three others were older white fellows, aged between forty-five and sixty. One was a young redheaded man, about eighteen. Another was a dark-haired man, approximately eighteen. An old, over seventy-five years old black male and an equally as old white man rounded out the dozen.

One of the young men called out, "Hey, old dude, whatcha in here fo?

J straight-facedly replied, "I let the air out of a young man's car tires at the airport." Gales of laughter followed. "Whatcha do dat fo, ole dude?" the young questioner followed up with. One of the middle-aged men yelled, "Don't answer that! You've already said too much! Never, never, never say you're guilty or you did something! You don't have to say anything!"

Another young verbally pointed out that there's always an outhouse lawyer in every crowd, and the last speaker was that group's. One of the older men said, "I've been in and out of here at least six times a year for the last twenty years, and I've never heard of somebody going to jail for letting air out of tires. Come clean. That can't be the whole story." Outhouse Lawyer warned again, "Don't say anything. Sit down in the corner and wait till tomorrow and get out. You've got your rights." J ignored the advice and shared the story, much to the delight of the group. Before long, each person gave a brief summary of why they were there. The first inquisitor answered why he was there by saying, "Me and Joree here was gettin' in a little tussle" and was interrupted by Joree. "Tussle my ass! You wuz trying to kill me!" Then laughed. A third man spoke up, "Yeah, it looked kinda serious to me too. Guess I shouldn't of pulled out my pistol because that's how I got here." J asked innocently, "Why were you and Joree fighting? You seem to be friends."

Speaker number one laughed and said, "Well, it's like this. Me and Joree be seeing the same lady and he found out about it and loss he temper and was being rude so I had to tek him down a little."

J shook his head and asked when supper would be served, which resulted in another peal of laughter. "Why don't you order us up some poke ribs and chittlins, ole dude? I'm sure they would be happy to take your order." Mr. Sarcastic suggested.

J replied, "You know, I think I will place an order. How do I do it?" Laughter again. One experienced person advised J to make a noise against the bars to get the jailer's attention and added that the jailer would come right away and be happy to help. (Mr. Sarcasm number two).

J did make a noise, and sure enough, the jailer did come. J asked what was for supper and when it might be served. The jailer advised that it would be served when the cook thought it should be and the fare would be to the cook's choosing. What followed amazed everyone. J suggested that he thought his son was still around, making cell phone calls (no pun intended) to Pat, Tom McLeish, and others and that he had given Jack his billfold and to please Jack to get something special for all of them. The cell occupants laughed and booed because the jailer just shook his head and walked away without a reply.

When the jailer returned to the desk, he found Sheriff Spears was there. He was still shaking his head and was telling the sheriff he had seen it all, that one of the prisoners wanted him to send out for dinner and he would pay for it. Sheriff Spears says, "And I'll bet that prisoner was Dr. J." The jailer looked up in surprise and says, "You mean the old guy who looks like Dirty Harry? It was." Sheriff Spears gave him another surprise. He said, "I'll get his son. He's still hanging around—on the phone outside, I think. I think that's a good idea."

Jack was summoned and was, to the amazement of the other prisoners, allowed to go back and speak to his father. J suggested that Jack look in his cell phone directory and call Joe Don Danny Best and see if he could deliver a Big Joe and french fries and a large Pepsi for everybody, including the jailer, Jack, the sheriff, and anybody else on duty. When J heard there was another cell with another six men, plus a cell of eight women, he insisted they be included too. Jack received permission from the sheriff, then called Joe Don Danny and found him to be on duty at the West Columbia store. It seemed as if Joe Don Danny was the owner of the Hoggy Park Barbecue chain, had an MBA and a master's in philosophy, but still insisted on working a shift a week at one of his stores. After many questions about Dr. J and why he was in jail, which Jack deflected, saying he wasn't allowed to have that conversation at the time, Joe Don Danny began the preparation of thirty-seven Big Joes with the trimmings. There was new respect for the old dude, whose dastardly act was deflating tires.

After the unexpected somewhat-catered meal (nothing sharp to eat with, all wrappings had to be accounted for so they could not be used to stop up the toilet and other precautions required by jailhouse rules), the gang of twelve settled down. J spent the night getting to know each of the men individually. One of the last ones was the redheaded kid who sat in the corner and never smiled. J approached him and asked what he was there for. The young man answered that he had gone to a high school-sponsored dance that late afternoon and slipped out of a door, returned to his car where his friend was, and was about to take a sip of vodka out of his friend's bottle when he was caught by the female deputy on the school campus. He was turned over to the school authorities at school and, at the deputy's insistence, was charged with possessing alcohol on school property, was arrested, and was brought to jail. He too was scheduled to go before the magistrate the next morning. The young man began to say, "It was . . .," before being interrupted by J.

J says, "You were going to tell me it was your friend's fault, weren't you? But it wasn't. You and you alone are responsible for your actions. You took action on your own to leave your date and to find an unmanned exit to slip out of and probably jimmied the lock so you could get back in undetected." J took this thought, and the two talked for two hours about the recognition of the need to be responsible for a person's decisions and ultimate actions. At the end of two hours, the young man confided in J that he had spent the hours in the cell deciding that he was going to drop out of school and try to join the military now that his life was ruined. J nodded his head and then talked to him about providential happenings, particularly that of throwing the two of them together in an unlikely place. In another hour, J convinced the young man that he had a great future ahead and that quitting was not the answer or even an option. Together they planned an approach for facing the young man's parents and eventually his girlfriend and then the school authorities.

This was not the only person providentially touched by J. The two shoplifters lost their belligerence and their thoughts of entitlement. Joree and his one-time friend agreed that their mutual girlfriend needed to be dropped and that maybe moving out of town and temptation was the answer. The alcoholic asked for an AA group he could join, after J's explanation of the twelve steps.

Dawn came with the last of the twelve, falling on his knees and asking for a road map for a different life. Court time came. Only then did J learn that WIS TV presented a "Breaking News" segment about a popular university professor being incarcerated for letting the air out a senator's son.

Dr. Stanley Woods sat down for his morning coffee and had to redress because he spilled the Columbian blend down his shirt as he opened the *State* to the inch-high front page of the Metro section headlines: Distinguished USC Faculty Member Arraigned for Malicious Vandalism.

WIS TV News crew set up outside the courtroom, along with WOLO TV, the *Rock Hill Herald*, the *State*, and the *Orangeburg Democrat* newspaper reporters.

The judge entered, the bailiff demanded "All rise," and court began. When J's case was called, the judge asked if he was represented by counsel, to which he replied he had none, leaving confused looks on the six attorneys present—all ready, willing, and able to represent him. The judge opened his mouth but stifled the adage that he thought about, that being that when representing oneself in court is tantamount to having a fool for a client.

He did ask why J was handcuffed. The officer answered, "Sir, he told us that he was a person with a violent temper, triggered by his idea of another's inappropriate behavior, and that he might just do something wild and crazy. He wanted to be shackled, but we decided they weren't really necessary."

The judge replied, half under his breath, "I agree with that." The judge proceeded, "What is this man charged with?"

"Vandalism, sir" was the answer.

"Can you give me a further explanation?"

The deputy went into detail about the incident, what the trigger was according to J, and J's admission, even insistence, of being guilty.

The judge turned to J and asked, "Sir, what do you have to say for yourself?"

J declared, "Sir, I plead guilty. If I had immediately recognized the young man driving the car that took what I considered my parking spot and had signaled for it was a popular student at the university, whose father is a senator, a fellow Rotarian, a member of Trinity Cathedral, and a lawyer, I might have thought twice before I did what I did. My actions are not acceptable in this society. What I did was wrong. But to be very honest with you, after thinking it over carefully, I would do it again."

The laughter in the courtroom was finally quelled by repeated blows from the judge's gavel.

"Do you have anything else to say, sir?"

"No, sir."

"The sentence is $350 or fifteen days in jail," the judge declared and banged his gavel. With that, he summoned Frank Howell Jr. to the bench. "I understand you signed the complaint. Is that correct?"

Frank replied only with a barely audible "Yeah."

The judge winced and said, "Would that be a 'yes, sir?'"

Frank caught on and replied, "Yes, sir."

"Approach the bench."

Frank stepped forward, and the judge leaned over and told Frank in a low whisper, "This has got to be the damn dumbest thing I have ever heard a person doing. If the complaint had come from that man instead of from you and if there was a law that made rudeness and crass behavior manifested by taking a parking place that you knew someone else had their eyes on, even to the point of signaling, I would have sentenced you to the maximum fine *and* jail time. Now go over there and sulk and wait your turn to be heard."

Upon exiting from the courtroom, J was greeted and congratulated by the six attorneys, all of whom had represented J on separate matters, students, fellow faculty members. Dr. Stanley Woods was there too but was very serious. When Stanley becomes excited or agitated, he stutters. "G-g-g-g . . ." He tried to get out, but J stops him.

He lays a hand on Stanley's shoulder and says, "Stanley, don't say it. Don't take the Lord's name in vain. We're Presbyterian, and we don't do that." Still frustrated, Stanley begins again,

"Okay, J. But you're a d-d-d-d damn fool! Did something click in your head, or is this your idea of fun?"

J smiles and says, "Stanley, you yourself told me that I should do those things I had never done before but thought I should. I made a list of things I hadn't done, and one of them was being arrested and put in jail. I've been detained and imprisoned as a POW and held in captivity, but never arrested. It was a good experience to be jailed. Providentially, I think I did some good. As well as I can count, I converted at least eight, saved a suicide, and brought reason to the lives of the others. And I enjoyed the hell out of deflating young Howell's tires. Don't worry about me yet. I had all of my faculties during this whole time. Just took your advice a little too literally. Besides, Elizabeth approved." Stanley looked at J, shook his head, and walked off.

The hardened criminal, proven guilty of deflating tires, is turned over to the care of Jack and is escorted to the clerk where the fine is paid. Free at last!

Jack and J find their way to faithful Blue Baby and they travel home to Shalom. Pat and Hab are waiting on them. Pat and Jack hug as old friends plus should. Jack meets Hab for the first time, and Hab is duly impressed with this tall, handsome air force officer with the quick smile and infectious laugh. J interrupts and declares that he has not had a decent breakfast and sure would appreciate Pat stirring something up. He asks, "What can you fix us in a hurry? If we don't eat pretty soon, it'll be time for lunch."

Pat replied whimsically, "Well, Dr. J, I had in mind some jailhouse pie or some fried jailbird fingers. Will that be okay, Dr. Old Dude?"

During and after breakfast, the four of them sat around the plantation table and shared what had been happening in their lives over the past fourteen years. Hab had to tell Jack about his mother's graduation and how proud he was of her accomplishment.

At almost noon, Pat told J and Jack that she had prepared some lunch and left it in the refrigerator for whenever they were hungry again and excused herself. "It's Christmas Eve, you know, and there are a few things I need to do. Got to pick up a few more things for tomorrow. Remember, the limit is sixteen, and that includes the four of us. Please don't have any last-minute invitations because we talked about it being nice to have everybody sitting at the table, and I don't want to eat in the kitchen." J nodded in reluctant agreement.

J and Jack talked and sat on the rock while J smoked, after Jack found some more comfortable clothes left over from an earlier visit, warm enough to be able to sit on the cold rock. They nibbled on the things they were allowed to have from the refrigerator then dressed and rode into Winnsboro to attend the evening candlelight Christmas Eve service at the Presbyterian Church.

Christmas day blew in. The whole South Carolina Midlands is under a tornado watch, and winds blew up to forty miles an hour for minutes at the time. But as fast moving weather systems do, it all blew over; and the sun came out around eleven.

Pat and Hab joined J and Jack for breakfast and for gift exchanges. J's Christmas shopping abilities were sorely lacking. Jack was given a generous check, Hab was given a business envelope with cash, and Pat was given a box filled with shredded paper with the cancelled promissory note for her car in the bottom.

Jack was dispatched in Blue Baby to pick up Mrs. Elizabeth Baker and Mrs. Harriett Hollis from the Everlasting Assisted Living Facility in Blythewood. J used Pat's Oldsmobile to collect Dr. Bubba, Charlsie Varnadore, and Eulalia Heffney from their respective houses in the rural areas. A second trip by Jack resulted in the collection of Sergeant

Christopher from the William Jennings Bryan Dorn Veteran's Hospital in Columbia.

J, as he had explained to Jack the evening before, has been hosting a South Carolina Christmas dinner to a dozen people, longtime acquaintances from a number of sources, all being people who would otherwise be alone on this celebration of Christ's birthday. Mrs. Hollis taught Sunday school and kept the church nursery years ago when Jack was growing up. Mrs. Baker is a native of Connecticut. She met her husband, a South Carolina Midlands native, while he served on a submarine crew at Groton, Connecticut, in World War II. Before his last cruise, she moved to South Carolina to live with his widowed mother until his return, which never happened. The submarine was sunk by German torpedoes in the North Atlantic, she later learned. Elizabeth Baker was the daughter-in-law who assumed the role of Naomi from the Book of Ruth and stayed with the senior Mrs. Baker until her passing. Elizabeth was the seamstress at Patrones Dry Cleaners until Joe Patrone died. Charlsie Varnadore has outlived his family by about eighteen years now and lives alone. Charlsie made his living as a pulpwood truck driver during the week and the pastor of the Fourth Precious Memories African Methodist Episcopal Church located between Flopeye and Ridgeway. Eulalia Heffney also lived alone with her memories, minimum social security, and her black cat Comfort. Eulalia fortunately or unfortunately, depending on one's perception, possessed extrasensory skills and made her living as Madam Eulalia, soothsayer, palm reader, fortune teller, and spiritual advisor, working from her little house beside Highway 21. People recognized her abilities, which was fortunate, but because of this recognition, most people avoided her. Most of her clients during the day were tourists, but her local spiritual advise was dispensed late at night by locals who entered through the back door. Almost all of that was in the past now, except for responding to a coded knock on the door when there was no moon to accommodate a soul in torture. Dr. Bubba has been described earlier. Sergeant Christopher, from the Veteran's Hospital, spent his military career much the same as J, serving as the sergeant major in army combat units beginning with World War II and ending with Vietnam. Josiah Christopher played the part of Santa Claus before his combat wounds prevented him from continuing. His great white beard and rotund girth, combined with his deep, authoritative voice, added to his authenticity. His family was now decimated. One son, whose looks duplicate Josiah's, lives in Darlington and is busy playing Santa to nursing homes in Darlington and Florence. His grandchildren look upon Josiah as an old fool they are ashamed of who is living in his past fantasies and have not visited him in years.

Picture, if you will, this group as they assembled. Mrs. Hollis was dressed to the nines, with a beautiful red suit, a large pin on her left chest that had holly berries, glittering silver tinsel, green holly leaves, and a small impish Santa's elf peering out of the holly. She wore a hat, with the front brim smartly snapped down, resembling a hat that Dick Tracy would have worn, but trimmed with a tall, curling, red feather. Mrs. Baker maneuvered her green walker with wheels, complete with a fold out seat. She was dressed in a comfortable velour green leisure suit, big fluffy shoes, and a red boa wrapped around her neck. Madam Eulalia wore her working clothes. Her head was bound in a turban with a large crescent holding a plume of feathers together on the front, her large round earrings framed her dark skinned, finely chiseled facial features. She wore a shawl over her shoulder, with an artificial owl mounted on her right shoulder. She relied heavily on her walking cane adorned with a carved handle, depicting the face of a monkey. Eulalia walked in a perpetually bent over position, duplicating the stance of a vulture looking for a meal. Both Dr. Bubba and Reverend Charlsie Varnadore were dressed impeccably in their black double-breasted suits. The significant difference between the two is the size of the individuals. Dr. Bubba's suit was a size fifty-two while Reverend Charlsie's was size forty. Dr. Bubba wore his usual bowler hat, and Reverend Charlsie wore a fedora. Shoes were shined to perfection, although holes in the soles could be visible to the careful observer. Dr. Charlsie wore a large ornate cross on a gold chain around his neck. Sergeant Christopher was dressed in his hospital issued sweat suit but had his Santa cap covering his shiny bald head. The Sergeant also used a walker, one with front wheels and rubber-tipped rear legs.

This unlikely band of living history, plus J, Jack, Pat, and Hab, sat down to a South Carolina Country Christmas of sweet potatoes baked in their skins, rice with giblet gravy, collard greens, diced rutabaga, barbecue with mustard sauce, fried turkey, cornbread dressing, and dropped cat-head biscuits, pecan pie with whipped cream and full strength Yuban coffee. Charlsie Varnadore provided the blessing of great length, and Eulalia Heffney predicted a year of great adventure for the first eleven months and refused to comment further.

In midafternoon, the icons of an illustrious past were delivered back to their small probably terminal dwelling places, filled with the largesse of South Carolina simple cuisine and recollected memories to sort out and embellish. Each recognized that the scene of this dinner would probably not be duplicated. Most of them didn't comment on Madame Eulalia's predictions but all thought of the possible ways of when their lives would end, with the distinct, odds on chances that none of them would see another Christmas. All wished for a swift and painless end, or as close to that as possible. All had deep Christian beliefs of the promised hereafter, with the possible exception of Eulalia. Who knows about Eulalia? She remains a woman of mystery, even to the end. These are the things that old, infirm people whose interests and activities are limited by circumstances think about. The specter of reality is always with them.

At six in the evening, as agreed upon, J and Jack called Rebecca, J's daughter, who was spending her holidays with her in-laws. The long conversation contained the usual expressions of holiday best wishes and promises of more visits in the New Year. After that, J put on his heavy coat, took his pipe and the walnut/cherry blend, and headed for his rock for his time to recap the day's activities with Elizabeth.

Over the next five days, J and Jack spent most of their time together. Sometimes they would sit on the rock, sometimes walking in the woods and around the pond, sometimes in the comfort of J's study, where each could sink into the leather chairs in front of the fireplace. Among their discussions were Jack's career and his pending reassignment to the Middle East, Rebecca's career and husband, J's current situation (without any mention of his brain tumor), weather, local happenings, national and state politics, cabbages and kings, and other things in true Lewis Carroll style, including J's financial portfolio.

Jack was ending his tour of duty at the Air Force Academy and had been offered an assignment as an intelligence officer in the Saudi Arabian consulate and an associated promotion to lieutenant colonel. There was a short unproductive discussion of Jack's family plans, Jack having none. Jack asked his father for comments on what he had told him of his plans, to which J replies, "Jack, if you'll remember, I told you and your sister that I really don't care what you did in life as long as you were doing something that is of benefit to mankind and that hopefully you would earn enough income to live comfortably and that I would like to see you happily married and give me the pleasure of grandchildren. Those were, and still are, the only items of my advice. I am happy with your decisions, whatever they are."

December 30, the day of Jack's departure, came sooner than expected or wanted. Pat volunteered to take Jack to the airport, giving them a chance to talk of their own cabbages and kings and other things. J consented for several reasons. The first was that he hated good-byes, and it would be easier to say good-bye to Jack with Elizabeth standing next to him. The second was that he sensed there was a need for Jack and Pat to have some time together, and the third was that the chirping sounds in the back of his head were almost deafening this morning, and he had a hint of vertigo as he got out of bed. After throat-choking good-byes, Pat and Jack drove off, leaving J to his pipe, his heavy coat, and his rock.

December 31 produced cold temperatures, no programmed things that needed to be done, and a colorful Rose Parade preparation program on television. Thus ends the first year of the rest of J's life, however long that might be.

DR. J'S JANUARY 2008

THE CLEAR, COLD (for the South Carolina Midlands) peered out from its blanket of frost. This is the ninth day of Christmas, and according to folklore and Madam Eulalia, this day generally predicts the weather for September 2008. Interpreted, the month will be dry (good news for coastal citizens who watch and wait for hurricanes) and cool (also good news of respite from a scorching summer), and winds will be calm. The full moon is on the wane; therefore, hogs should not be killed because bacon made from their salt-cured bellies will shrink. This is the day that your true love will send you nine ladies dancing to go along with the accumulation of the eight maids a-milking, seven swans a-swimming, six geese a-laying, five golden rings, four calling birds, three French hens, two turtle doves, and the Christmas day gift of the partridge in a pear tree. The day of epiphany is approaching, so thought should be given to plans for the New Year to be announced on this day of preparation for a sudden intuitive perception into the essential meaning of something, precipitated by a providential act. Also, the Magi are on their way to view the newborn Jesus, having gotten lost and forgetting to ask their wives for direction.

J dutifully spent as much time as the temperature would allow sitting on his rock, sharing ideas for the future with Elizabeth. Pat and Hab spent hours on storing Christmas decorations securely, labeling each box as to the contents. They, of course, had been taken down before the end of the year. Bad luck will surely follow you during the New Year if one does not remove those things from their decorated positions before the stroke of midnight on December 31. (It's okay to *store* them later.) The smell of cooked collard greens, served each New Year's Day, along with black-eyed peas and rice, was just now being dissipated from the kitchen. Things were on their way back to normal, if there is ever such a thing as normal. Pat mused about that as she busied herself. "What's normal? What's ever normal in Dr. J's life? What to expect this year? When will the brain tumor manifest itself?"

All of these thoughts were interrupted by the observant Hab, who asked, "What you thinking about so hard, Mama?" It was indeed a day for thought.

Just before dark, an unfamiliar car made itself down the circuitous driveway. The cargo was Marie, delivered by a young man of about her age. As usual, and to Pat's frustration, J announced that they were just in time for supper. After the young man unloaded Marie's luggage, they entered the Shalom kitchen where Young Man was introduced to Pat and Hab. After the hastily and tastefully prepared meal, Young Man excused himself to return to the university campus.

While Pat and Hab tended to the meal cleanup, J invited Marie to his den. After the pleasantries of how things went during her absence, J asks, "And how did things go at home?"

Marie replied that things had gone extremely well. She had not varied from her plan and had told her parents nothing about her pending motherhood.

J, in an unusually frank manner, asks after acknowledging her report, "Marie, what can I do for you now?"

Marie's equally straightforward answer was "Provide me a place to stay until the baby comes. I'll do what work I can for you and others, and I'll repay you in some manner at some time in the future."

J asks, "Do you feel you will feel comfortable living in a house in the country with an old man?"

Marie smiled and says, "I don't think you would do me any harm."

J's response is "I guess you're right about that. Let's do this. Let us sit down together in the morning and sit down with all of our proposals. I'll have to come up with some idea of paying you for your work, where it might be done, and so on. Take this writing pad and write out your thoughts and hopes and I'll do the same on this pad." Each took their respective yellow legal pads, agreeing on the plan. J called Pat and told her that Marie would be spending the night in the downstairs guest room and to please check it for any last-minute items of comfort. Marie was standing facing J, and Pat was standing behind her when she received this request. She moved her head slightly, and her eyes flashed. Dr. J responded by one of his looks easily interpreted to mean "I don't want to hear about it now. We'll talk later."

Pat called for Hab to help with Marie's luggage and walked heavily down the hall without a further comment. When finished, she and Hab drove home.

J thought, "The song says, 'nine ladies dancing,' but I've managed to get two ladies dancing in different expressions. Not what I was hoping for."

The tenth day of Christmas was much like the ninth, but with the promised addition of ten lords a-leaping. "God help me," conjuring up the mental picture of Henny Youngman's *men in tights*.

After breakfast and J making a mental note of speaking to Marie about her cleavage, "Or maybe I'll get Pat to talk to her about that," the two prospective business partners retired to J's den.

J began, "One important thing that I usually forget to do so I'm doing this first is to have you fill out this IRS withholding form, which will allow some social security funds to be credited to your account for some time in the future."

Marie followed the instruction, filled out the form, and returned it to J. J looked at it and then back at Marie with the question, "Sister Marie Tradonio?"

"Yes. When my mother was giving birth to me, there were a number of complications. Our local priest and a nun, Sister Marie, came to sit with my father. The doctor would enter the hospital waiting room occasionally and kept giving negative reports on the prognosis of the birth and even my mother's life expectancy. My father turned to the num and told her that if she would pray for them and help get his wife safely through this crisis and deliver a healthy child, he would name the girl after her. All did go well after a rapid, unexpected turnaround. And therefore, I am Sister Marie Tradonio. I'll admit it's a little unusual, but thankfully the priest brought Sister Marie. Otherwise I might be named Brother Francis!" Both Marie and J got a good laugh from that story.

J told Marie, "I'm glad you can laugh. It's the first time I've seen a smile on your face, and I hope in days to come that I'll see many more of them."

J takes the lead in the business discussion. "What do you expect to be paid?"

Marie replied that she didn't know, but would like to accumulate enough to pay for the delivery of her expected child, with a cushion for possible complications.

J said, "There's something I need to tell you. I received a call from your former boyfriend's father a couple of days ago. He is concerned about the direction his son's life appears to be taking and has had some comeuppances in his own life in the past month, and he and his wife agree that they should take some steps to save their future plans for him. They have conveyed through attorneys that they will appreciate it if I would talk to you and tell you he is willing to assume all doctor and hospital and any other medical costs associated with the delivery of your child and give you a sum of money to compensate you for the time you must take out of your life regarding the carrying, birth, and care of your child. In addition, he, his wife, and his son will provide you with a legal document that they will not divulge any information about your relationship with their son and asked that you provide them with a similar document that declares that you will never divulge your relationship with their son, never name him in any paternity suit, never use his name in the child's name, and agree to the confidentiality of the receipt of any money from them. I told him that I would discuss this with you and would pass along your answer."

Marie, of course, vented her anger and frustration, declaring that she didn't appreciate being bribed, that she didn't want anything from any of them, that she would take care of herself and her child and that the whole family could go to hell and she wasn't going to sign or promise anything.

J acknowledged the validity of her response, but added, "Marie, I totally understand. However, let me warn you and advise you that Frank's father won't be at all happy with your response. He wants desperately to sweep all of this under the rug, so to speak. He wants to get this whole thing behind him, regardless of the monetary cost. You see, he has plans for his son. He has mapped out a career for him in politics. As soon as he graduates from law school and gets a couple of years in a law firm of his father's choosing, he will have him appointed to important boards then orchestrate his running for the state house of representatives, and then senate, and then the governor's office, and then the national offices. Maybe I shouldn't tell you this, but he told me that his son has a promising career and life ahead of him and he doesn't need to be married to or associated with a Yankee Wop. I guess you know that refers to those of Italian descent."

"I'm all too familiar with that term, thank you. I grew up with it. I was referred to as 'Wop Baby' by many people I could have called polocks, spiks, slantheads, chinks, japs, and niggers but didn't. My father uses those terms on a daily basis, but I can't stand to disrespect people like that."

J added that he was glad to hear of her abhorrence of derogatory words like that because they were not tolerated in his presence.

Marie continued, "I don't think I could live with myself if I thought I had hooked Frank by getting pregnant and that I had misused him. I got myself into this mess, and I'll get myself out of it by the grace of God and help from you. You can assure Pop that I don't want anything else to do with his pretty little son who can't keep his pants zipped or his hands off people who want to get away from him."

J acknowledged the tirade but reserved the right to return to the subject. J didn't tell Marie that he had been brought up to speed by Tom McLeish, who told him about Frank's father being visited in his luxury suite in Greenville by an angry wife with a hangover, complete with the handgun she had figured out to use. It seems as if there was an unforgettable confrontation with Pop's new soul mate in audience, quavering under the sheets. Promises of redemption and behavioral changes were made by him, and action was taken on the scene to escort the person in question out of the door with an obligatory sheet wrapped around them, in return for immediate personal safety, prompted by staring down the hole of relatively short barrel that had an individual message in place. One omission, however, was the revelation of Frank Jr.'s real parentage. All eggs don't need to be tossed out of a basket at the same time, you know. This near death encounter resulted in the benevolent gesture proposed to Marie via J. J didn't share with Marie that he has received advice from an attorney friend he had consulted, who, after calculation of "very fair, reasonable and conciliatory considerations," a minimal settlement sum, which would be complete with confidential signatures when delivered, was in the ballpark starting range of a little over $1,000, 000. Estimates could perhaps go higher with any protests or displays of indignation on Pop's part. These "reasonable and minimal" amounts included prenatal care, hospitalization for childbirth, the cost of food, clothing, shelter, education, medical insurance, daycare, travel for educational experiences, compensation for loss of identity, damages to the psyche due to separation from a parental figure, loss of genealogical records, pain, suffering, loss of companionship and compensation for humiliation, as well as some more esoteric needs over a span of twenty-five years, considering a benevolently minimal inflation rate of 10 percent per year. There would also be a clause guaranteeing that none of the money would have to be paid back in the event the child died at any time after conception.

"Let's leave that for now and revisit it when your indignation has cooled," J offered. "But let's go ahead with what I might want you to do. I understand that you have your own laptop and that you, through your college courses, have knowledge of publishing, correct grammar, acceptable language, and that sort of thing. Is that correct?"

Marie agreed that she had that knowledge and that the dean of the journalism school had recommended her for part-time jobs doing just that.

J continued, "Well, my twin children and I wrote two children's stories together. I sent them to three or four potential publishers and received rejection slips. I would like for you to take these stories, read them, rewrite as you see fit, review the revision with me, and see if we can get them published. Check the illustrations. We may need to find another illustrator that more nearly depicts what we want. One of the books is entitled *The Man Who Wanted to be Santa Claus*, and the other is *Responsibility, That's a Big Word*. I think they are good stories and are worthy of publication. The other thing I want you to do is more complicated. A day or so after we met, I talked to the dean of philosophy and tendered by resignation or, maybe more appropriately, retirement. Just today I received a letter from him in which he informs me that my letter of retirement was not accepted, but I will enter a period of sabbatical. During this time, I am to write a book, with the tentative title of *Profound Philosophies from the Working Man*. I guess he knows that over the course of my professorship, I have recorded interviews with a variety of people, such as a farmer, a plumber, a carpenter, a schoolteacher, and a couple of merchants. I have fifteen or twenty of these tapes that need transcribing and editing so the book can take shape. After that, we can begin work on the book. I want to have it completed, at least in final draft form, by the fall. Are you up to that challenge? If so, you can begin work tomorrow."

As to compensation, Marie suggested that she would exchange her work on the books and assist with housework for room and board and for the payment of her medical expenses, including prenatal care and delivery. J agreed, and they placed an estimated value on the package, to which J added $100 a week. J knew he would be revisiting the settlement issue from Frank Sr. but let it lie for the time being.

After lunch, J suggested that it would be helpful for Marie to become familiar with the neighborhood because some of it had been used as the basis for the children's stories. He could also tell her the background of some of the local subjects whom he had interviewed for the Philosophies of the *Working Man* book.

They dressed warmly to fend off the January cold and rode off in the pond scum green Toyota in the direction of Cedar Creek. On the way out of the property, J explained that Cedar Creek was a geological peculiarity that resulted in temperatures being lower there than in other spots in the South Carolina Midlands. Marie comments that she remembers watching the weather report on WIS TV and the weather person always reporting the condition of Cedar Creek, but she had no idea where it might be and why a place not located on most maps would be mentioned as if listeners were greatly interested. The first stop outside the gates to Shalom was what appeared to be a baseball field, but with a fringe of wilted and dried sunflowers at the end of the outfield. Marie jokingly says, "And perhaps you own a baseball field? Maybe the Cedar Creek Freezers team plays here?"

"As a matter of fact, I do own this field. However, it's not big enough to be called a baseball field, but a softball field. There's a reason for it being here. Let me tell you about the providential event that caused its birth." The story was this: Years ago, J, his wife, and children were riding home from a Labor Day picnic sponsored by the Uniroyal Tire plant and saw a group of black men playing softball as best they could in a makeshift playing field. The ground was unlevel, the grass barely knocked down, and there was no backstop. J remembered his youth when the teenagers in the community, both black and white, would play softball on Sunday afternoons using the same sort of makeshift arrangements. Those were pleasant memories that built lasting friendships to this day. The resident deputy sheriff discouraged such integrated gatherings, fearing racial troubles that would trigger cross burnings and other KKK antics. If he happened up on such, he would break the game up and send everybody home, threatening to tell their daddies. However, most of the time, the deputy didn't show up was because he devoted Sunday afternoons to a clandestine meeting with his lady friend at the furthermost end of the county. With those memories, J turned into the one lane, deeply ditched dirt road leading to the field. As he turned a corner, he saw six or eight black men sitting on the ditch bank, passing around a two-quart mason jar. In their drunken state, deteriorating rapidly, they displayed their hatred and anger of their territory being invaded by white people. One man attempted to stagger out of the ditch to step in front of J's car but slipped and fell in the ditch. As they passed this unkempt group, there were catcalls to the effect that white folks had no business there and things would get ugly. J's wife pleaded for J to stop and back the car out—to no avail. J proceeded to the area of the softball game, thinking that he would simply drive out the other side. After looking, there were no other exits. J asked one of the spectators who verified that there was only one way in and one way out. The play of the game stopped, and J's wife began to cry so J carefully maneuvered his car around ditches and pine stumps, finally turning around as several men began to move toward the car. As they approached the only exit, the moonshine drinkers were waving their arms in anger and were preparing to stop the car. All but one was armed with a stick or rock or some other missile. That unarmed person seemed to be trying to calm the situation and ordering the others to drop their weapons and get out of the way. J decided this was no time for negotiation or conciliation and opted to put his car in first gear and floorboard the accelerator. He consciously tried to avoid hitting any of the haranguers, but that was the chance he would have to take. His Buick responded, and he somehow managed to avoid frontally running over any of the group while staying between the ditches, but there were thumps as he drove through. He saw through the rearview mirror that three of the group were either on their knees or on their backs, and the other two were in one of the ditches.

J continued by sharing with Marie that this episode was very disturbing to him. He had grown up with black friends as he described the softball game players earlier, and he had finished his tour of military service without racial troubles. He had been very careful to instruct his men that racial slurs would not be tolerated and did severely discipline those few that did cross the line he imposed. Now this incident happened close to home, although not in his neighborhood. That sort of hatred by either race should not happen, and something should be done about it.

J and Marie were parked at the entrance to the field, and J continued to tell her that he came up with the idea of turning this two-acre field into a ball field that could be used by the community. He involved Reverend Charlsie, who met with the families using the makeshift ball field where J and his family had their unfortunate experience, urging trust instead of hatred for the rest of the area citizens. J knew just about everybody in the community and called on a man who owned a road scraper he had purchased from the county for his personal use in maintaining dirt roads on his property. This fellow agreed to donate his time and his machine to manipulate the former cornfield into a flat, level disk, complete with a mound in the center. Neither of them knew the exact dimensions of a softball field so the local surveyor was brought into the mix. The surveyor did the research on the angles required, the distance between bases, and the height of the pitcher's mound. Before long, the entire neighborhood got in the act. The neighbor with a horse farm provided several bags of lime to mark the baselines with, left over from whitewashing his fences. South Carolina Electric and Gas Company was approached and convinced they should donate a few poles and erect them around the back of home plate so a backstop could be built. Just about every Saturday during that spring found a group of people doing something to get the field shaped up for the summer. The decision was made to make the field and the accompanying rules a little unorthodox and plant sunflowers around the outfield. If a batted ball barely reached the sunflowers, the result was an automatic double; and if the ball went into the sunflowers, a home run must be declared. Parking was provided in the rough. There were no bleachers or seats, other than benches for the players. Spectators must bring their own folding chairs or sit in the back of pickup trucks. Teams were formed without regard for racial balance. Churches in the area formed teams from their congregations, and this necessitated the forming of a central body to handle scheduling and to ensure umpires with some sort of credentials, which in turn necessitated some fund-raising so the umpires could be paid.

J confided that "they even let me pitch until I got tired once or twice."

Their tour of the community continued. J drove north to the small community of Rion to meet Joe Buchanan. They passed through Rion and took the first right just outside the community limits. An attractive, well-kept one-story house adjacent to a very upscale kennel. Marie asked, "Is this your house too?" J hesitated and answered, "Well, yes and no. Let me tell you the story about Joe. Joe served in the army as an explosives demolition specialist and was among the first to be sent to Kuwait in Operation Desert Storm along with the bomb-sniffing dog he had trained named Bum. Joe went out one day with another soldier without Bum, and his soldier companion detonated a bomb, killing him in Joe's presence and injuring Joe to the extent that his right leg had to be amputated. His psychological bruises, however, were worse than his physical injuries. He returned home with deep depression, guilt, and frequent suicide plans. Joe's wife came to me, being referred by one of my friends in the community as someone willing to work with folks down on their luck. She told me that she was sure that Joe would eventually follow through on his suicide threats unless something happened quickly. It seemed all that would ease his mind was his friend Bum, who he was able to return home with. I met with Joe the next day, telling him that a friend of a friend told me about him and I wanted to meet him and to thank him for his military service. He was an extremely unhappy person and I could certainly understand why. He seemed to relate to me because of my military experience.

The one thing that Joe seemed enjoy was taking care of dogs and was proud of the training he had given Bum. I talked to him for some time and shared with him a dream of mine to provide a really good, upscale, modern, clean boarding kennel for dogs. The community needed one. Blythewood is a bedroom community of Columbia for many people who travel and frequently have the need for boarding their furry friends. Those kennels that were available are located on the south side of Columbia and, quite frankly, have a lot to be desired. Some of the animals return from their stay in those kennels upset and distrustful, taking several weeks for them to recover. I've been told that when their owners start packing suitcases, they hide, being fearful they will be boarded in those places again. Joe was excited and more than a little interested. I finally asked if he would be interested in being responsible for such a kennel that would have, let's say, ten pens for working dogs and then a boarding facility for up to twenty lap dogs. He at first said an enthusiastic "Yes!" but then remembered his physical disability, telling me that he was pretty much wheelchair-bound and that would be a problem. I then told him that I thought I could buy the land next door and build it there, and he broke down and cried. I knew I had to follow through, even though I would have to mortgage Shalom.

I had already checked that the land next door could be purchased so I went to see the owner and bent his arm, so to speak. I formed a LLC, with me, Joe, and the property owner as principals. I called on another friend, a landscape architect, who drew up the plans, and I will say he did a great job, using a lot of imagination and input from Joe. Word got out about what we were doing in the community and after the plans were complete, there were twenty volunteers—white, black, young, old—who came to pour concrete and install water lines and do the grunt work, leaving contractors to do the complicated stuff. The total cost ended up at one-third of the estimate. We poured a concrete walkway, actually a driveway, from Joe's house to the kennel. A retired lawyer friend of mine even drew up the easement agreement, although I question whether we needed it or not, but it was his way of contributing.

This endeavor has been tremendously successful. People know that if they bring their dogs, they will be well cared for, fed, and exercised. Joe's gone a step further and has gone into the grooming business too. Dogs even have a choice of scents used for shampoo and conditioner! So remember, if you or someone you know have a dog that needs to be washed with love, boarded and exercised, and needs nail trimming, send them to Joe."

"I must confess that I'm proud of this," J confided. "From the first week, there has been almost a full house of dog customers. I'll have to admit that I'm glad the kennel's close to his house and not mine because sometime, something will set the dogs off and such barking and howling you've never heard comes out, but Joe and his family don't seem to mind. It sure has given him peace of mind, hope, and a will to live. From the very beginning, he's been able to care for his family with the money earned and for the venture to make money to pay me back for the amount I borrowed to make it work. One of these days, I'm going to turn it all over to Joe and talk the other principle into doing the same. Don't know exactly when, but now that I think about it, it has to be pretty soon."

DR. J.'S FEBRUARY 2008

D URING THE MONTH of February 2008, there were many conversations held around the dinner table about joys and tragedies and perhaps too many conversations about basketball. National politics was heating up, and there was quite a bit of discussion about those offering themselves for candidates for one party or the other. After dinner, the foursome listened to debates and then took a vote as to who did the best in debates and then as to who would be elected as the final candidates.

J and Marie continued their rides, this time around the property in the golf cart, with dogs running ahead. This time they take a small lane on the west side of the property. After a quarter of a mile or so, a three-acre pond appears out of the wilderness. The pond was fringed with a border of grass, neatly trimmed, with a border of well-established azalea bushes. The border was wide enough for a car to drive all the way around. A dock extended out for some twenty-five feet.

J told Marie, "Marie, if you really want to see something beautiful, come down here in the spring when the azaleas or irises are in bloom, reflecting in the water. It's a wonderful place just to come and sit and fish or sunbathe or just think. I think you'll find it a delightful place to be."

They continued on their ride, reversing direction and then taking a left turn into a winding road taking them to the back of the property, ending at a bay of large trees.

"Do you like the woods?" J asked. Without waiting for a reply, he pointed out that there were thirty-nine black walnut trees, remarking that the chances are that at least three cuts could be gotten out of each tree. He explained that he had had two of the trees cut to make the paneling in the Shalom den. They climbed out of the golf cart and walked around, admiring the trees, when Marie exclaimed, "Wait a minute!" and pointed to a deer antler lying on the ground. "What's that?" she asked as she picked it up. J tells her, "You are lucky. Deer antlers lying on the ground are as scarce as hen's teeth. Usually, when a deer drops an antler like that it isn't long before a squirrel or some other creature gets it to gnaw on for its mineral value. I've lived here a long time, and I've only found two or three of them and none as magnificent as the one you have. That has six points on it so it must have come from Big Jack."

"Who's Big Jack?"

"Big Jack is the number one resident deer. He rules the deer herd in these parts. He knows who is in the woods and when dogs may be on his trail. I think he enjoys embarrassing them when they chase him because he can really move. I've seen him many times just standing, looking at me when I least expect it. If I look away, he disappears without a trace or a sound. I hope you'll be able to see him one of these moonlit nights when he comes close to the house. Like I said, he likes to keep up with who comes and goes."

"As a matter of fact, there are a lot of things on this piece of land that I hope you'll get to see. We have turkeys that are commonly seen at the edge of fields. Geese migrate through here and use the pond for overnight stays, sometimes longer. There are several coveys of quail in the woods where I've planted patches of lespedeza. That bush grows to over eight feet tall, and the branches bend over. I planted the bushes about six feet apart so that there is a sort of alley in between to give the birds some protection. The seeds are just right for quail too. It's a food chain sort of place. Foxes feed on quail and rabbits, and bobcats feed on the foxes and other things. If anything is left over, buzzards come and clean it up. If you just sit back and watch, the whole forest is alive and is a wonder. I hope you'll develop a feel for just sitting and listening quietly. You'll be surprised at the action."

As they returned to the Shalom house and parked the golf cart, Marie asked, "May I ask you a question?" J replied that of course she could, and she continued, "What is the relationship between you, Pat, and Hab? I asked Pat a month or so ago, right after I got here, and she gave me a quick rundown. But I'd like to hear it from you. I don't think she told me the whole story."

J looked off into the distance for a short while and then related, "Our relationship is long and very, very complex. I know you find it unusual for an old man, such as I am, to rely so much on a young black woman, especially in the South Carolina Midlands. Actually, I congratulate you on trying to delve into the complexity of the South. It shows you're truly trying to understand what makes people like Pat and I tick. I also know that you feel that Pat resents your being here, and perhaps she has reasons for that, but she is a fair person, and I think that given time she would share the entire story with you. Let me begin by saying that Pat is like a daughter to me. She is also my friend, and in many ways, she's my caregiver and my guardian. Knowing that it might be some time before she feels close enough to feel comfortable, let me tell you about us. But first, let's go inside and make some tea. It's getting cold outside. These February days can show you temperature changes that vary greatly, considering whether or not you're in the sunshine."

Over their cups of steaming tea with a side order of cookies J picked up at the Piggly Wiggly grocery, J began.

"My mind goes back fifteen or sixteen years. I remember when my son Jack was in the eleventh grade, and he frequently talked about a young woman in his class by the name of Patricia. He mentioned that she was so much brighter than most and was attractive as well. She worked at the local community store after school. Mr. Ralph Jordan, the owner, had sort of taken her under his wing and encouraged her. In many ways, he was a father figure to her even though she lived in a household with both parents. I ran across her name again when I was serving on the Carolina scholars committee, and her name was brought forth and her records reviewed and were found extremely outstanding. Without hesitation, she was chosen to be given the opportunity to become a Carolina scholar. This was just before her graduation from high school, in the same year that Jack graduated. However, to everyone's amazement, I read the announcement that she had married Joe Frazier Brown. Everyone's thoughts were that this was such a waste. But in time, the reasons for not accepting the scholarship became quite evident because she was pregnant.

"A vicious rumor got started. There's a woman in the community by the name of Molly Moore, with an appropriate name of Motor Mouth Molly. It seems as if one day Molly stopped by the store and, finding no one visible, walked to the back door of the wooden building and saw Patricia and Mr. Jordan sitting there, he with one arm around her, and they were in head-to-head conversation. Molly slipped out of the front door and spread the rumor that it might just be that Mr. Jordan was the father of the child she was bearing. The rumor was widely circulated, as is the unfortunate case in small towns. Months went by, and Patricia became larger and larger. It was midmorning when a call came to my wife explaining that the one ambulance in the community was on its way to Charleston, carrying a patient, and that the local doctor couldn't be found, and would she please do midwife duties for the girl Patricia Brown. Without hesitation, my wife put the twins in her car and arrived at the Brown house within five minutes or so.

"As she entered the back door and was heading to the bedroom, the child was coming into the world unassisted. Elizabeth was a professional and delivered the baby boy. She had swatted him on the behind, and he responded with a loud cry just in time for Joe Frazier Brown to walk in. Elizabeth told me he didn't look like a particularly happy camper. She found out later that as he left work, being called to come home for the delivery, one of his so-called friends told him, 'Joe, look at that child good and see if it looks more like you or more like Ralph Jordan,' and the rest of the crew at the sawmill laughed. This was on his mind when he walked in the door of his parents' house. He walked up to Elizabeth as she was holding the child, wrapped in a towel. He said nothing to her but pulled the towel away from the child's face to see what his color was. He had light complexion, much lighter than his mother's and considerably lighter than Joe's. He walked over to the bed where Patricia lay, and everyone in the room thought he was going to kiss his wife; but instead, his balled fist struck against her face, smashing her nose and making her eyes bloodshot. She was struck with such force she was knocked unconscious.

"Joe said, 'Where's Daddy's pistol? Where is it? I'm going to kill both the bitch and the bastard!' Fortunately there were several elderly men in the hall, and as he came by, they tried stopping him and were scuffling back and forth when Elizabeth picked up the infant, still wrapped in the towel, and yelled, 'Help me!' The two women in the room, standing by the bedside, managed to get Patricia to Elizabeth's car. The baby was shoved into the arms of the twins in the backseat, and Patricia was helped into the front seat. Elizabeth drove as if possessed, running the stop sign and disregarding all the traffic laws as she drove to Ridgeway. She arrived at Dr. Pulaski's clinic and raced in, managing to literally drag one of the two nurses out to the car. The other nurse followed, and they helped Patricia inside. The twins, left to their own devices, consulted each other and decided to take the baby into the clinic too. The doctor was not in, being out on a house call somewhere in town. One of the nurses called the one-man police department. And in a few minutes, Chief of Police Joe Simmons arrived, flying up with Dr. Pulaski in the front seat of his personal pickup, bearing the magnetized Ridgeway town seal on the doors. Dr. Pulaski's words were 'Child, what in the world happened to you?' Without getting an answer, he gave her a shot for pain, treated her wounds, and taped her broken nose back in place. After checking all the vital signs and examining all the damage, he announced that she would be all right but would have to have care for the next few days because of the pain she would have.

"Elizabeth announced that Patricia was going home with her, and that's what she did. That's how it came about. After several weeks, her face looked normal, and her pains subsided. The question then came—what now? The twins gave the answer—'They stay with us.'"

DR. J'S MARCH 2008

MARCH. FOR THOSE living or have lived in the South Carolina Midlands, all will attest to likening the month of March to a seductress. March beckons the promise of spring. Maple trees begin to bud, lining the creeks and rivers with a reddish tinge in the horizon. Yellow forsythia blossoms burst out. Days hint of warmth, luring mankind out of their houses, only to be driven back in by cold winds and sometimes snow. Men, along with some women, rush out to the golf course and then curse the weather. March promises good things, rile you when these promises fall through, and then thrills you with emerging color. March is a true charmeuse, spellbinder, enchanter, mystic; but compared with February, she's heaven.

There is an old adage describing the month of March, which says in words to the effect that March winds come in like a lion and go out as quietly as a lamb. March 2008 came in with winds likened to lions' roars, steadfastly blowing. Leaves that had been hiding in out-of-the-way places were now swirling, caught up in the lionlike roar, sending them into the next county, or at least into the woods that surrounded the house.

After breakfast with Marie, J announced that he and the girls were going to take a walk through the woods. He whistled for Princess and Victoria, who headed for the door with perked ears and switching tails, ready for an adventure. J reached into a corner of the kitchen and grasped a well-worn stick. He explained that over several years he found nice-looking sticks and brought them home and made some modifications to them. "Snake sticks. If you look closely, you'll see that I've left several in various parts of the house, mostly by one of the exit doors. I take one with me when I walk. Now I'm not likely to encounter a snake today because we haven't had enough warm weather, but it will keep me from stumbling through any briars I might encounter, and it's a good idea to maintain the habit of carrying one. If you are taking walks in the woods from May through

December, it's a good idea to carry a stick. Most of the time, snakes get out of your way, being more scared of you than you are of them. But sometimes when they feel threatened or don't have a good escape route, they will attack. My advice is to aim for the head and use the stick with force. I know they're one of God's creatures, but they're still no favorites of mine. An attacking snake is much more attractive with no head, in my opinion."

"Thanks for that great piece of information" was Marie's reply. She added, "I'll take that instruction under advisement while I'm running in the opposite direction. But I understand, and I'll grab a stick when I get the urge to walk in the woods."

J and the girls headed out, J bundled up with a heavy jacket and hat. The girls' breath formed little clouds of condensation as they barked with anticipation. Just as J's feet left the top step, Marie called out, "Dr. J, may I ask a favor?" J asked what that might be, and Marie explained that she noticed he had a Jacuzzi in his bathtub and wondered if she might take a soaking, swirling hot bath while he was gone. He, of course, agreed and continued on his way, urging her to enjoy but to remember to lock the door while he was gone.

Marie took her time, recalling that when J took his walks in the woods, they were usually a couple of hours long. She placed some things in the washing machine, including the clothes she had on, and wrapped herself in a large towel then headed for the Jacuzzi. She was ready to step in when she heard the washing machine making a racket, indicating something was out of balance. She loosely replaced the towel and returned to the washing machine. The one thing that she had forgotten to do was to lock the doors. She didn't realize she was going to come face-to-face with a middle-aged woman dressed fashionably in high heels and with just a little too much jewelry. Both women gasped and stared at each other for a long moment, and without exchanging words, each scurried in different directions—Marie back to the bathroom, and the woman to the door and to her car. Marie watched as the Cadillac slung gravel and raced down the driveway.

Not knowing what else to do, Marie took her bath without a great deal of enjoyment, dressed, and waited for J to return. As soon as his coat was removed, Marie relayed the experience. J laughed a little nervously and explained that the visitor had to be Millie. He also explained that Millie was an old friend who was used to entering the house when the door was unlocked and nosing around. He also explained that Millie was the Midlands' gossip and J's self-appointed protector against sin and that he was sure he would hear from his children before the day was over because Millie was sure to call them and report his apparent aberrant behavior. He was sure she would express concern to his children that he was having a late-life moral crisis, having a pretty dark-haired, mostly naked young pregnant companion running around the house. Marie apologized for all the things that went wrong, including the looseness of the towel and her failure to lock the doors.

She asked what Millie might do, and J answered that Millie would have a telephone meltdown all day today and would call all her friends and some who were borderline as well as his children and would embellish as she saw fit. He explained that Millie had "been after him" for a closer relationship for years, which he had successfully rejected. Millie was a widow with megabucks and had promised him a life of leisure and untold pleasure if he would only give in. Millie was, he admitted, a fun person to be around and to escort to special occasions because she was attractive, was a good conversationalist and knew everybody worth knowing in Richland, Fairfield, Chester, and York counties.

One of the expected phone calls came just after lunch from J's daughter. Rebecca began the conversation by asking, "Daddy, are you all right?" J feigned surprise at hearing from her and answered, "I'm fine, honey. I'm having a wonderful time, feeling younger every day. This March wind means that spring can't be far behind, and I always feel rejuvenated in the spring. I'm delighted to hear your voice. Is there any special reason you are making a call at this time of day and week?" Rebecca stammered, "Well, uh, no, I, ah don't really have a reason . . . Just wanted to hear your voice . . . I, ah—"

J interrupted, "Oh, just go ahead and say it. Millie called you, didn't she? I don't know what she said, of course, but there's a long story to be told, sweetheart. I tell you what, I'll write, well, no, when I call at the end of the week like I usually do, I'll bring you up-to-date on the happenings around here. I'm sure you'll understand then, but until then, let me assure you that I haven't lost my mind, at least completely, that nothing bad has happened to me, that I've done nothing to be ashamed of or that will get me in trouble with the law, morally or legally. But how are you and that man of yours getting along? I do miss you, and I hope that you can plan to visit this fall. If not Thanksgiving, then Christmas. I want us to have a very special family time together. Jack was just here, and I think he can make it around that time too. There are a lot of things happening, and time is always short."

After asking about a number of things and people, the gist of the conversation was turned around and evolved into more mundane father-daughter stuff.

J urged her to get back to work and not worry about him and his reported wayward behavior, leaving Rebecca with a lot of unanswered questions but satisfied that there was no crisis that had to be dealt with.

No sooner than the conversation with Rebecca ended, the phone rang again, this time with Jack on the line. His conversation began much the same as Rebecca's had. "Dad, are you all right?"

J answered by laughing and said, "I just talked with your sister. I think Millie got the shock of her life, meeting Marie with very little clothes on. She has been running her phone hot. I would have loved to have been here to see it. I'm sure she didn't leave out any details or gave you a chance to tell her that you have met Marie. I'll call Millie tonight when she's exhausted and talk to her, and I'm sure she will understand. I'm also sure she won't backtrack and talk to all those people she has talked to today, but I'm also sure they all know her and will get the story straight sometime in the future. Millie knows me well enough to accept what I tell her."

Jack agreed and they began to talk about other things, being assured that nothing had come up causing his father to go off his rocker.

After that conversation, J headed for the heavy jacket and the door to do some rock thinking but abruptly changed his mind, got in his slime green truck, and headed for town. He returned shortly and invited Marie to get her coat and go with him. They rode to Pat and Hab's house and found them home and announced that he had a surprise for them. With that, he reached behind the truck seat and pulled out four kites, complete with four balls of twine. "We're going to have a kite-flying contest!" Get in the truck and let's go down to the ball field and fly them!"

In almost the same breath, both Hab and Marie declared that they had never flown kites and had no idea how to do it. Pat recalled that she and her Dad had flown kites a couple of times, but that was years ago.

Pat and Hab jumped on the tailgate of the truck, and away they went to the ball field where there was plenty of room to prevent entanglement in trees. After a lecture on the principles of kite-flying, complete with safety instructions, all busied themselves with readying their kites for flight. J made sure they were all separated by about thirty yards and then demonstrated by running as fast as he could until his kite was lifted upward. Hab had instant success (probably by being able to run more swiftly than others). Pat had to try four times and Marie almost lost count in her attempts.

Eventually, there were four beautiful kits flying in the air, being buoyed by the twenty-five-mile-an-hour March wind. Each declared that their kites were flying higher than the others, with protests from the others.

Motorists driving along the highway adjacent to the ball field saw the kites and some of them stopped to watch. It truly was a beautiful sight for the forty-five minutes to an hour they were flying. Marie was the first to declare "Uncle!" and began to reel in her kite. The others agreed because darkness was closing in and the temperature was rapidly dropping.

All agreed that this spontaneous idea of J's was indeed good, one where much was learned, the exercise was good, and the fresh air was a rejuvenating change.

No one was looking when J took a tumble. The only obvious damage was a red clay scuff mark on his trousers, but J had to wonder what caused the fall. Was it something in his brain that malfunctioned, or was it the rough surface causing him to stumble, or . . . ?

When the ride back to Shalom was completed, J had another announcement. "Supper's on me tonight, and we're going to have my favorite, and I'm going to fix it all by myself!" (Remember that in most of South Carolina, meals are served at six in the morning, noon, and six in the evening and are called breakfast, dinner, and supper.)

Marie asked, "And what might that be?"

Without hesitation, Pat answered for J. "Hot dogs!"

J added, "With all the trimmings too. We'll have Castleberry's chili straight from the can, buns from Piggly Wiggly, potato chips by Lay's, and slaw also from the Piggly Wiggly deli section—all served on paper plates. Won't be long in the making, either. As a matter of fact, if the rest of you would wash your hands and work together by setting the table, I'll have it ready. Oh yeah, I forgot to mention that these are not just any hot dogs. They're all beef ball park hot dogs. Best they make."

With that offer no one could turn down, all pitched in and were seated when J brought forth his gourmet meal. In addition to all the rare items, the adults were treated to ice-cold RC Cola, leaving Hab to the milk, as directed by his mother.

After the feast, J announced that the ladies were free to rest, that he and Hab would do the dishes, which consisted mainly of throwing the paper plates into garbage bags and putting away condiments.

Marie motioned to Pat, and they left quietly for the den. Marie asks, "Pat, I have two questions. But before that, I'm sure you've heard about my encounter with Mrs. Millie Banks IV, or whatever she is."

Pat smiled and confessed, "Yes, I have."

"Tell me something about the lady."

"Well, her husband, John Mitchell Lynch Banks IV, died about six years ago. He unfortunately died before her passions did."

"What kind of relationship does Dr. J have with her?'

"Actually, it's a friendship. I think—no, I'm sure—that Mrs. Banks would like for it to be something more, but J has insisted that it remain a friendship. He asks her to go with him to certain things, and she asks him to escort her to a lot of events, mostly high-end fund-raising soirees where everybody who knows everybody that's worth anything attends."

Marie offered, "She's a beautiful woman, and I'm surprised that nothing has happened."

Pat mused, "Yes and no. They live in the same world, and yet they are different in their goals and values and outlooks. Dr. J shops at Piggly Wiggly, and she shops at Publix and the Fresh Market and wouldn't be caught dead in a Piggly Wiggly. She would probably throw up at the sight of chitterlings and pigs' feet and backbone, and J would think of who would enjoy those things with him. He likes country and Western music, and she likes opera or thinks she does or thinks she should. They have much in common, such as knowing a lot of influential people throughout the state and enjoy mingling with them, but they live in two different worlds. J, in particular, would not like to cross into her world and knows he would have to if their relationship was any stronger. If you have time when you're in Columbia, ride by her house, and you can see the outside of the world she lives in. She knows and is known by everyone of importance, particularly in Columbia. She is the center of the social world there. As you've noticed from seeing the rear end of her vehicle leaving Shalom, she travels in a Cadillac, never one that's over two years old. And J travels in a slime green Toyota pickup. There's a world of difference, and yet they like each other well. In fact, there's a love relationship there. Not a romantic one because J has not had one since Elizabeth died, but a deep relationship that I don't really know how to describe. In a sentence, let me say of Millicent Weston Adams Banks—widow of the late John Mitchell Lynch Banks IV, known as Millie by all who know or know of her—is an extremely well-educated, extremely wealthy, and extremely social-minded, politically sought-after lovely lady. Now what's your second question?"

"My second question is—how did Dr. J get over the death of his wife and children?"

Pat raised her eyebrows and answered, "Oh, he hasn't gotten over it. Their presence, especially Elizabeth's, is still with him. As long as a month after the tragedy, I was wondering what was going to happen to him. He had experienced something that it would be easier to die than to get over. For several weeks after the funeral, he didn't shave, and I don't think he bathed most days. He didn't go to the university at all and barely ate. He would go and sit on that rock in the front yard into the wee hours of the morning. There was deep concern about his well-being by many people. Many people came by to see him, but he was not there for them. When he wasn't sitting on the rock, he and his dogs would be somewhere down in the woods. People would leave notes, which he read, but made no replies to. Then a strange thing happened. Hab and I were staying here at Shalom, and it must have been two or three o'clock in the morning when he came in from sitting on the rock, showered, shaved, and returned to the rock. I got up and went out there and asked, 'Dr. J, you all right?' He said, 'I'm fine, Pat.' I asked, 'What's happened?' Dr. J said, 'I've been talking with Elizabeth.' Of course, I said, 'What?' He said, 'I've been sitting here on the rock and talking to Elizabeth, and she told me she was disappointed in me, the way I've been neglecting myself and all those who care about me.' There for a minute the only thought in my mind was that he's gone over the edge and is entering a total mental breakdown. He reached over and took my hand and told me, 'Don't think I'm crazy. Elizabeth and I did speak, and she simply said she wanted me to get on with my life. She said that all was well with her and the children and for me to remember that I had two other children who needed a father. She also mentioned you and Hab, saying that both of you needed an influence in your lives, and it was time for me to stop feeling sorry for myself and get about doing those things that I do best, such as return to the classroom, take care of family and friends, influence young people positively, and enjoy life the best you possibly can. I agreed, went inside, showered, and shaved and dressed decently. And now I've come back out here to show her and to thank her for her advice and tell her that I love her and respect the guidance she's given me. I'm also going to ask her not to stay away but meet me on the rock when I need her.'

"The next morning, he got up, cleaned up, dressed up, and returned to the university. It was like he was lost and now was found, like the prodigal son had returned. There was celebration in the department. Now from time to time, he'll share with me a conversation he's had with Elizabeth. And it makes perfect sense, like he is relating a conversation he's had with an old friend, and I don't think he's crazy at all. Something is happening there that is very real, even though out of the ordinary, to say the least. To him, it's very real, not a delusion of any kind. From what I understand, the conversations take place while he's out on that rock. Sometimes the conversations are about me and Hab, and he tells me about them. I think I've told you before, but let me tell you again. If you see him out on that rock by himself, let him be. It's a very special place for him—his remembering place, his communication place."

Marie said, "One of these afternoons when we have time, I want you to tell me more about Elizabeth. You told me once that you would tell me about their romance, and I'm looking forward to hearing about it."

With that, something happened that had not before. Pat took Marie's hand and squeezed it, before walking back into the kitchen to inspect the kitchen cleanup.

J asked, "What's the gossip of the day, and can I get in on it?"

They said in unison, "You wouldn't believe it!"

He said, "I might."

With that, the phone rang. J was sitting the closest to the wall-mounted telephone in the kitchen, so he arose and answered. After a few seconds, the others in the room hear, "Tommy! What a delight to hear your voice." After several minutes of "Of course," "Please do," "Uh-huh," and other words indicating understanding and pleasure, followed by "Good-bye," J announced to the diners that the call was from his old friend and one of his favored friends. "Hab and Pat know Tommy, Marie, but Tommy is a Presbyterian minister whom I've known for at least forty years. I have told him on many occasions that he knows me better than I know myself. I've told him that if my time comes before his, I want him to conduct my funeral. He's done several funerals for our family over the years (neglecting to say that among those funerals conducted by Tommy were for J's wife and two children). He's coming to Columbia tomorrow to attend a conference at the Radisson the next morning, and he's bringing his wife Mary with him. I invited him to come out between two and three tomorrow afternoon to catch up on our news and to have dinner with us."

Marie laughed and directed her voice to Pat, "Pat, you have to be a saint! You absolutely do not know from one minute to the next when there's going to be something happening in this house and you're expected to come up with a memorable meal on very short notice! And it's like this all the time! How do you cope with this man?"

Pat shrugged her shoulders and looked away. "The Lord gave me strength and the ability to cook, and Dr. J gives me the budget. We have adventures like this all the time. Dr. J knows thousands of people and unfortunately knows them all well. I've never known a person to have scores of close friends, and all of them feel comfortable enough to come in and kick off their shoes and get snacks out of the fridge and even uncork a bottle of wine. But that's what we like, and we can handle it. What'll it be, Dr. J? Tommy loves chicken and rice and strawberry ice cream. Seems like he would get tired of chicken and decaf coffee, seeing that he gets such all the time at church functions."

J agreed that chicken and rice would be the mainstays of the menu and agreed to do any extra chores that might be necessary to prepare for the visit.

Marie asked, "Would it be good for me to stay out of the way tomorrow rather than you having to try to explain me?" J's quick reply was "Oh no. I want you here. As I said, Tommy knows me as well as any other person on earth, and I'm sure he will understand and will agree that our decision was the best one and will not judge either of us for something that isn't there. No, please stay and be a part of this reunion. You'll enjoy Tommy and Mary."

With that being settled, J, Marie and Hab set about cleaning the table and the kitchen while Pat made the grocery list. J reminded her to remember the strawberry ice cream and some Earl Grey tea for Mary. It was apparent that J was delighted at the prospect of seeing the couple again. Light seemed to radiate from his face.

When the chores were done, J invited everyone to the den to watch a basketball game, but Pat quickly replied, "You watch. We study," turning her eyes to Hab, whose eyes fell to the floor. After leaving her list on the kitchen table, Pat and Hab go home, and Marie and J go to the den.

When the game is over, Marie turned to J and said, "You have not asked me about the progress I'm making on my assignments. I'm doing really well, I think, with the children's stories and with the book. After reading through the lectures, I have a question for you."

"And what is that?"

"Did you ever consider becoming a minister?"

J smiled and said, "Well, as a matter of fact, I did."

"And why didn't you act on it?"

"Well, in that time of my life in which I should have made that decision, I had a problem. I enjoyed smoking, which I still do, and I enjoyed being with the lady friends. I enjoyed dancing and concluded that maybe those things and some others wouldn't be acceptable in a conservative church, such as Presbyterian churches are. I wouldn't consider any other denomination, and besides, other denominations would probably frown on my actions if I were a preacher."

Marie offered, "I'm not saying that your writing is preachy but it strikes a high moral tone."

"I hope it's not too much, though."

"Oh, no! I find it delightful."

"Okay, when you get to the point that you're ready for me to, I look forward to reviewing your work."

"It looks like I'll be finished with what you've given me so you'd better be lining up some other things for me to do unless you want me to sit around the house all day watching television and getting fat."

"I don't think there's going to be much danger in that," J replied and laughed. "I've got just about a hundred years of stuff in my collection and rest assured I haven't given it all to you yet."

The next afternoon, Tommy and Mary arrive. Dr. J seems as happy as a child on Christmas morning to see them. After greeting them at the door, with hugs and squeezes, Marie is introduced. Although extremely cordial and pleasant, Marie could detect the immediate quizzical look on their faces.

After an hour or so of conversation, Mary admitted that the trip had taken a toll on her and she would like to be excused to take a nap. J insisted that she do just that, and asked Marie to show her to his bedroom and while she was napping, he and Tommy would take a walk. This March afternoon was very pleasant, just cool enough for a light jacket.

During the walk, when they paused briefly at the fishing dock on the pond, J reminded Tommy that, during a conversation of several years back, he promised to officiate at his funeral and that he really wanted him to do it, considering it to be a great honor.

Tommy replied as expected by saying "Well, I hope you're not planning on leaving us anytime soon, but if I'm up and able, you request will be granted."

The conversation turned to other things, such as mutual friends, updating each other on what they knew about persons who had crossed their paths in past years, politics, the world situation, what each of their children were about.

There was a pause in the conversation, broken by Tommy, who asked, "J, it's been ten years since Elizabeth left us. Have you ever thought about remarrying? It's not right being alone with no one to share things with."

J shook his head and said, "No, Tommy, and let me tell you something. I expect you'll think me crazy, but Elizabeth and I still have a very meaningful relationship. We talk often. She tells me all is well with her and the two younger children. I talk to her about my daily work or happenings or news, and she knows all about what I'm doing as if she was by my side. Most people would think I am out of my gourd, but these conversations are so real. They seem to be the same as we had when I could reach out and touch her. Of course, I only do this privately, and that was at her suggestion. She tells me she looks forward to our times together but realizes that others won't think it sane. Tommy, these conversations are meaningful, and I look forward to them. She initiates many of these conversations, and I am always receptive to them. I've never been afraid of death, but I'm at the state now where I look forward to it. I look forward to understanding the mysteries that have plagued me through the years. I look forward to being with family. I do believe that we will know each other as we did here on earth and that we'll be reunited in some fashion as family."

Tommy slowly replied, "That's an encouraging thought. Most of the people I deal with every day are scared to death of death. Be sure you and I know what's coming. It's coming to all of us. J, is there anything particular that you would like me to say at your funeral? Any particular passages of scripture you would like me to read?"

J turned to Tommy and said, "I've got it all written out. Before you leave tonight, I need to give it to you. Please remind me if I forget."

With that the two old friends continued to sit in silence and watched the lengthening shadows of the trees that fringed the fish pond. Every so often, one of the big bass fish would turn over near the surface, causing a series of ripples. At times, each would take turns reaching to the other and giving a pat on the leg as a nonverbal expression of love and appreciation for each other.

J broke the silence by asking, "Should we go back and join the ladies?"

Tommy agreed, "I think so. Mary's nap is over by now, I'm sure" then added, "J, when are you going to tell me about the young pregnant lady in your house?"

J's answer was a little cryptic and short on details. "Oh my, Tommy, it's one of those providential things. She found herself in deep difficulty. The man responsible wants to have nothing to do with her pregnancy. And I believe, providentially, that she has been brought into the Shalom lives. I believe she will be a blessing to us, and I hope that we will be a blessing to her. She is very intelligent. She's a good worker, and believe it or not, that's what she's doing here. She is working for me. She's editing a lot of old papers and taking care of things that I've neglected over the years. Oh, incidentally, I'm on sabbatical. I've been requested to write a book, and she is in the process of editing it. When it's finished, I'll send you a copy."

Tommy didn't press for more information. They continued to walk in silence, finding Pat and Hab arriving. Mary had indeed arisen from her nap and was chatting with Marie, who excused herself to help Pat and Hab in the kitchen. The visit, mostly with Mary now, continued. Chicken and rice with veggies, topped with strawberry ice cream and the corresponding conversation, was enjoyed by all.

The after-dinner conversation turned to the politics of the day. In March 2008, Hillary Clinton and Barack Obama seemed to be in a virtual dead heat in their bids for the presidency. The consensus of the group was that the Democratic Dream Team ticket would include both Clinton and Obama in president/vice presidential roles, in either order. The talk drifted to the news that the governor of New York was in a terrible political, moral, and legal mess after being linked to visits to prostitutes. J asked, "Tommy, don't you think $5,000 an hour is a little high?"

Tommy diplomatically and wisely declined to answer, but Mary chimed in with the opinion, "Well, I think that's about right. You get what you pay for, you know."

Nobody countered nor answered, and Tommy pointedly changed the subject, turning to Hab. "What's happening in your world, Hab?"

"Everything moves along, sir." All the adults thought that was an extremely well put noncommittal answer.

Tommy persisted, "Who are your present-day heroes, Hab?"

Without hesitation, Hab answered, "LeBron James is one of them."

Nods around the table agreed that James was indeed a magnificent basketball player.

J offered, "He is a superb basketball player, but there's just something about our values that troubles me. Here's a young man just out of high school who signs endorsements worth $91 million before he even signs a probasketball contract. Now I agree he's the best I have ever seen on the court. He's absolutely amazing. I don't know what his salary with Cleveland is, but I expect that's more than a little too."

Marie observed that Hab had tensed with the oblique rebuke about values, so she changed the subject again, recalling that she had read that week of England's Prince Harry being recalled from his military duties in Afghanistan, contributing that it would be ashamed for him to be killed in that conflict. Tommy and J pontificated about the conundrum of the Afghanistan war, commenting on the differences of political opinions and the futile attempts of other countries in that country.

The conversation drifted back to sports again, and particularly basketball. Hab spoke up saying, "Dr. J pulls for Davidson."

J's responded with a tongue in cheek smile on his face, "Yes, I pull for them. They're such a liberal team."

Someone in the group questioned, "A liberal team?"

"Yes. They let a few white boys play!"

Hab felt compelled to speak up and offer, "I knew you were prejudiced!"

J confessed, "Yes, and I expect we're all prejudiced to some degree. But it is good to see a few white faces out there on the court as it should be in any contest. I must confess that the black youth have earned their places on the court. I ride through town and I don't see white children out bouncing basketballs and competing with one another, but the black children are out there playing and practicing from early ages, therefore earning the positions they play."

Tommy symbiotically looked at his watch and announced that it was time to go, enjoyed the visit, got to get together more often, give our love to the children and eventually good-bye after hugs.

And thus ended the month of March 2008. The March winds blew with a little less force than they blew in with. The Ides of March had come and gone, and no Roman emperor died, but blossoms were swelling and getting ready to burst forth to join the yellow bell and the dogwood.

DR. J'S APRIL 2008

THE MARCH WINDS quit blowing and April arrived. What a delight! Spring flowers are in bloom, so much so it looked like the whole world was smiling. The band of unlike was in a festive mood as they gathered around the dinner table. Marie led the conversation with boldness. "I have an announcement to make. I went to see Dr. Robert smith today and, he said that I should prepare myself to be the mother of quadruplets!" Cries of surprise and shock exploded from all those around the table then turned to total dismay when Marie said, "April Fool!" After a good laugh and admission that they had been had, the conversation turned to other subjects.

Dr. J asked Hab, "I have a question for you, young man. Who's in the Final Four?"

Without hesitation, Hab answered, "Memphis, North Carolina, UCLA, and Kansas."

"That's exactly right. Another question for you, sir. How many points did LeBron James score last night?"

"Thirty."

"How did Davidson do?"

"Lost to Kansas by two."

"Well, you're really up on your sports today, but how are you doing in school?"

"You'll be proud of me."

J spoke up quickly and said, "Hab, I'm proud of you no matter what your grades are. All of us are proud of you."

Hab shot back, "That's good. I'm glad to hear that. Now I won't have to run away."

All laughed at the quick comeback. J smiled and said, "Looks to me like you're the local hero, especially around this table. But tell me who your heroes are."

"LeBron James would be high on my list. And Tiger Woods would be up there too."

"Who in the political world would be high on your list?"

"Well, Barack Obama would be. Who else is there?"

J baited, "How about Jesse Jackson? And would you include Al Sharpton?"

Hab confessed after a slight hesitation, "The last two aren't too high on my list. I think they have a sixth sense and know when a camera flash is about to go off in their direction or a TV camera is going to be present and they are on their way to be filmed. I used to think Jesse Jackson was high on my list but I think he's gotten away from what he used to stand for. I don't like his criticism of Bill Cosby because I think Bill Cosby really has the interests of black folk at heart, like Jesse Jackson once had."

Leading the conversation, J continued, "Fast forwarding into the world of politics, did all of you read in the paper that our Governor Sanford is on the list of possible running mates for John McCain?

After nods of recognition from all around the table, J continued, "Well, what do you bright people think of the proposed stimulus package? Right now, it would amount to $100 per person, I think."

Pat offered, "From the sound of your voice, I take it you don't like it."

"I think it's foolish, personally. The money will go out in the millions or billions and half of the people will spend it, and the other half will simply put it in a checking account or add to it and make an investment with it in some way or other. I don't think it'll have an impact on the local economy at all."

"There's something else I read today that bothers me. That was the report that thirty colleges are adopting gender neutral rooming assignments. I think that would be disastrous. My opinion, anyhow. Maybe I'm just getting old."

Hab held his gaze on Dr. J while Pat and Marie swapped glances and smiles as if to say, yes, Dr. J, you're getting old.

J continued, directing his conversation to Hab, "Hab, let me speak about one of your heroes. I think that Tiger Woods is, without a doubt, the golfer with the greatest natural ability that the world has ever seen. But I also believe that, in addition to his tremendous talent, he has a guardian angel that brings him a certain amount of providential gifts. In more common terms, I think Tiger Woods could step in a cesspool up to his neck and he would find a ladder at the bottom of so he could climb right out, and when he did, would be perfectly clean and spotless, smelling like roses, smiling, with another $10 million endorsement check in his back pocket."

J moved around the room but still addressed Hab. Did you hear that he's always buying up companies or distributorships?" Hab nodded and continued to listen.

"I heard that he bought up the company that makes the cups for the golf course greens that he plays on. At the bottom of each of these cups, he has caused a very strong magnet to be placed. When he's making an extremely long putt, he turns to his caddy who gives him a special ball. What people don't know is that there are special balls that have a center that includes another magnet, a plus charge compared to the negative charge in the magnet in the bottom of the cup. When the ball comes with two feet of the cup, the combination of magnets work and pulls the ball right into the cup."

Hab practically jumped up and Pat's mouth fell open in disbelief. Hab burst out, "Where did you hear such a thing! Tiger wouldn't do that!"

J answered, "That's the word going around on the local golf courses."

"I don't believe it! It's not fair to make up stories like that!"

J smiled and looked at Hab and said, "I'm glad you don't believe it." I was leading you on to see how you'd react."

Pat looked at Marie then at J with obvious disapproval, shook her head, and proceeded to handle the night's dishes without comment.

J told Hab, "Oh, Hab, when you get home from school tomorrow afternoon, come over. I want to talk to you about something and get you to do something for me. We'll talk about it when you get here. Right now, I'm going to the den and catch up on my reading and maybe watch one of your heroes play basketball."

The following afternoon, Hab came in and found J in the kitchen, sorting his daily mail, having just returned from the mailbox at the end of the drive. "What you want me to do, Dr. J? Got some bush trimming you want done?"

"Yes, I do have something, Hab, but as I think about it, it'll have to be on a weekend and not on a school night."

"Night?"

J nodded his head in agreement and continued, "Yes, at night, Hab. I want you to do some detective work. Maybe this Saturday night after dark, about bedtime. I'll tell your mother enough that she'll go along with it. Don't know exactly what I'm going to tell her yet."

"Detective work?"

"Yes, Hab. I don't know if your mother mentioned it or not, or if you overheard it, but Marie told me that she had a feeling that somebody was looking at her when she undressed for the night. Sort of got the idea that somebody was looking through the bottom of the window to her room. I told her I didn't think that would happen here. We haven't heard the dogs make any racket, which they usually do when somebody strange comes in to the yard. Now they don't do anything but turn around and go back to sleep when we come around unexpectedly. What I want you to do is to put on some heavy clothes because it still gets cold on April nights and wear dark-colored clothing and watch to see if there's really anybody creeping up and peeping in the window. I'll give you a good flashlight and a whistle; and if you see anybody, blow the whistle and wait for me and the dogs to get outside before you turn on the flashlight."

Hab looked at J and asked, "You think it's happening and it's me, don't you?"

J looked at Hab for several seconds and then said, "Well, you are high on my list of suspects. Let's walk out to the rock and talk some more."

They walked out to the rock, with J's arm over Hab's shoulders. When seated and J's pipe was lit, J began, "Hab, you're at the age when your body is going though some tremendous changes. You're at the age when boys talk and you have to find about things yourself because you don't want to discuss them with older people. I know . . . been there. I see so many of girls in your school becoming pregnant when they're twelve, thirteen, or fourteen, which means that many more must be sexually active because a girl doesn't get pregnant the first time usually. These girls have a lifetime of struggles before they're ready for them. Most of them have to endure hardships that we men can't comprehend. Another bad statistic that goes with it is that there are a lot of sexually transmitted diseases among your age group. I guess what I'm saying is that if someone approaches you and offers you a gift of sexual gratification, please think about it before you accept because they might be giving you something much greater than a moment's pleasure. They might be giving you something that'll haunt you for a lifetime. You are a handsome young man and I expect you'll get offers you won't want to turn down. But back to Marie and the peeping Tom—yes, I do suspect you. I can imagine she has a body that would be beautiful to look at, even though she is pregnant."

"But let's let that lie right there and I won't mention it again unless I have to. You realize that I have to maintain the security and well-being of any of the guests in my house. Right now, her person, her space, her privacy that should come automatically to a guest in my house, have been violated."

"Okay. Enough of that. Let's get back to the sex part that I need to talk to you about. Let me tell you about a conversation I had with my friend Rayfield when I was sixteen and Rayfield was a couple of years older. I think you know Rayfield. He's your mother's uncle. My father used to hire Rayfield to work with me in the fields and woods. The difference in the employment was that I wasn't paid, but Rayfield was. As I recall, the going rate around that time was $3 a day for farm labor. There were no hourly rates. The work day began when all the household chores were done, like helping with the dishes, taking care of the garbage, making sure the dogs were fed and all the equipment we'd be working with was gathered up, checked over, sharpened, or repaired, and this would be between seven and seven thirty in the morning. We always returned home for lunch somewhere between eleven thirty and noon and then get back at what we were doing by one or one thirty, depending on how hot it was.

"Anyhow, Rayfield and I were working together, talking about everything under the sun, when Rayfield asked me if I was getting any. The question took be off guard for a minute. So I told him no, that too much of that stuff would make you blind, and I had the need to see a long time. Rayfield just laughed and told me that activity was not the cause of blindness, but taking care of your needs by yourself would surely cause blindness. He went on to say something about blood pressure going up or some such wisdom. Rayfield then told me that I shouldn't worry about blindness, but I should be worried about making children. You see, the incidence of sexually transmitted disease wasn't as great a threat as getting your girl pregnant. Rayfield admitted that there might be—just might be—a couple of children in the neighborhood who looked like him, but he had changed his ways and now always used protection. He told me I should always be prepared and get some packages and stick them in my wallet. (He also told me that it was helpful, in some cases, to make an excuse to pull out your wallet so the circular imprint could be seen. Shows you're ready, and you know what you're doing.) I asked Rayfield where you got such, and he told me that he regularly shopped at the local country store, taking the male clerk or owner aside. I told him that it would be impossible for me to go up to Mr. Garrison and tell him I wanted you know what. Rayfield insisted by telling me he would shop for me if I would give him a quarter. I reminded Rayfield, probably a little too quickly, that he was the one with all the money, he being the one paid out of this twosome. Rayfield thought a minute and nodded his head, and the conversation shifted to something else, being interrupted by a black snake charging through the cornfield.

"One day the next week, Rayfield presented me with a small paper bag that contained three coin-shaped things. Using the term he always referred to me, Rayfield said, 'Hyuh, Captn Jawn, put dese ting in yo pocket an keep one in yo wallet aller de time. I ain't wanna see yu hafta get marry to sumbody 'cause yu mek haste.' I thanked Rayfield for his generosity, and we went on about our business of the day.

"When I got home, I very nervously and cautiously took the package in and hid two of them under a loose board in the floor of my room and did as Rayfield instructed—put the third in my wallet.

"Later on, probably a couple of years later, I landed a job with the county spraying for mosquitoes. I had this truck that I drove around and fogged plum thickets and overgrown shrubbery around people's houses. I had to ask permission to spray shrubbery or anything close to houses, and in one house was a very pretty girl, about seventeen. She and I talked for a while, and I finally got up enough nerve to ask her if she had a steady boyfriend and found she did not. That led, as you are suspecting, to asking her to go out with me that coming Saturday night. And she accepted.

"Well, I borrowed my father's Studebaker that night and went to Juanita's house to pick her up. When I drove up to her house, she was waiting on the outside for her. It was my usual habit to go inside and meet the girl's parents and receive the usual inquisition about who my daddy and mama were and to be told in no uncertain terms about when to return the daughter home. Not the case here.

"She jumped in the car. And as we drove out of her driveway, she told me to take the next left after getting on the highway, which was a little used, woodsy road. She said that they had a fish pond down there, and her daddy wanted her to make sure the chain across the road was locked. Okay by me. When we got to the pond, which was several hundred yards from the highway, sure enough, the chain was down and the lock was on the ground. She told me to drive in and get out and look at the pond. She would get out and be ready to lock the gate when we drove out. I did as she suggested, noting that it was a good-looking pond, obviously well stocked. I turned around and returned to the car but found she was already in it. I opened the door, and to my surprise, Juanita did not have a stitch of clothes on and was lying on the backseat of the Studebaker. Talk about backpedaling, but that was what I did. I made every rational and irrational excuse in the world until she sort of indignantly started putting her clothes on. After leaving the pond site, we went in to Columbia and saw a movie, and I took her home.

I didn't see Juanita again. I went off to college that fall and met some of the boys from her hometown. I mentioned that I knew her, and the boys laughed and asked how I liked it. I told them that nothing happened, and they all showed their disbelief. One of the fellows dropped out of school before the semester ended, having to return home to marry Juanita and support them and the expectant child. Hab, I'm so glad I didn't take up that offer! I'm proud of the fact that I did finish college without having to take on obligations like that. Also, knowing her history of doing it with practically anybody, you would always wonder if the child was yours or if the next one would be yours. It would be a horrible way to begin a family.

Anyhow, that's the story I wanted to tell you. Also, you know I have a pretty extensive library at home—you've used some of the reference material. When we go back to the house, let me tell you about a couple of books on anatomy and such that you might be interested in. Got some past editions of *National Geographic* magazine too.

"Let me tell you that if the urges get too great, come to me, and I'll do what Rayfield did for me. I can't support a habit of more than a dollar a week for such, though (laughing)."

"Your life is ahead of you. You are a good-looking, well-proportioned young man. Your skin color renders you to be attractive to whites, blacks, and Hispanics. I don't want you to get yourself in water over your head when it comes to sexual activities. There will be a time and place, and if you wait long enough to develop clear thinking, all will be good and proper. "Now let's get off this rock and join your mama, who just drove up. Keep your britches zipped when you're around Marie, and we'll be in good shape."

J returned to the house, and Hab went in another direction, ostensibly to do some chore or other.

Pat said as J approached the house, "Well, what was that manly conversation about?"

J looked off into the distant and told her, "We spoke of cabbages and kings and oh so many things, world situation, nuclear fission, stock market, and how to catch and relocate the beaver that's damming up the creek."

Realizing the improbability of a straight answer, Pat simply said, "Sounds good. I hope you included birds and bees while you were at it. I'd a whole lot rather he hear about that subject from you than from my uncle Rayfield. Listening to Rayfield would probably result in a whole crop of children with a lighter shade of skin."

J nodded in agreement and proceeded to tap out the residue from his pipe while he was outside. End of conversation.

They entered the house and found Marie reading recipes at the kitchen table. After the usual exchange of pleasantries, J asked, "Pat, how's your schedule looking? I have all my income tax stuff together, and I'm wondering if you'll have the time, or should I find an accountant?"

Pat replied, "Dr. J, the tax information you've always given me in the past has been pretty complete, and all I have to do is enter the figures and wham-bam, it's done. No big deal. If I have questions about anything, I'll ask. Sure, I'll be glad to do that" and turned to her household tasks.

That night when Pat and Hab returned to their home, Marie commented to J, "I see that Pat does your taxes too. Has she been doing that a long time?" J explained that up until the time of my wife's accident and death, he had done his taxes. However, when it came time to do taxes after that, he found himself floundering, making one mistake after another, forgetting to take into account a lot of things dealing with Elizabeth's estate but fortunately catching them before sending the return in. I complained about losing the ability to do that chore and Pat told me she knew how to do taxes, having the software and having had a course in tax preparation. She does a great job, and all I have to do is sign it."

Marie continued, "You put a lot of trust in her, don't you?"

J answered, "I surely do. She not only does my income tax returns, she does my banking, and she pays all the bills. She is a trusted friend and a competent person. She knows more about my financial situation than either of my children. In fact, I sort of consider her one of my children. In many ways, I'm a surrogate father much the same as Ralph Jordan, the grocery store owner, was. Between the two of us, Ralph and me, we've had about as much fatherly influence on her as her biological parents, and they don't seem to resent it at all."

Their conversation turned to what Marie was doing for J, reporting progress and mentioning needs for more information and other cabbage and kings things.

At the end of that conversation, J turns to Marie and says, "Marie, as you have seen, it's my habit to go to church every Sunday, and I really haven't offered to take you. Would you like to go to my church with me, or would you like for me to take you to St. Gregory's for the Catholic services?"

Marie confessed, "I am reluctant to do either right now, Dr. J, but I appreciate the offer. I think my presence at either place would raise more questions and detract from the purpose of my going. I have found a television program on Sunday mornings when you're at church, and I think it's best for me to continue my worship in that way."

"If that's what you want to do, it's fine with me, but anytime you feel the need to go to mass, let me know, or if you would like to talk to a priest, the Catholic chaplain at the university is a dear friend and I'm sure he would be glad to come over and pay us a visit. Or I can get you to meet him there, whatever suits you. We'll have to feed him if he comes here, but that's not a problem."

Marie agreed. She was not accustomed to the "lost sheep" that seemed to drift in and out of Shalom.

The next day was Sunday, and J goes to the early service at church and stays for Sunday school. When he returned home, he was surprised to see Pat and Hab driving in just as he entered the Shalom driveway. Pat and Hab attend the Mt. Zion African Methodist Episcopal Church, and those services are not over until two or three in the afternoon.

The first question after "how are you" dealt with food. Pat asked if anybody had made plans for lunch, and the suspicion that it had not been thought of was confirmed. J offered something different. He recalled that there were some New York Strip steaks in the freezer and suggested that they be given a quick trip to the microwave for thawing, which would give him a chance to properly light charcoal. This was met with total agreement so he and Hab worked with the charcoal. His actions were such that indicated he had something to tell the close group but was holding it off for the proper time.

Marie detected this proud anxiety, saying, "Hab, I have a feeling that you want to tell us something, do you?"

Hab gleefully spilled the beans, so to speak, "Indeed I do. Y'all shoulda been at church this morning. I bet they're still there, talking about it."

With slight prodding, Hab relates, "Mama got up and walked to the front of the church right at the beginning and said, 'I need to say something to this congregation.' She said, 'some years ago I had a child and there was a rumor as to who might be the father, other than my husband, and the person they named in the rounds of gossip was Ralph Jordan, one of the sweetest men I have ever known in my life, and many of you knew he had had testicular cancer and wasn't able to have children but you didn't raise a hand to stop the gossip. Nobody stood up to say the gossip was absolute foolishness. It seemed like everybody in this congregation had itchy ears to hear things and tried to believe the very worst about a person. A lot of years have passed since then. I've finished my degree at the university, and I'm teaching in Winnsboro. I am thoroughly enjoying it, but I was told yesterday that there is another rumor going around, and that is that I'm having an affair with the principal of the school and I know who started it and she should be ashamed of herself. What happened is we were attending a workshop in Columbia and for the noon break, a number of us decided to go to California Dreaming Restaurant and have a good lunch. Well, it so happened that the principal and I were the first to arrive. I'm sure the person who started the rumor saw the two of us together, but what she didn't tell everybody else that within five minutes, there were ten other people sitting around the table. There were twelve of us at the meeting and yet according to the gossip monger, the principal and I were having an intimate lunch at California Dreaming. This kind of unfounded gossip is not good for anybody. It is not fair to my parents, it is not fair to our principal and his wife and family, and to be honest with you, I've had it with this church. I can't take any more of this, and I am going to get my son and I'm going to be walking out of this church and it is not my intention to come back unless it's for a funeral for somebody I respect so that will not be many.'"

"With that," Hab allowed, "she turned and looked at the preacher and said, 'You think you can find some time some Sunday to preach on the evil of gossip? I wish you would, and I wish these gossiping persons would listen and heed what you say.'"

Hab continued, smiling with pride, "She turned and motioned to me to stand up and out the church we walked. I 'spect the preacher might call us this afternoon or maybe one of the deacons. But Mama let them have it and I was proud of her."

There was a round of applause from the group, and Pat sort of nodded. "I didn't think I would have the courage to do it, but I've been waiting to do just the same thing for fourteen years."

After the much deserved steak dinner and the subsequent group cleanup, Pat was excusing herself when Marie asked if she could go with her, that she had some limited, simple income tax questions. Pat agreed, and the two of them left for Pat's house.

When it was time for questions, Marie confided that she really wanted to ask some more questions about J and his family. She said, "Pat, tell me about Elizabeth's fatal accident. The twins and I have questions about Rebecca and Jack. Start with why there are no pictures of these people in the house."

Pat took a long breath, and began. "First, let's talk about the cemetery located on the side of the driveway to Shalom. It's arranged, as are all Christian cemeteries, with the headstones facing east. This is in keeping with the Biblical promise that on Resurrection Day, the day Jesus returns to earth, all of the dead shall rise and all will be reunited. The deceased is placed in the grave facing the east so that the sunshine on that great getting-up morning will be in their face.

There is a stone on the front row bears the name of Elizabeth Christian Taylor Stewart. To the left of that one are two more, with the names James Christian Stewart and Margaret Christian Stewart. Those are the headstones for J's wife, Elizabeth, and the twins.

When the twins were fourteen, Elizabeth had some errands to run and took the twins with her. Dr. J wished them well that morning and they started out. Elizabeth took a back road into town because she wanted to drop off a couple of late Christmas presents to people she knew through her nursing duties. In that area, logging, the cutting of trees for timber, was going on. Robert Foster and his sons ran a very efficient logging operation and were well-known for the condition of their equipment. They had done so well they had just bought a new truck and trailer. It was delivered to them where they were logging. Robert and his boys were as excited as children with their new rig.

The salesman for the truck backed it in to where they were loading logs, and with great pleasure, they loaded the new trailer. When they were about finished, the truck started lurching forward without explanation. Bobby, the oldest son, jumped into the truck, thinking the emergency brake could not be activated, which it was. He applied the foot brakes with all his might, to no avail. It began lurching and skipping forward, with Bobby yelling that he couldn't stop it. The truck had been backed up an incline in the newly cut logging road, and it continued out of control until it reached the bottom, where it intersected with the country road Elizabeth was travelling on. The truck collided with Elizabeth's car and rammed it across the road and into the woods on the other side before becoming so entangled that the rig stopped. Elizabeth, the twins and Bobby were all killed instantly. The funeral for Elizabeth and the twins was held two days later, and those are their tombstones in the Stewart Family cemetery. That was a little over ten years ago now. Even after that long, he's still in a state of mourning to a degree. He's confided in me that things are just now settling down because when he sits on the rock, he's talking to Elizabeth, and she's assuring him that all is okay with them.

Within days after the accident, J received calls from attorneys from all over the country, offering to represent him in a suit against the truck manufacturer. He finally turned to his old friend, a lawyer from Camden, John C. (Jack) Westerfield. Jack was probably the best choice that J could have made because of Jack's connection. He has connections from all over. One of the stipulations was that J would not testify in any hearing or court proceeding and was not going to be involved in any negotiations personally. Robert Foster also used the Westerfield firm to represent him for his losses, also, but I don't know anything about that settlement.

J's settlement was huge, into the multimillion dollars. He, of course, had to share a substantial portion with the Westerfield Law Firm, but needless to say, J is very well off. To look at him, you would not be able to tell he has money to wash his car with, but that's the way he wants it.

I need to tell you about J, Elizabeth, and the children. It is a love story that would make a great movie, and it still continues, ten years after her death. Maybe with my telling you details to such a person as you with writing skills, it would be a best-seller.

Now about the lack of pictures of these people in the house, following the accident, J just could not look them. It reduced him to tears and he would simply walk out of the house and sit on that damn rock. After a few days, I took them all out of sight and I have them here at my house. As a matter of fact, I have several albums of photographs, not only of Elizabeth and the children, but of his parents and him as a kid.

As to his son Jack, I have a photo of him when he was president of the student body, and I was president of the senior class where we went to school. Jack and I graduated from high school the same year. Shortly after his high school graduation, he entered the U.S. Air Force Academy. He would return home maybe once per year for the whole four years he was there and graduated with an outstanding record. I have photographs of him when he was accepted into the Air Force Academy and news clippings of honors he has received during his air force career. He went on active duty with the air force after his graduation, and after only one year, the air force gave him an opportunity to go to graduate school. He has a master's of science in aeronautical engineering. But for his doctorate, he chose philosophy, oddly enough. He served a tour of duty somewhere in the Middle East. But after that tour of duty, he was asked to return to the Air Force Academy as a member of the faculty, where he has been for the past four or so years. When he was here for Christmas, he told me he was entering a new assignment with the air force.

"Now as for Rebecca, I have wedding pictures of Jack's sister Rebecca. She is two years younger than Jack. She was living at home for about a year and a half after I moved in. When she finished high school, she went to college, as all expected her to do. She's extremely bright and did exceptionally well in academics. She majored in history and was offered an outstanding scholarship to work on her PhD, which she did, and graduated first in her class. During the last year of her PhD work, she started dating a young man, and after a year's courtship and their graduations, they were married. Incidentally, his major was philosophy also. The wedding was held in Colorado, where he came from. His family has been there for years, and they had a long list of people they wished to invite to the wedding, so J agreed that the wedding should be held there. After their marriage, they both received good job offers from the University of Oregon, and that's where they've been since. Rebecca is now thirty years old, and Jack is thirty-two. Jack has never married, and I have never heard of any rumors of him every being seriously involved with anyone. There is no evidence whatsoever that he has a sexual preference other than the usual one. J would be delighted to have a grandchild come into this world before he goes, but it doesn't look like that's going to happen."

Marie gave Pat time to get her breath and collect her thoughts and then asked, "Now please tell me about Elizabeth. You told me you were going to tell me about her sometime, especially about how they met and such."

Pat bit her lip, which began to curve downward. She shook her head and said, "I don't know if I can do this. I wish she were here to tell you herself, but let me try. Elizabeth majored in nursing at the university. In her junior year, she had an opportunity to take an elective, and she took philosophy under the young Dr. J. When the first class was over, J said, 'Ms. Taylor, if you would, please stop by my desk.' And of course, she did. He asked her, 'I have a question of you. Why are you taking philosophy?' When she looked at him quizzically, he continued, 'I've never had a nursing student select philosophy as an elective.'

"Her answer was a simple, 'Well, I have my own reasons, but at this time, I prefer not to tell you.'

"J agreed and the subject was dropped."

Pat continued to describe Elizabeth. "She was oh so fiery. She was brilliant. She was one of those people who are blessed with a photographic memory and nothing escaped her. The reason she took that philosophy class and was not willing to share the reason was that she had heard him speak at some event and when she saw him, she said, 'That's the man I want to marry.' It was just that quick and sudden. The next year, when she had the need for an elective, she was there in J's class.

J, upon seeing Elizabeth Christian Taylor had enrolled in the second philosophy class, asked her again why she was choosing his class as an elective, adding that nurses just don't do that.

Her reply contained words to the effect that she would tell him in May. Still puzzled, J simply said, "All right, I'll wait till May."

On the last day of classes in Elizabeth's last semester, she appeared at J's office and tapped on the door. She was beckoned in so she came in and stood. J waved to a chair and offered, "Have a seat." She declined, saying her visit wouldn't take long.

"What can I do for you?"

"You can be my escort at a dance that going to be taking place next week."

"Young lady, how old are you? Twenty-one? Twenty-two? I'm many years your senior."

"That doesn't bother me, and I hope it doesn't bother you."

"Well, I'm flattered that you asked, but you should know there are rules against a faculty member dating a student."

"I'm well aware of that, Dr. J, but by that time I'll no longer be a student. My graduation is just before the dance."

"Well, Ms. Taylor, you have caught me completely off guard. May I think about it?"

"I was in hopes you wouldn't have to think about it."

After a moment's silence, J said, "No. I don't need to think about it. I'd be delighted and honored to be your escort. Give me the time and the place and all the details."

Ms. Elizabeth Christian Taylor pulled a sheet of paper from her philosophy textbook, smiled, and said, "And here it is, sir," turned and went out the office door.

Pat paused and smiled and said, "I said she was brilliant but I didn't tell you that she was also beautiful. Here's a photograph of her in her wedding dress. But I'm getting ahead of my story. Dr. J did escort her to the dance, and one month later, he asked her to be his wife and the wedding took place three months after that. They were made for each other. I wish everyone could have that kind of love affair that never cooled. They worked together and played together. Everything was just about in a state of perfection. After graduation and marriage and the honeymoon, she went to work for the County Health Department, making home visits. Her parents weren't particularly pleased with the timing of the marriage. Oh, they were very pleased with having J as a son-in-law but thought Margaret had many other opportunities she could explore. For example, the dean of the School of Nursing at the university told her that if she would get her PhD, she had a teaching position at the university, or if she would get her master's she had a job on the dean's staff. Elizabeth supposed to have said, 'The only other degree I want is Mrs. J Stewart.'

"I told you they worked together and for each other and that she had very definite ideas of how things should go. As an example, after they had been married about a year, J asked an insurance salesman to come to see him and to discuss a $500,000 life insurance policy on himself. The salesman was of course delighted to be able to write such a policy, but being a good salesman, he asked what size policy he was planning for Mrs. Stewart. J told him that he hadn't planned on that, just insurance for him.

Elizabeth was furious. She told him right then and there, 'Listen, if something happened to you, we could get along fine. If something happened to me, you would be in a state of turmoil and wouldn't be able to make a living. If anybody in this family needs life insurance, it's me and not you.' The salesman took the cue and presented some excellent facts, with the result being they took out a $250,000 policy on Elizabeth and a $250,000 policy on J, and $50,000 for each child, with automatic insurability of the same $50,000 for children yet unborn.

Pat went through the photo albums and went through them, identifying the people and the occasion, with tears streaming down her cheeks. Pat walked into her bedroom and left Marie with the albums, telling her that when she had finished, leave the albums on the dining room table.

DR. J'S MAY 2008

E VERY DAY IN the last two weeks of April was beautiful, beautiful in temperature, beautiful in clear skies, and beautiful in blooming plants and trees. May 2008 continued the pattern. Flowers of all sorts were safe from spring frosts. Azaleas were in full bloom in the South Carolina Midlands and it seemed as if every household had at least one bush, with many having banks of the voracious blooming plants. Azaleas and the other flowering bushes were showing themselves off.

Speaking of showing themselves, but with a different meaning, Marie was showing with her pregnancy. Maternity clothing had to be purchased and adjustments had to be made.

In yet another light of showing themselves, Marie reminded J of his date with Millie, scheduled for that evening. Millie, after recovering from seeing the mostly nude Marie in the staid Stewart home and thinking it was her duty to pass that information on to J's children and anybody else she could think of that might be concerned with J's welfare, had been calmed after an explanation of why Marie was there by J. What J told her made perfect sense and would have expected those actions from Gentleman J.

Now there was a black tie fund-raiser scheduled at the McKissick Library on the university campus and Millie called and asked J to escort her, J being the pillar of respectability and representative of the university and the fine old families of the South Carolina Midlands.

Marie suggested that J's hair was getting a little long, and he just might want to get a little trim before picking his tuxedo shirt from the cleaners.

J agreed, saying that he owed Millie a fresh look, which she deserved, knowing her station in life.

J has not yet developed a relationship with a female hairdresser professional or one with much of a barber professional either. He traveled down to Paul's on Main Street in Blythewood and was able to walk right in and sit in Paul's number one chair, manned by Paul, himself. As Paul was doing the best he could, Arlis Jeffrey, one of the neighbor landowners, came in for his monthly trim. The usual barbershop banter began, suspended temporarily by Paul announcing he had done all he could do. J suggested that maybe he could get a shave too, stating that it was one of those things he hadn't witnessed. Paul backed away, saying, "Oh no! I don't shave live people. I get called on by the Kornegay Funeral Home to shave dead people sometimes so they'll look good in the casket, but I wouldn't dare attempt shaving a live soul for nothing!" Paul added that the last live person he'd shaved was when he was in barber school at the Area Trade School in West Columbia about forty years ago.

Under the circumstances, J did not press the issue. He said, "I guess I'll have to do it myself," giving a mock display of dissatisfaction and disappointment.

When getting out of the chair, J felt a sharp pain in the right side of his head, which remained. He walked over to one of the waiting chairs and resumed his conversation with Arlis Jeffrey. Arlis mentioned to J that he must have an overstocked fish pond, and how were they biting. J countered by saying that he, himself, had not been fishing in his pond lately, but had given Clara Johnson permission to fish there a week or so ago. "She told me she was having family in and wanted enough for eight or ten people. I asked her after she'd been there as to her success and she told me they were biting slowly and she was barely able to catch enough for her company. She said she wanted to come back and try again today."

Arlis said, "J, that's not what I heard. I must have seen her husband, Tom, the same day she was over there, and he told me that Clara just brought home sixty fish, mostly Bream, but three or four Bass. Might want to look into that, J. Your pond isn't that big and when you take out that many fish at one time, it takes a while to regroup."

J's facial expression apparently indicated to Arlis that J hadn't expected to hear that and added, "Did I say something wrong? I was just telling you what Tom told me. I know both of them lie like snakes, but I also know they're all out for themselves. I didn't discuss it with Tom, but I don't allow them on my property. Something always comes up missing when one of them's been there."

With the pain in J's head raging, he assured Arlis that what he had told him was okay, and he appreciated it then got up, checked to see if his walking and balancing abilities were acceptable, and then got in the slime green Toyota and drove home, faster than he usually would have, because it was approaching noon and he knew that Clara Johnson would be leaving the pond shortly. He drove directly to the pond, and saw Clara's brown Ford pickup parked in the shade with a large cooler in the truck bed. J went over and opened the cooler and found thirty or forty large bream that had just been placed there. He looked to his left and saw Clara sitting on a bucket near the pond's edge, still fishing. He walked up behind her and called her by name. She jumped, being startled, and showed extreme discomfort that he was there. J asked, "Are you having any luck?" Clara hesitated a second and told him she was having a little, but they were biting slowly, but it was time for her to go. J walked closer and pulled a stringer from the edge of the water next to her, to which fifteen to eighteen bream were attached.

They looked at each other for a second or two, and J said in a quiet but unmistakable tone, "Clara, I have known you for a long time and I have always taken you at your word that you were being truthful with me. I really expected better out of you. Now before I call the sheriff, get your fish from this stringer, put them in the cooler with the other thirty or forty in the back of your truck and get your . . . your . . . yourself out of here and I never want to see you on this property again. You have lost my trust. You have taken advantage of my property and you have lied to me, not only today but last week when I asked how they were biting. Now go and be quick about it."

Clara left, mumbling something under her breath that J could barely detect, but they were words to the effect that she was being treated without the respect she deserved.

J sat in the driver's seat of his Toyota with his door open while he watched Clara leave. The pain in his head was beginning to dim slightly, but not enough to make much difference. After Clara left, J started the Toyota and returned to Shalom. J thought to himself, "Oh god! What have I done? I've probably alienated the entire white trash population around the county. Should've just kept her from coming back."

J returned to Shalom, walked into the kitchen to receive Marie's approval of his haircut and was distracted by a late model Buick entering the driveway. He said to Marie, "I don't know who this is, but I hope we have enough leftovers for lunch for at least three people."

His suspicions were confirmed when he welcomed Jason McIntosh, III, dubbed by J to be J Mac 3, to Shalom and introduced him to Marie.

J Mac 3's first words were, "I hope you have enough scraps leftover for one more traveler!"

J explained to Marie while the three of them were in the kitchen, Marie working diligently to round up leftovers, that J Mac 3 and J had shared an apartment during their graduate school days.

Lunch was consumed at the kitchen table, and the conversation and the participants drifted in to the den. As time went on, J apologized and told the others that he felt he had to lie down for a while because his headache was not getting better. Marie reminded J that his time in the bedroom needed to be pretty short because he had a date that night. J Mac 3 jumped into the conversation, insisting that J tell him about this even and who his date was. Curious, gossipy old men, thought Marie. And we get accused of gossip!

J reveals that his date is none other than Millie, who J Mac 3 remembers, but not well, from years ago. J excused himself and left J Mac 3 and Marie talking. In an hour, J returned, saying that his headache was not getting better and that he had an idea. "Why don't you go in my place?" he asked J Mac 3. After protests that such would not be appropriate and that he hadn't planned on doing anything like that and didn't have the proper clothing with him, J observed that they were about the same size. The result was that J Mac 3 agreed to be a substitute, further being an unannounced substitute, without letting Millie know. J described the event, gave Millie's address, and told J Mac 3 to stop by Publix or some grocery store other than Piggly Wiggly and pick up a dozen roses to take with him and show up at Millie's house at seven in the evening. Marie protested the decision of surprising Millie, thinking that it would be awfully unfair to send somewhat of a stranger, someone she hadn't seen in thirty years and probably didn't remember him then. J vetoed the protest, just smiling and saying, "Let the old gal be surprised."

J returned to rest while Marie helped round up the proper attire for a formal occasion. Within the time allotted for a quick trip to the Fresh Market, a substitute for Publix, J Mac 3 left on his mission of mercy.

That evening, J shared information about his old friend with Marie and Pat. He told them that four years ago, Jason's wife died after a long battle with cancer. J and Jason have communicated off and on since her death, but not much in the last year. At the end of their dinner, J proposed an ice tea toast to his old friend, wishing him the best of a good evening. The wish must have worked because Jason did not return the entire night long and not until eleven the next morning, walking in with a sheepish grin.

J pontificated, "I think it best not to ask what happened, but from the look on your face and the fatigue in your walk, it apparently was an extensive fun-filled evening!"

Jason began the details of his evening, night and morning out talking about the marvelous company of Marvelous Millie. She did in fact remember him from years back and had spent the greater part of the night talking about old acquaintances, people, places, their former spouses, and probably much he omitted. He did ask J if he could stay a couple of days at Shalom while he got to know Millie better. J agreed, and little was seen of J Mac 3 because of spending time in Columbia. At J's insistence, he even raided J's closet and borrowed clothes because he had brought only an overnight bag with him, expecting to spend only one night with J. On the fourth day, he announced that he was returning to Virginia—this time with Millie, wanting to show her where he lived, meet his children, and so forth.

That evening, the family of four enjoyed their evening fried chicken meal and reviewing the current events. They all took turns with their reports, much as reporting a classroom assignment. In the news of the day, John Edwards announced he was supporting Barack Obama for president. And then there were the great China earthquake and the cyclone in Darfur. Marie talked about Ted Kennedy's hospitalization, suffering with seizures. Pat contributed news of foreclosures and the decline of the housing market. When the conversation seemed to come to a close, on J's suggestion, they all held hands and individually prayed for one disaster or other.

The group was about to break up, with Pat and Hab returning to their home after the kitchen cleanup, and Marie back to some of her work on J's children's books, when J received a phone call. Everyone watched as J's voice became serious, and the expression on his face became troubled. He kept saying to the caller in disbelief, "You're joking! You are kidding, aren't you?"

The caller insisted the news he brought was not, indeed a joke. As the conversation ended, J thanked the caller and reached for the telephone directory, saying, "I thought those days were over and gone forever, but I guess not." The group watched with interest as he dialed the number and asked to speak to Sheriff Culclasure. The conversation went like this—the caller was his friend Arlis Jeffrey, who he had met in the barbershop that morning. It seems as if Clara Johnson's husband was visiting all of the less-intelligent white men in the area and telling them that J was living in double sin at his "mansion," that he had had a black concubine living with him since his wife died, and that now he had taken on a young white woman, who was obviously pregnant. He harangued that the Christian men of the community had an obligation to show this infidel some manners and was enlisting them to join him tomorrow night dressed in white robes. They would burn a cross on his front lawn, next to the cemetery; and if there were enough of them, they'd burn his mansion too. J related to the sheriff that his friend Arlis told him the white fellow that worked for him on his property came to him and told him, assuring Arlis that he wanted no part of that action himself and that he thought Johnson would not be able to rally much support. Jeffery's man told him that Johnson had gone into the local mill village and started talking the same thing, ending with Anderson being chased out. The conversation ended with J thanking the sheriff for listening and that the plan outlined sounded like a good one.

J turned to his bewildered group and told them the whole story, much of which they had already been able to piece together. He told them the background of the action that he found that Clara Johnson had taken advantage of his generosity by fishing in his pond, depleting his stock, and selling some in the neighborhood, that he had pretty adamantly told her to leave and not come back. He then gave them a history of Klan work in the area, noting that the last such cross burning occurred back in the late 1930s, that he was surprised that such evil still persisted. He told them to say nothing of the planned activity but plan to return before dark tomorrow night to see the outcome.

Part of the next day was spent at Sheriff Roy Culclasure's office. The sheriff sent his deputies out to interview possible accomplices and found that the news picked up by Arlis Jeffrey's man was accurate. Johnson had been trying to solicit support for this cross burning or worse endeavor but, from all evidence, had been turned down. J returned home in the early afternoon and called Pat when she returned home from school, insisting that she and Hab come over as soon as feasible. J told Pat that a deputy was going to be stationed near here house from about four in the afternoon through the night, just in case there were any unknown accomplices.

The four assembled with quiet deliberation. Dinner was done with little conversation. Hab alone burst out, decrying the injustices of hate and the unfairness of fostering untruths, gossip, and innuendos. Pat shushed him, and J outlined the plan for the night. Pat, Hab and Marie, if they chose to, could watch out of the den window. No lights were to be turned on at dark that night. Sheriff Culclasure and J would be sitting together, hidden, in the front yard, while deputies would be hidden on all sides of the house. All of the law enforcement people would be in touch with each other by radio. The sheriff and deputies were equipped with night-vision binoculars.

The wait began. In the latter part of May in the South Carolina Midlands, dark does not come until just before nine in the evening. The men outside swatted mosquitoes and tried to get as comfortable as they could.

Sure enough, around ten in the evening, the first radio report came in from Deputy Coronado, who was stationed near the entrance to Shalom. A few seconds later, Sheriff Culclasure, looking through his night-vision glasses, said, "Here he is. He's in his brown Ford pickup with the lights off. Guess he can see the ruts in the road, even though it's dark. Looks like he's got somebody with him too. I'll be damned! It's Clara!"

The truck moved slowly to a point about in the middle of the rock and the cemetery.

"He's getting out," reports the sheriff. From then on, he kept J posted on what was apparently happening. Johnson walked around to the back of the truck and removed a skinny cross that appeared to be wrapped in hay or straw of some sort. Johnson walked a few feet with the cross and took a hammer from his overalls and beat a rod sticking out of the back into the ground. "Must have a piece of rod fixed to the bottom of the cross somehow because he's driving it in the ground," reported the sheriff.

Johnson returned to the truck and put on his robe, which covered his body from the shoulders down like a dress, almost to the ground. He reached into the truck cab again and pulled out a ridiculous looking hood, with a peaked top, but complete with eye holes, and proceeded to put it on. The next thing he did was to reach into the back of the truck and retrieved a gallon metal can, removed the cap, and sloppily threw the contents onto the cross but failed to pour a trail away from the cross which would have provided an escape route for him. He threw the can to the ground, reached under his robe, and pulled out a Bic cigarette lighter. "That fool's going to kill himself!" Blurted the Sheriff. "He's going to light the damn thing standing right next to it!" He grabbed his radio and ordered a deputy, stationed even closer, to move in and prepare to extinguish the fire. Just as he gave those instructions, Johnson lit the gasoline soaked cross, and the flames leaped over to his robe, setting it on fire too just as the sheriff suspected he would.

He said, "I knew he was dumb as a stump, but for God's sake, nobody is that dumb, to set themselves on fire!" at the same time ordering a second deputy to assist. Before the first deputy arrived at full run, Clara Johnson screamed and jumped out of the truck and ran over to her husband, trying to knock him down and roll him over. The deputy had to lift her out of the way before he could rip the burning white cloth from Johnson, who was not only trying to extinguish the flames but run away. The second deputy arrived and restrained Johnson while the first deputy extinguished the remaining flames. A third deputy arrived in time to catch Clara as she ran down the driveway to the highway.

Within minutes, the whole show, if it could be called a show, was over. The Johnson's were placed in separate patrol cars and were being whisked away to the hospital to be checked over and treated if needed. Deputies remaining used a fire extinguisher to put out the blazes on the skinny, malformed cross, which was taken away.

J thanked the Sheriff and returned to the house and reported all to those there.

Johnson faced charges of trespassing, destruction of property, perpetuating a hate crime (which is a relatively new statute adopted by the South Carolina legislature), resisting arrest and who knows what else. Clara was charged with aiding and abetting and trespassing and resisting arrest. Their nine-year-old son was found at home alone and was taken to a foster home by the Department of Social Services.

And so ended the month of May 2008 in J's limited life.

THE FIRST FEW days of June found J working with Sheriff Culclasure and the Johnsons. J did not file charges of trespassing or destroying personal property. He talked to the Sheriff about dropping all charges, but Culclasure refused. Hate crimes in South Carolina are taken seriously and cannot and will not be tolerated. Johnson's burns were not that severe and, after treatment, healed well. The Department of Social Services did keep their child safe and in a better home environment. After investigation, neighbors verified that Johnson was an alcoholic and neglected his family, frequently beating his wife and son during drunken frenzies. J made a mental note of the son's situation, silently vowing to assist the child in some way if at all possible.

The first day of June also marked the last day of the school year for Hab and Pat, with Hab now preparing to enter middle school the next school year. Pat's job as a substitute teacher came to an end.

One morning in the first week of June, as J watched Marie fixing herself breakfast of coffee, toast, and jelly and told her, "You know, Marie, you need more food than that. Let me at least get you some cereal and milk. Got to get milk into your system. Got to get those strong bones going."

Marie reluctantly agreed, and after a few minutes of conversation, J suggested they take a ride through the neighborhood. In less than an hour, the slime green Toyota and two people exited the Shalom driveway.

The first stop was Jordan's country store, the place where Pat was befriended by proprietor Ralph Jordan, shortly after her graduation from high school and marriage. Marie commented on the sign outside that declared, "If we don't have it, you don't need it."

They went inside and J introduced Marie to Ralph and his wife Sybil. The store owners were very friendly and talked on various subjects for almost an hour. The only purchase J made was a set of Snickers bars for his friend, Bubba, the road greeter.

Marie asked J as they left if the store was a prototype for Walmart, in that it had a little bit of almost anything a person would want. The sign outside was technically correct. If the Jordan's didn't have it, a shopper could find something vaguely similar or they really didn't need it.

Marie also commented on the plethora of McCain-for-President signs and the total absence of Obama signs in the neighborhood. J sagely pointed out that this community, as was most in the entire state of South Carolina, solidly Republican, which was a constant source of criticism by the mainstream, but not the local media. He explained that it did not necessarily mean that much support for McCain, but it indicated that the devil you know something about is better than the devil you don't. He agreed that Obama's rise to power and the ideas that he espoused were in serious need of explaining, and just change for the sake of change is not a good thing.

The conversation shifted to Bubba because they were coming up on his station by the side of the road, where he took his waving and smiling position. Marie asked if Bubba would be there, and J's answer was "If the sun's shining, Bubba will be there."

Sure enough, Bubba was there, smiling in all of his radiant glory, keeping all the passersby happy with his ebullience. They talked for several minutes when Bubba reached through the passenger window, touched Marie, and said, "It's gonna be a fine boy." Marie almost recoiled and said, "And how do you know that? I don't even know myself."

Bubba replied, "Oh, I just knows. It's a baby boy and he's just as pretty as me!" All laughed at that comparison, and Marie said a nonverbal prayer, "Dear God, let the child be better looking than that!"

All said their good-byes and well wishes, and J and Marie returned to Shalom.

As they entered the house, the telephone rang. J didn't recognize the voice on the other end at first, which brought on a friendly accusation that he sure did forget old friends fast. In a few seconds, J identified the caller as William Johnson, one of the fellows in the community whom he knew well during his high school and early college years. Johnson's voice was serious, and he asked if he could drive from just inside the South Carolina line, near Charlotte, and talk to J, which he, of course, agreed to.

Upon hanging up, J told Marie that an old friend was coming to talk to him about something, something apparently serious to him, because he was going to drive over, taking around two hours then drive back home. J asked Marie to get something together for lunch, which she readily agreed to.

Marie said, "Tell me about your friend."

J laughed and said, shaking his head, "Bill Johnson and I were best of friends in high school and the first few years of college. He's had his ups and downs, and unfortunately, many more downs than ups. I don't know what's on his mind now, but it must be weighing heavily on him. We haven't seen each other in over a year now. It may concern his care giving efforts to his wife, who has muscular dystrophy, or something might be going on with his children. I don't know, but I feel privileged that he thinks enough of me to drive all this way in one day to see me.

"But let me tell you about some of our experiences. Bill was the quarterback on our football team and I was playing an end position. I'm sure he was the brightest student in our class, maybe with the exception of Barbara Smith. I can't remember who was valedictorian and who was salutatorian, but between the two, they filled both slots. Like I said, Bill was the quarterback. He has mentioned many times about the night we were playing a rival team and during the huddle told me to go out fifteen steps and turn and the ball would be there. I went out the fifteen steps and turned, and yes, just as he said it would be, the ball was there, but it hit me right in the face. It was of course my fault. During that same game, and I don't know how it came about, but Bill was running with the ball and I was running beside him to block and he lateraled the ball off to me. There was one person between me and eighty yards of the goal and I knew I could fake him, and I did a fairly good job of faking and stiff arming but he caught me by my sleeve and planted his feet to the ground. The sleeve stretched and stretched and finally came over my hand. This, of course, was before the day of tear-away jerseys. He put his feet into the turf and I couldn't go. I tried to circle him to break him loose, and it was just like pop the whip that little kids play. I wouldn't turn loose, and he wouldn't either. Finally, he did let go. And when he did, I was totally off balance and went plowing into the ground. The thing that added to the embarrassment was a young lady in the stands who was visiting that night who had sent a note that she was coming to town especially to see me play.

"Bill and I ran around together during his school and the first few years of college. A group of us boys would get together some Saturday nights and ride over to the Barn, which was located in the country between Lancaster and Pageland, about forty miles away. I don't know whether you're familiar with the term 'snake' or not, but we were all snakes. We were too cheap to take girlfriends or didn't have any at the time but would go without dates to this country dance hall. We relied on dancing with the dates of the other fellows who were there. Snakes are regarded as being the lowest form of life that would steal dates. By going in numbers in one car, we really didn't do that. We just danced with the women whose husbands or boyfriends were too tired or more interested in talking or drinking. Sort of a dangerous thing to do. The odds of getting your tail whipped by a jealous boyfriend were pretty high. Going in numbers helped there too. If we saw one of the group getting in a fight or if it looked like one, we would grab him up, and away we'd go. I remember one occasion when Bill and I, along with two more fellows, rode over to the barn. We were sitting in our booth when a man walked in with this very, very pretty young lady, about three or four years older than we were, who looked almost as pretty as you do, and sat down two booths away. We commented on her looks, assigned her number very close to ten, and went on with our conversation. In a few minutes, we noticed the man had disappeared and that the young lady was sipping on a Coke, clearly agitated, with her legs crossed and one of them swinging impatiently. A reasonable length of time passed, probably thirty seconds, and I went over and asked her if she wanted to dance. Ms. Gorgeous—or rather Mrs., as it turned out—shook her head, thanked me, but said no. In about a half hour, I asked her again, and she declined again. Around an hour later, after we had "snaked" dances with several girls, I looked up after having sat down after dancing, here was Mrs. Gorgeous placing her hand on my shoulder and asking me, "Would you like to dance?" Naturally, I said, "Why not?" and we must have danced for the next hour or so. Shortly after that, she leaned over and asked me, "Would you like to go to Ocean Drive with me right now? The pavilion at OD is just starting to get going, and we can be there in an hour or so." I explained that it sounded good to me. But I didn't have my car, that there were four of us, to which she replied that she had hers and would bring me back some time around daylight. I thought about all the consequences for about ten seconds and agreed, but warned her that I really didn't have but about $15 with me. No problem for her, so there was no problem with me. She told me to give her about five minutes and then come outside and she would be in a new Ford convertible. I watched as she went up to the counter and asked for her purse, which was the custom at the barn. People had the option of paying when served or running up a tab, if a purse or billfold was left with the person behind the counter, who guaranteed safekeeping. Anyhow, she received her purse, reached in, and pulled out a roll of bills, peeled several off for her bill and a tip, and walked through the door.

JERRY HAMMET & HAROLD GUERRY

"I waited like I was supposed to for about five minutes and as I went outside I saw the convertible, with the young lady and a man holding a pistol, talking.

"The man was shouting, 'What in the hell are you doing? Are you running off again?' The lady calmly answered that she was just getting some fresh air, that it was getting a little stuffy inside. The man looked up and saw me, looked me over and was about say something to me, but I looked away as if I had seen nothing and walked over to one of the cars parked down the row and pretended to get something from it. I turned around and walked back in, paying as little attention as I could to the couple. In a minute or so, the couple returns and sits down again. I sat there in silence with my buddies, who were dying for an explanation, but I signaled for silence and we changed the subject. It wasn't long before the man came over to me and said, "Buddy, how about doing me a favor?" Naturally, I said "Sure," and he told me, "How about keeping an eye on my wife. Here's ten bucks. Buy yourself a beer or whatever you want and keep her in cokes and if she wants to dance, dance with her. Just make sure she doesn't leave the building again. If she does, just knock on that green door, but don't go in. I'll be sitting right inside, and I'll hear your knock." With agreements all around, the man left and closed the green door behind him. In a few minutes, I went over and sat down and asked what the hell all that was about, and she told me that they do this every Saturday night. "He makes me come with him and sit out here while he goes in to join the poker game. I'm tired of it. About a month ago I left him here and went to OD and didn't come back for three days and he didn't like it. But I'm not going anywhere tonight so let's dance."

And dance we did until about two in the morning when the poker game broke up. Bill and I have talked about that many times, especially about me saying I was seeing imaginary headlines in the *State Newspaper*, declaring "Fairfield student killed in Lancaster County Dance Hall Parking Lot."

Bill and I had a lot of experiences like that. He finished his bachelor's and went on to earn an MBA. From there he got a good job with a large company and was moving up the ladder pretty quickly. Bill was one of few boys in high school who drank and, after college, began heavy social drinking. This came crashing down, however, when he was in charge of a banquet for the company's major customers. He started drinking early that day, and when the banquet was to begin, he stood up to make announcements but passed out at the head table and fell over onto the floor. The company fired him the next morning when he recovered. From there, he knocked around in a series of jobs, none of which were doing him or them any good. After a while I was able to convince him to attend AA meetings regularly and luckily, he responded well. He realized his children were getting to be of the age they notice alcoholic antics, and his wife was threatening to leave him.

Around that time, I learned of a high school football team that needed an assistant coach, and on my recommendation and promise to intervene if he fell off the wagon, Bill was hired. He coached and taught there for a few years then became the head coach of a larger high school near the North Carolina line and served there until his retirement.

Bill and his wife, Caroline, have three children, two of them living in nearby towns. Bill retired early because his wife, who did stand by him through his difficult times, came down with muscular dystrophy. He is her caregiver, and I think their love for each other grows every day. Once he gave up drinking, his bad temper and caustic remarks went away. He's accepted the fact he is an alcoholic and always will be and knows the consequences of his actions, should he decide to drink again. He accepts things as they are and makes the best of them. I don't know what's on his mind, but I'm looking forward to seeing him and encouraging him and hearing what he has to say.

Bill arrives sharply at eleven in the morning. J introduces Bill to Marie, who excuses herself to work on lunch, leaving them to talk.

Talk they did. Bill stayed for three hours, and then announced it was time to go. Most of their conversation dealt with remembrances of the past, of high school football, home town, politics, the world situation, and other miscellaneous topics. When Bill was driving out of the driveway, J thought to himself, *What the hell was that all about? I enjoyed spending time with Bill, but he didn't mention one relevant reason why he wanted to come to see me. Oh, well. Guess I should be grateful for old friends who want to stay in touch.*

The rest of June seemed to rush by. The lazy days of summer were kicking in, so to speak. Hab asked J to help him go into business. He knew that the summer baseball games would be starting up soon, and his entrepreneurial idea was to operate a concession stand at the community ball park. His plan was to have hot dogs, chips, candy bars and drinks for sale at the games. His plan was to keep the math simple, thus facilitating the speed of making change, much less the complexity. Everything would be $1.00, with no tax added. He asked J if he and his mother could borrow the slime green pickup to transport the supplies in, which J agreed to, as well as financing the first purchase of goods. Hab didn't make a million but did well with his venture, unencumbered by government regulations. He had no business license, no food handlers or preparers health certificate, no inspection of his prep kitchen, and completely forgot to reimburse J for gas in the truck.

South Carolina community baseball games are something everyone should become involved in, whether it is joining one of the teams, volunteering to umpire, or just being a spectator. The team members work at regular jobs and never practice, unless one would call throwing and catching the ball in the backyard with one of the family children practice. Team members are usually very good about showing up for games, but they never start on time. If too many show up for one team and not enough show for the opposing team, one or two from the overstaffed team moves over to the opposition, or a player is drafted from the audience. A young man from the neighborhood, home on leave from the military, is always allowed to play. Uniforms may or may not be required. Some retired person usually serves as umpire, unless there is an injured player who takes the role. Rule infractions are of course argued, but without the vehemence of the major league confrontations, mainly because no one is exactly sure of the rule in question. Tempers sometime flair and there is an occasional fight, but these altercations are short-lived. The resident deputy sheriff oftentimes attends, sitting in his car, listening to the crime reports over his radio as dispatched from the sheriff's office. There may be bleachers, but that's not a requirement. There is no admission charged, but if there is a person in need in the community, the "hat" is passed. There is no medical backup, and if someone is hit in the head with a stray ball and really needs attention, someone will volunteer to take him or her for treatment or home for an ice pack. If there is a strain or a charley horse, there is encouragement from the team to "shake it off."

After supper one Friday night during the waning days of June, J moderated the usual current events discussion at the supper table. What's been happening? What have the big events for the month been? Even in this small group with common bonds, it was amazing to hear what each person thought was important as well as the major news stories that were totally missed.

Pat began by saying, "Well, it's very clear. Barack Obama is going to be the presidential candidate for the Democratic Party. I'm fond of Hillary

Clinton, but I see that she isn't going to get the nod. I sure hope the two of them can work out some sort of deal. She needs to be in service for the country."

J lamented the death of thirteen boy scouts that had been killed in a tornado and talked about the great loss of the singer Bo Diddly, who had died at the age of seventy-nine. He mentioned that he had had the opportunity to hear him in person once, calling it one of his life's great experiences.

Marie added that she had heard about a tell-all book being written about Vice President Dick Cheney revealing the identity of Valerie Phlame as a CIA agent, resulting in putting her effectiveness useless and perhaps her life in jeopardy. She also commented on how our South Carolina Senator Lindsey Graham was very upset over the Supreme Court decision giving Guantanamo Bay detainees the right to legal representation.

J spoke of the sad death of television reporter Tim Russert and how much he respected him. One of the others heard that Tom Brokaw would replace Russert on the TV program, *Meet the Press.* J added that if he were President of the United States he would like for Tom Brokaw to be one of his advisors, and would also bring Bill Moyers back into the fold, having great respect for both men.

Pat discussed her displeasure of the news of CEO pay for large corporations, quoting the average pay for such a CEO as being 8.4 million a year, and that the CEO of Merrill Lynch being paid eighty-three million. She added that she was pleased with her teacher's salary, but to think that the Merrill Lynch CEO would make in one year the amount paid in a lifetime for eighty-three teachers. J agreed that the balance seemed terribly wrong and that his way of protesting was to vote against all of the candidates for boards of directors.

Another contribution of Pat's was mention of a news article that the Baltimore Museum was establishing a unit to celebrate body art, meaning, tattooing. She turned to Marie and asked if she had any tattoos, to which Marie only replied, "No," without elaboration, leaving the question in Pat's mind as to whether she really did or did not have some discreet tattoo but certainly raised the question of whether her tattoos, if she had any, were acceptable permanent decorations.

The conversation returned to politics again, with the question thrown out as to who Obama might choose for his running mate. Marie thought it would be Hillary Clinton, but Dr. J countered with, "There's not a chance in the world that Hillary will be chosen because she would threaten the

Dickens out of Obama. She feels very strongly that she would be presidential candidate and if weren't for the fact that Obama is of color and the press is in love with him, he wouldn't be in the running at all. There are hundreds of other people that are far better qualified to be president. This is not just my opinion. I think it was Pat Schroeder, the former congress lady from Colorado who made a similar statement that Obama was the leading candidate because of his color and because of the liberal press. After she made the statement, she resigned as an advisor to Hillary and her campaign the next day. Nods of reluctant agreement were observed all around the table, and the conversation turn to sports.

Hab said he had watched the 108th U.S. Open and was surprised that Tiger Woods couldn't pull it out at the last minute. All agreed that Woods was an exceptional athlete. One of the members of the roundtable asked J if he had as high of an opinion of Woods as they did, to which J replied, "I do believe that Tiger Woods is the best golfer that has ever lived, but as to his greatness, I would have to look at his checkbook. He is a great athlete, but as to whether he's a great human being, a lot of that depends on how he spends his money. I hope he is a very generous person. I hope many people benefit from the fortune that is his. I saw some photographs of his home and his yacht. He does live an opulent lifestyle. When I start to think of great people, I think of people like Paul Newman, who has made millions and given millions away. People don't seem to realize that we are only here for a short period of time and we really don't need that much."

Pat questioned, "What do you think of the Williams sisters?"

"They're fantastic. I reckon it shows narrowness on my part, but I've never pulled for them and maybe I should have. The reason I haven't is that years ago, their father was their spokesperson and he just made some statements that irritated me and I have to say that is an indication of narrowness on my part. His remarks were accusatory and unnecessary for the occasion and that has stuck with me. But speaking of tennis players, I'll tell you who my hero was, and that's Arthur Ash. He was the first man of color to really break into professional tennis in a big way and I always admired him. I was saddened when it was announced that he had a fatal illness. I think it was some form of cancer and I don't remember whether it was in an interview I heard or what, but he was speaking and was talking about facing death. His main regret was that he was not going to be there for his children to grow up. He was a man full of grace and hope. In short, he was a person I admired tremendously."

J assumed the role of moderator and asked if there was anyone having the need to say anything else, and Pat mentioned California wants to pass legislation legalizing same-sex marriage.

Marie asked if anyone had read Tim Russert's book that was dedicated to his father. J spoke up saying, "I have not read it, but I would like to. I have read a review and it's the kind of book that I'm sure would be uplifting. I don't know how many of you are aware of this, but Tim's father drove a garbage truck and worked other part-time jobs to see that his family was cared for and his children were educated. It's amazing to me the number of young people who are embarrassed for their parents' occupations. Tim Russert wasn't. He recognized his father as a great man and paid tribute to him in this book. I really would like to get the book and read it. If somebody's looking for something to give me for Christmas that would be a good choice I would appreciate."

Marie speaks. "When you mentioned parents, I just now realize that June 13 was Father's Day and I didn't send my father anything and didn't even call him."

"Maybe you should call him belatedly."

Pat admitted that she didn't send her father anything either and didn't call.

Hab caught everyone off their guard by his statement that he had read somewhere that American happiness was declining, despite the relative wealth of this nation.

J, realizing that it was time to wrap up these newsy observations, said, "I have one other comment to make, and then I'm going to my room and vegetate. I read in the paper the other day that seven people were arrested at a high school graduation because they stood up and applauded as one student was receiving their high school diploma. I understand the need for decorum and order and why the school administration and maybe many of the audience didn't like the interruption, but there must be another side of the story. It might just been that for this family, the person being applauded was the first to graduate from high school or maybe they had overcome some obstacle or impediment or disability. If that were the case, their excitement and joy would be understandable." With that profundity, the group was dismissed with good nights to all.

DR. J'S JULY 2008

J ULY 1, 2008, blossomed early, with daylight streaming into every east facing window in Shalom. This day will be a hot one, a good one for an afternoon watermelon, particularly if time was taken to cool it in the large water trough the dogs drank out of. Hummingbirds were hard at work, sucking the sweetness out of all of the flowers. Bees were hard at work too. The flowerbeds seemed to be literal factories with humming sounds.

Around nine in the morning, after spending an hour on his thinking rock, J enters the Shalom house, looks up Marie, and tells her, "Get some outside clothes on, Marie. We're going somewhere."

The obvious comeback was to question why and where.

J announced, "We are going to the courthouse in Winnsboro."

Still curious, Marie inquired, "And for what purpose?"

"To the clerk of court's office to apply for a marriage license so we can get married. That child of yours will be coming soon, and he has to have a father's name on the birth certificate."

"Are you out of your mind? I can't let you do that!"

"No, I'm not out of my mind, at least not today. And I can legally do this, and I've thought about it and discussed it in my mind [meaning that he had just had a candid discussion with Margaret while sitting on the rock and they came to their mutual conclusion] and that's what I think should be done."

Marie sat in silence with her head down for several minutes, followed by crying. J consoled her, and she finally got up and moved to her room to get ready. "Give me a while, please, Dr. J. I'll get dressed, but I also have to get myself together." J agreed and returned to the rock for more deep thought and pipe smoke.

In a little less than an hour, Marie was ready. When J returned to the house, he found her sitting at the breakfast table with some papers and a pen next to them.

"There's something that I'm going to have to insist on, Dr. J. I've gone to my computer, and through the Internet, I've found sample prenuptial agreements. I copied and altered one of them that seemed to have the best legal language. In order for you to do what you're proposing, I insist that you read and sign it before we go. You're an angel for the care you've given me and continue to give me, but you have to have some legal protection for you. Now please sit down here, read what I've put together, and sign it." J nodded his head in agreement, sat, and read but didn't sign, mentioning that their signatures needed to be witnessed and the paper notarized. Marie agreed, folded the paper, stuck it in an envelope, and put it in her purse.

J asked with cheer, "Ready to go?" and received the yes he expected.

Since this was a special day, they rode in Blue Baby, a considerable step up from Slime Green. They pulled up to the Fairfield County Courthouse and walked in. The sight of a pretty young woman in her twenties, obviously near the end of her pregnancy, being escorted courteously by a gentleman in his seventies, headed for the clerk of court's office, brought smiles to some and frowns to others. This was an obvious, lately thought out action, being very close to the legendary shotgun wedding that happened all too many times in past years. The current thinking is that marriage isn't necessary, and there's no stigma or shame or discomfort for a child to be born without a father's name on the birth certificate, or at least the father and the mother having the same last name.

J announced to the clerk behind the opening with decorative bars that they needed to apply for a marriage license. Those engaged in filling out other paperwork heard this, and one old—older than J—black man came up to J and whispered in his ear, "You're doing the right thing, brother, and God will bless you for it."

J replied, "Thank you for your blessing. I feel God is with us." When the application for marriage license was completed, Marie asked the clerk if she could provide a witness to their signatures on the document she gave her and if she would notarize it. The clerk quickly agreed and rounded up two witnesses from the other clerks in the office then notarized the prenuptial.

After receipt of the license, which could only be used twenty-four hours later, according to South Carolina laws, the awkward couple headed back to Shalom.

After several miles, Marie turned to J and said, "Do you really know what you're doing, Dr. J? You're altering the record of your life just to do a favor to somebody who got wrapped up in sex with somebody else and is paying the price for it. Your generosity toward me and with all the other people you come in contact with is unbelievable. I appreciate it and hope to repay you in some way some time."

J remained silent, only nodded his head in acknowledgment.

The next morning, as they discussed the day before, "out of the house" clothing was donned, and the two headed toward Winnsboro once again. This time they drove to a feed and seed store at the edge of town. J motioned for Marie to join him as he went in and called out for Jack.

Jack was in the back of the store, attending to some new merchandise he'd just received. J introduced Jack to Marie, and J began, "Jack, I want you to do me a favor, please, sir."

"And what might that be, Dr. J? You know I'll do anything I can for somebody I've known as long as you."

"You're a notary public, aren't you?"

"Yes, been one for over forty years, but I don't do much with it. Notarize three or four papers a year, I guess."

"Well, Jack, I want you to perform a marriage. That's within the notary law, and I'd appreciate it."

"I've never done one of those before."

J told Jack, "It's really pretty simple. I just want you to ask me if I'll marry this lady and I'll say yes then you ask her if she'll marry this man and she'll say yes, and we'll all sign this marriage certificate and that'll be that."

Jack was incredulous. "You mean right here, right here in the middle of the store?"

J said, "Well, I guess it would be more comfortable and smell better if we moved away from the pesticides and stuff."

Jack and Marie agreed and the trio moved over to the aisle where the rabbit and dog food was kept, Jack looked around, rose on the balls of his feet, and asked the proper questions. In less than a minute, a new couple, bound in matrimony, was one. Jack thought of congratulating them but thought better of it. J pulled a fifty-dollar bill from his billfold and handed it Jack as the last signature had been collected. With a simple "thanks" from both J and Marie, the couple departed and Jack returned to his newly arrived trailer of pine stray.

J and Marie rode in silence back to Shalom. Somewhere along the way, Marie made the comment that she always had different visions of what a wedding day would be and mentioned that the baby was kicking and jumping. "I wonder if it's a leap of joy or of faith."

Since they left Shalom so late in the day, Pat and Hab were there, and Pat asked, "And just where have the two of you been, cruising around in Blue Baby. Must have been important to bring out Blue Baby."

J just smiled and said, "Just taking care of a little business in Winnsboro. Nothing big or fancy. Thought we would take little fellow that's on his way for a ride. He's restless and jumping around.

Hab asked, "Can I feel it jumping?"

"Of course," said Marie.

Hab stepped over as if he were walking on eggshells and slowly put out his hand and laid it on Marie's bulging midriff. In a few seconds, he quickly pulled his hand away and exclaimed, "Yes! I feel it! I feel it! It's kicking!"

The next day was the fourth of July, and J demonstrated his barbecuing skills by spending the greater part of the day fussing over his "secret" barbecue sauce recipe. (As a matter of fact, it was so "secret" that he didn't remember what the ingredients were.) J added, tasted, adjusted and asked for Pat's opinion, and repeated the process three times until Pat suddenly took her apron off and announced that she had something that he needed to add at her house and would only be a few minutes. J obeyed, reducing the heat from the second pot of sauce, the first pot overflowing with possibilities. Pat returned as promised and thrust a large bottle of Maurice's barbecue sauce into his hands, and said emphatically, "This is what you need, Dr. J! No more fooling around, no more tasting, no more messing up the kitchen, no more waiting. Just add Maurice's and you'll have sauce that everybody likes and everybody will use and lick their chops over. Now take this bottle and head for the grill and use what's in it. I'll take care of the kitchen because I need to get the rest of the stuff ready. Go!"

By way of explanation, if one is necessary, the German immigrants to the South Carolina Midlands are credited with developing a mustard based barbecue sauce that is widely used in the middle of the state. Maurice Bessinger is known for his barbecue at least from Columbia to the coast. Bessinger opened a drive-in in West Columbia in the 1950s and still serves his barbecued chicken and pork drenched in his mustard based sauce. He bottles and sells the concoction in many grocery stores.

The grilling went well, now that the sauce use was established, and the usual crew sat down for a traditional Fourth of July midday meal. Marie excused herself after picking at her plate. It wasn't clear to the others whether she was not feeling well physically, or if she realized that her child was due in two days was causing her mental anguish. J suggested that they all ride into Columbia and watch the fireworks display at the Fort Jackson Army Post, but Marie declined. Pat picked up on Marie's concerns and told her, "We won't leave you here alone. There's going to be all sorts of fireworks on television and we'll watch what we want from there."

They did watch a TV program originating from Columbia, narrated by Joe Pinner, local TV personality, produced by the First Baptist Church of Columbia, and then flipped channels to glimpse the plethora of fireworks displays. When they had all marveled at the beauty of the fireworks, Pat and Hab headed for home.

Around midnight, J heard Marie calling out in distress. He grabbed his robe and rushed to her room, where she told him that she thought she was going into labor, but she wasn't feeling the child move and she was scared. J instructed her to put something on and he would meet her at the back door, then hurried to his telephone and dialed his old friend, Dr. Robert Searcy, at home on his private number. J and Dr. Searcy agreed to meet at the hospital in fifteen to twenty minutes but advised J, to no avail, to call for an ambulance.

The closest vehicle to the door was the Toyota. J and Marie were soon speeding down the driveway, onto the secondary road in a matter of seconds. J pushed the Toyota to speeds it was not accustomed to, as high as eighty to eighty-five miles per hour on straight-a-ways. Marie was crying, and occasionally clutching J's arm. J repeated, over again, "All right, try to settle down. Everything's going to be fine. Everything's going to be fine."

Around ten miles into the twenty mile trip, Marie raised her head, trying to interpret what J was saying, which was two loud bursts of "Duck! Duck!" J caught the glow of ten little balls of light just ahead before he saw the light brown contrast with the black pavement and realized that there were five deer staring at him just beyond the hood of the Toyota. His instinct was to protect Marie which resulted in him pulling the steering wheel hard to the right, thinking that any impact from the deer that would be flying through the air would enter his side of the windshield and maybe through his passenger door, but there was no time. The laws of physics prevailed, hurtling stationary deer upward in line with the magnitude of the force being propelled against them. One of the bucks entered the windshield squarely in the middle of it, was propelled between J and Marie, with its body being stopped by the small backseat and the small opening of the rear window. One doe was lifted upward and over the cab of the truck, landing in the cargo space of the pickup. Another doe's body clipped off the driver's outside mirror and continued off the highway into the steep ditch on the other side. The second buck's head stuck grotesquely through Marie's side of the windshield. The first buck that landed between the two people was kicking and writhing, striking anything and everything in the path of its sharp hooves. The Toyota rolled, landing on J's driver's side, striking the pavement near the top of the cab. Glass cracked into thousands of pencil eraser sizes, some leaving its protective plastic inner layer and flying through the truck cab. The momentum created by the speed and weight of the truck caused it to roll again, ensuring the flattening of the roof of the cab. The spare tire that J kept in the bed of the truck because the frame it was usually housed in had long ago rusted was propelled as if shot from a catapult high into the air, landing some sixty feet in front of the truck, bounced twenty feet in the air and continued up the road. From its forward motion and the sudden jerk on the steering wheel to the right, the truck rolled down the middle of the road, providentially resulting in coming to a rest on its wheels on the pavement instead of down one of the steep embankments on either side of the road.

Also providentially, three young men travelling in a pickup in the opposite direction had just crested a hill in time to first dodge a speeding tire coming over the hill on their side of the road and to then see the entire scene and stop in time to avoid a collision with the cloud of dust with a Toyota inside it. These young, muscular granite pit workers jumped and tried to open the doors to the Toyota but to no avail until one ran back to his vehicle and came back with a stout crowbar. Smoke began to rise from the wreck. By pure brute force, aided by adrenaline and fortified with pain-killing beer, the three fellows literally ripped the door from Marie's side of the truck. One began to talk to Marie while the other two ran to J's side and finished demolishing the door on his side. By this time, the two deer stuck in the truck cab, one with its nose only inches from Marie's, were both wiggling in death throes. As the old adage goes, where there is smoke there is bound to be fire, proved true. A flicker of flame began and was quickly spreading through the truck's engine compartment, which was exposed because the engine hood had crumpled and was almost torn off. The young man assisting on the passenger side was getting Marie out, taking care to note her obvious wounds and her obvious maternity situation. The other two dragged J to safety and carried him in the direction of their truck, which was parked in the middle of the road with the lights on.

"We ain't got no cell phone to call a ambulance" one cried out, to which J replied that it would take a long time for one of them to get to a phone to call for help and asked that they place them in the back of their pickup and take them to the Winnsboro hospital. There was a little reluctance on the driver's part, but he quickly agreed and began to help put the two in the pickup bed after hastily rearranging tools. The driver drove while the other two did their best to keep Marie and J still and sheltered during the harried trip. One of the fellows cradled Marie's head in his lap, holding her head steady between his legs. He knew enough to try to keep her head still in case she had some spinal injuries, yet realizing that if she had had such, the pulling and lifting would have already made it worse. J was bleeding profusely from a head wound, with blood running down into his eyes.

The driver knew his way around town, a very fortunate thing, not having to stop for directions. When he approached the emergency room entrance, he began blowing his horn to summon help. The passenger tending to J jumped out of the truck and ran inside and yelled for help, and help responded quickly. Dr. Searcy was there waiting on Marie to arrive but had almost given up, thinking that J had changed his mind and had gone to another medical facility. He was shocked, to say the least, to see the bloody scene. He took a quick look at J and noted that a scalp wound can be scary looking and bloody, but if there was no cranial damage, that wound could wait. He turned his attention to Marie and directed her safe removal from the pickup bed. As soon as J and Marie were inside the emergency room, the driver called his buddies and summoned them to get in the truck and leave. He had accumulated enough trouble in his life up to that point, including drunk driving and driving without a license, and there was no sense in sticking around to prove a parole violation. His other two friends saw the wisdom and jumped in, leaving the hospital grounds with burning rubber.

The triage revealed that Marie had some minor cuts from flying glass and flying deer hooves but miraculously resulting in nothing serious. Dr. Searcy turned his attention to the delivery of the child. After more labor pains and pushing and pain, the child was born but was found to be dead, having been strangled by his umbilical cord. Without regard to the pronunciation of death, the child was placed on a ventilator to revive its lung function.

Dr. Searcy broke the news to Marie, who burst into more tears that mingled with the blood from her superficial wounds. After a very few minutes, he asked if she would be willing to have some of the child's vital organs harvested. Marie at first shook her head indicating no, but Dr. Searcy persisted. "Marie, you need to know that there are at this moment three newborn babies in the Baptist Hospital in Columbia who will die before morning without your child's body parts. One needs a heart, another needs a kidney, and one needs lungs. If you would agree to what we refer to as a harvest, at least one, and maybe all three, of these babies will live to grow up and have meaningful, fruitful lives. The decision is yours, of course. I'll leave you for a few minutes while I check on J, but time is critical." Dr. Searcy left, seeing that the emergency room doctor was tending to J, and returned in less than two minutes. Marie was unable to say anything but nodded in agreement that she would give her consent. With tears flowing, she motioned for Dr. Searcy to come closer, and she said in the only whisper she could muster, "May I see him first? And may I hold him for just a minute? I'd like that." The request was granted while chest compression was continued on the child. The ubiquitous paperwork was presented and signed, and the necessary transportation was arranged. In a matter of minutes, the siren of the departing ambulance transport was heard leaving the Winnsboro hospital, headed for Columbia, carrying the promises of life to the Baptist Hospital and the surgical teams that were being summoned.

After a night, day, and another day of hospitalization observation, Dr. Searcy called Pat and asked her to come to the hospital to transport the two badly bruised and sore patients home and to be present for discharge instructions.

Pat arrived early and went to J's room, finding him, as she suspected she would, complaining that he would be better off at home and that he had other things to do besides lie around in a damn hospital room, etcetera, etcetera. Pat was listening dutifully when Dr. Searcy arrived.

The doctor barely acknowledged J's presence, and turned to Pat, saying, "I'm glad you're here, Pat. I'm going to give J some discharge instructions. Some are the standard ones regarding mobility, activity, wound care, and that sort of thing, but the more important ones are more essential to preserving and prolonging the life of this stubborn curmudgeon. You know that I've known J and his family for over thirty years, and J has been very generous in allowing me to fish in his pond and wander around his property so I can get mentally refreshed. We've been together at the few sporting events I've been able to go to, and my wife and I have enjoyed his company at many social things over the years. I say this because I genuinely care for J as a friend, over and above the concerns I have for him as a patient. Some of the instructions I'm going to give J will seem radical, and I hope you'll see the wisdom in them because I know that J will dismiss them as soon as he gets out of the door or even sooner. So I've asked that you be here and I hope you'll agree with these instructions, which are really recommendations that can be taken in the spirit given or not. I hope you'll see that the prescriptions I'm going to give J will, if followed, prolong his life and perhaps the lives of those around him."

Pat was smiling and nodding in agreement with her eyes sparkling. J was solemn but listening intently as he was being bypassed altogether, thinking that he was being treated as if he were a piece of meat lying in the bed, with cooks discussing how he was going to be prepared. His thoughts were to the effect—*This ain't going to be good.*

Dr. Searcy began. "First, let me get the immediate things out of the way," turning to J for the first time. "You have stitches out the wazoo, J. I don't know if you've looked in the mirror, but you've had cuts on your face and head. I don't think they'll affect your handsome charisma long-range, but these places do need care. After a day, Pat, you can change the bandages, clean gently, and watch for any signs of infections. There are places where the emergency room doctor had to remove little pieces of glass, and he hopefully removed all of them, but there may be some that will work their way out over time and require physician removal. Bruises will go away after a couple of weeks. J, I know you are sore, and for good reason. As far as x-rays show, you have no broken bones, which is nothing short of a miracle. However, you may find that you have strained or torn some tendons. I want to see you again in a week, and we'll go from there." He wrote a prescription from a pad, and gave it to Pat. "Here's a prescription for Lortab to be used for pain. I don't think he'll use it because he's into masochism and suffering, but it's here in case he gives in." Turning to J, Searcy says, "J, this is standard modern medicine. There's no sin in taking this medication, and it will not cause you to be addicted even if you take all of them. You'll heal more quickly when pain is under control." J nodded as if he were a Pavlov dog, giving at least the appearance of understanding as agreement or at least acquiescence.

"Now come the nonconventional prescriptions." Searcy wrote on his pad, tore off the page, and gave it to Pat. "The first is for a cell phone. I have not written telephone carrier names on it, but I recommend one that will give you good as close to national coverage as possible. Please don't go cheap. When you do subscribe, consider getting a phone for each individual in the household. I know that this man who clings to the rugged past, haunted by the days of financial burdens, will resist. It will require charging every night and will require whoever it is assigned to the duty of carrying it with them. Let me tell you that it is absolutely necessary for you, J, to carry a modern, up to date phone with you and to have it turned on. Do not, and I repeat, do not, turn it on just when you want to call out on it. Those that love you and care for you need to be in touch with you *all the time*! Pat, I want you to get this done today if possible. It's going to take a while to get used to all the things these devices can do, and this second prescription is for lessons on how to use it," tearing off a second page.

J suffered in silence while Pat stifled a chuckle but could not contain a smile nor could hide her laughing eyes.

Searcy returned to his pad, wrote a few sentences, signed it, and gave it to J this time. "This prescription is more information than medication, but it can save your life and the lives of others. Please look at it while I read it to you. It says, 'When a medical emergency arises, call 911 and ask for an ambulance and qualified medical personnel.' Let me explain. This is 2008, like it or not. Through lavish government spending, we now have in this county, and throughout the state, strategically placed fire departments with qualified medical first responders. They know how to handle emergencies. I also know there is a considerable amount of anxiety generated while waiting on help to arrive, but the results are infinitely better. It is a miracle that you and Marie weren't killed. I know your thinking and know that your thought was that you could get her to the hospital in less time than it would take for an ambulance to come from wherever it was coming from and then go to the hospital. The upright ride in a pickup truck was enough to cause permanent damage to the child, had it not already been in jeopardy, as well as to Marie. Let me quickly add that I don't think there was much anyone could have done to save the child, but if this would have been a normal delivery, it was not appropriate to transport a pregnant lady by pickup truck. I hope you know that I'm not criticizing your motive. You did what you thought was the right thing to do and I respect that. I don't think you have had the need to know about the modern medical facilities we are fortunate to have."

J nodded his head in agreement once again, but said nothing.

Searcy turned to his prescription pad once again and continued to scribble.

"This prescription is the most expensive one, by far." He tore off the page and gave it to Pat. "I'm giving this to you, Pat, because I fear that

J will tear it up or use it for toilet paper the first chance he gets. J will probably tell you, and maybe me, that I've stepped way over the boundaries of professionalism and friendship by issuing this. However, I think it is time to make a change in lifestyle and enter an age of comfort. By filling this prescription, old bones, and new ones for that matter, will have the feeling of comfort and safety, which all of you deserve." Pat read the words on the prescription, studying words that needed to be deciphered because of the habitual hasty, time saving writing. The words of the prescription were written in very general, flexible terms, but the meaning was clear. J was to invest in luxury transportation. The prescription was for not just a new car, but a large, comfortable one. J was to shop for and purchase an automobile of his choice but confined to the luxury models of a Lincoln, Cadillac, Lexus, or a SUV, such as a Suburban, Tahoe, Navigator or such.

Pat could not remain silent any further and exclaimed, "Amen, brother! Hallelujah! Praise God! This doctor got brains! Thank you, Dr. Searcy, thank you!"

Pat passed the small prescription on to J, who had a bewildered look on his face. J read it with predicted difficulty because of the handwriting and the unexpected content and finally smiled and returned the prescription to Pat.

"Doc, I expect you're right on all counts. I know your heart's in the right place, and I know I'll appreciate it before long. I am, believe it or not, coming to the conclusion that I've lived in the past and have resisted new things and technologies and services and that I need to get with the program. You are a good friend, and thank you for this jolt of reality. Now please go downstairs and sign the damn papers that'll allow me to get out of this house of horrors so I can go home!"

Searcy laughed and arose from his chair, preparing to leave for his apparently much-needed or much-desired administrative duties. "Thanks for taking it better than I thought you would, J. We've known each other for a long time and you've been through a lot—I know because I've been close by and was involved with a lot of your tribulations. Please take my advice seriously and get on with your life in comfort and get rid of this façade of roughness and 'I can do it myself' stuff. There comes a time in everyone's life, believe me, that the old days are best put behind you. It's a natural cycle. I see it every day in the old patients whom I see. They try to keep up and do those things they have been doing, things they think they, only, can do or those things they want to do, but their bodies or minds won't let them. Enjoy your life, J. It's going to end sooner than you think and at the very end, unless you change your ways, you'll be mentally kicking yourself and what you didn't do. But enough lecturing. I'll see you in a week, but call if there are any signs of infection or serious or new pain or evidence of internal bleeding. I'll go sign the papers."

Marie had some scrapes, mostly resulting from being dragged from the wreckage and from lying in the back of the rescue truck but no cuts that needed stitches. Her wounds were more mental than physical. She asked Pat to call her brother, who began his arrangements to travel. She was sedated, and kept repeating, "Please tell me that this is all a bad dream. Please tell me that nothing has really happened and that I'm about to have my healthy baby." The most Pat could do was to hold her hand and urge her to succumb to sleep. Marie finally drifted off to a fitful sleep, still muttering words that were unintelligible.

Meanwhile, the remains of the infant were kept in Columbia at the Baptist Hospital, after the harvest of body parts. Dr. Searcy conferred with Marie first and then with J when they were both in the hospital, and the two, talking on the telephone to each other, decided that the child's body should be turned over to the local mortician and prepared for burial at the Shalom Cemetery.

The trip back to Shalom from the hospital was a solemn one. Pat transported both J and Marie to Shalom in her car, stopping briefly at the burned spot in the paved road where the slime green Toyota and four deer met their end. Marie sobbed, and J remained quiet, both realizing that this spot could have been their exit station for life here on earth. After several minutes of silence, J asked where the Toyota was. Pat told him that it had been taken to the storage lot used by the local wrecker service and reminded him that he should be in touch with them as soon as he felt up to it, to advise what to do with it. The only real option was to sell it for junk, but there might be some items left in it to be recovered. J also asked if the young men that rescued them had been located, and Pat told him that she didn't know. J made a mental note that he could put out the word to some of his friends that he would like to know who they were in order to properly thank them for their valiant efforts and to assure them that they would remain anonymous.

Once home, the sore patients made their way to the den and tried to find comfortable positions. Pat reminded both of them that it would be helpful for them to take their next scheduled dosages of Lortab and rest for the remainder of the day. When they finally walked, with assistance, to their respective bedrooms, Pat gave a sigh of relief and began her mindless housework duties until interrupted by a call from Marie's brother who had arrived at the Columbia Airport and would be arriving as soon as he could arrange for a car rental. Tom arrived before the patients emerged from their drug-induced rest, giving Pat time to fill him in on the details while sitting at the kitchen table. The meeting of the siblings was a tearful one, with Marie attempting to fix blame on herself, insisting that the cause of this dilemma was her sinfulness, the product of her lust, and that God was angry with her and therefore punished her, with J being an innocent bystander yet reaping His wrath. Marie repeated this several times before J arose and joined the trio in the kitchen. J heard this lament of Marie and quickly said, "No, Marie, not the God that I know. He's not punishing you. This thing you have gone through is just one of these things that happen in life. I don't see it as being the result of God's displeasure, but I do think it is a part of His plan that can be painful to some people until the entire purpose is revealed to us. The unfortunate part is that we may never get to know or, for some reason, cannot comprehend what the purpose is. As to the value of putting a guilt trip on yourself, that's not going to serve any purpose, any purpose at all. Just wait until we get to the place that we can get some answers, which may or may not come. For now, let us simply ask for strength to see us through this tragic time in our lives." Tom agreed and took up silent consolation by holding Marie in his arms. After the tears subsided and the redness in her cheeks cooled, Tom asked if she had thought about a name for the child or would he remain nameless. Marie said that she had thought about a name on many occasions and had selected Michael, which was their father's name. The conversation continued to include what the arrangements for a burial should be. Marie, with encouragement from J, preferred a traditional burial instead of cremation. J offered to make the arrangements for the private burial in the Shalom Cemetery while Tom was still here. He excused himself and made telephone calls from the den to have his friend Tim from the university to conduct the service the next day. Marie began to talk about the debt she was mounting for J, considering the hospitalization and now the funeral, which J refused to allow continuing.

The following day was a typical South Carolina Midlands summer day, with temperature in the upper eighties and the sky filled with large fluffy white clouds. A midmorning service time was selected to take advantage of the coolest part of the day. J insisted that it would not be irreverent for the men to dispense with ties or coats. J made a mental note to call on the local tombstone dealer to install a small stone made of Winnsboro blue granite and for Buddy Hirschfeld to inscribe it.

That afternoon, J received a call from a person asking to visit Marie. After some questions, J advised that such a visit would be granted, would be appropriate, and would be very helpful and suggested a time the following day. After the conversation, J mentioned to Marie and her brother that there would be a visit from some people that he felt would be very helpful for Marie but offered little else, in his usual close-to-the chest manner.

Around eleven in the morning, an SUV drove up, and three couples who appeared to be in their late twenties or early thirties got out and walked up to the front door. They were welcomed in by J and escorted into the Shalom living room, which had been freshly dusted by Pat that morning. (Presence in the living room meant special guests. Most of Shalom's visitors were people that had been there many times, who entered through the kitchen and sat around the kitchen or dining room table.) After introductions of names, one of the young men explained that the three couples were the parents of three infants that had received a vital organ from infant Michael. The young spokesman stumbled through his words, frequently stopping to regain his composure and his emotion-choked voice, but told Marie that they realized the great loss Marie had suffered and expressed their sympathy and their grief for her, but at the same time thanking her for her decision to allow body parts to be harvested from baby Michael after his death to that their children could live. The visitor explained that one child received Michael's heart, another lungs, and the third a cornea. One of the young women said, through tears and halting speech, that these children would now be given a chance at relatively normal lives, all because of Marie's generosity. The visitors assumed, without asking and without receiving a correction, that Tom, Marie's brother, was Marie's husband. Everyone in the room sobbed in unison tears of sadness, joy and thanksgiving. J mentioned something about providential happenings and the inability of human thought to comprehend the will of God.

Marie excused herself at an appropriate time to return to her room, followed by Pat with another Lortab in hand. Pat stayed with her for enough time to be sure she was safe and was about to drift into a druggy sleep.

After the visit, J found his pipe and made his way to his rock for a talk with his wife. There was much to talk about, and the visit lasted until almost dark when Pat and Tom insisted that he come in before mosquitoes made a meal of him.

Hab was conspicuously absent during this time of grieving. When he did come in, several days later, he and Marie spent several silent minutes in a hug, Hab saying nothing, and Marie saying, "Lord, be with this your child. Keep him from harm. Help him to live a life that will be pleasing in your sight."

Tom returned to his duty at the end of the week, staying long enough to watch Buddy Hirschfeld place the rubber mat he used to inscribe letters in the granite headstone so that the inscription read only "Michael, a child of God" and the single date of his birth and death would be sandblasted into the stone.

As soon as J could travel by himself, he drove his blue truck to a bookstore in Columbia and purchased the book *The Will of God* by Leslie Willohan for Marie. He also went to the wrecker service yard and visited the charred remains of Slime Green. Nothing of any value was visible, so arrangements were made to the now rusting mass to be sold to the local junk dealer.

The rest of July was spent in quiet rest and contemplation and many imaginary talks while sitting on the rock. During evening meals, everyone was trying to make things as normal as possible, but it was a difficult task. There wasn't much conversation around the table, but after a few days, J began to facilitate the current events discussions. J began by the news that Speaker of the House of Representatives Nancy Pelosi vowed that there would be no off-shore drilling for oil. Hab brought up the news that Brett Favre was asking the football league to reinstate him and to his surprise his former team members didn't seem excited about the prospects. Hab speculated that even though Favre had been an exceptional quarterback his team mates must feel that once he resigned, that's the way it should remain. Hab added that he saw where negotiations were ongoing that would result in Favre being released and there was conversation that he was talking with the New York Jets.

Pat mentioned that, over the protests of many, our president was going to be present at the Olympics, at least for the opening festivities. She also mentioned the tidbits of a large mortgage mess looming.

Marie finally joined the roundtable reports by saying that she watched the Wimbledon tennis matches and if sisters Venus and Serena playing in their outstanding manner, chances are they would be the two finalists.

A discussion of death did enter the conversation, with a report of the death of Jesse Helms, longtime senator from North Carolina and former newscaster. She noted that it was sad that despite his long service and obvious dedication to serving his country, there didn't seem to be any particular admiration for Helms from the new media. She added that the press reported that Helms and Strom Thurmond were like two peas in a pod.

J noted, especially to Marie because of her Roman Catholic upbringing that some group in that church had ordained three women priests but were encouraged by church authorities to recant their action and if they didn't, there would be the possibility of excommunication. He added that his Catholic friends say there will be no changes in the Catholic Church as long as the current pope sits on the chair of Peter.

Pat chimed in with the report that Alaska Senator Ted Stevens had been indicted for perjuring himself before a grand jury.

J concluded the reports by saying that he understood that there are twenty-seven helicopters assigned to the White House at a cost of some six or more billion dollars a year. He added sarcastically that he was thinking of buying one when they became obsolete, probably within a year, when they go on sale. "Do you think I could find four hundred people who might be willing to pay a million dollars to take a joy ride in a presidential helicopter?" Hab replied, "Maybe you'd better buy two."

DR. J'S AUGUST 2008

O N THE DAY the calendar announced the month of August had begun, Pat announced that it was time to fill Dr. Searcy's prescriptions. J looked at her with pursed lips and was about to say something when Pat, Marie, and Hab all looked at him to see if a protest was forthcoming. With the looks he was receiving, J knew he was defeated and agreed. "Tell me what we need to do."

"I'm so glad you asked," countered Pat with a note of sarcasm, as she arose from the dining room table and retrieved a set of file folders. The first was her collection of information on cell phones. Over the past few weeks, she had taken the time to visit the offices of all of the cell phone service providers she could think of and poured the literature out on the table that had been hastily cleaned by Hab and Marie. One promised low rates. Another promised trouble free operations. A third promised help with technical stuff if you needed it. A fourth offered almost-nationwide calling at the same monthly rate. All offered to deduct the monthly fee from a bank account. Three of the four allowed up to four phones with different numbers for the same monthly fee. Each of those not using cell phone offered their horror stories on the shortcomings of the various services. In turn, each offered their knowledge of the various things that cell phones could do, which included e-mail service, photography, calendar, voice mail, texting, and on, and on.

After a lengthy discussion and a trip the following day, the end result was that J, Pat, Marie, and Hab found themselves equipped with the latest and finest means of communication in the South Carolina Midlands. Each had their own Blackberry and was able to do all the wonderful things that the instrument allowed.

Pat wisely allowed a full day to pass before bringing out the second prescription, this being the one for the new vehicle. J sort of sighed and only asked, "When?" The next day was the long shopping day, ending with another roundtable discussion at the kitchen table. Hab favored the sporty models, Marie was more interested in color, J was an advocate of utility, but all were brought into focus by Pat. "I think we need to think about the intent of the prescription. Dr. Searcy's advice was for Dr. J to have a vehicle that provided comfort and space, above all else. It's a proven fact that full-sized cars are safer when involved in a collision. Even the *Real Age* survey that people can take via the Internet gives you more years to live if you travel in a full sized or luxury car. So let's not forget the doctor's advice. Secondly, Dr. J is going to pay for whatever he gets, and he should make a final decision. Color might result in availability. In addition, Dr. J needs to be comfortable with the dealer's service department, and he knows everybody in the world, especially in the world around Winnsboro and most of Columbia. With those thoughts in mind, Dr. J, what's your choice?"

Acknowledging that there could not be any argument with Pat's soliloquy, J began to recall the virtues of all the makes and models and finally chose a Lincoln Navigator because it provided space, comfort and a reasonably large cargo area. The only compromise was the age of the vehicle. J insisted that his reputation was at stake in this selection and he could never justify the purchase of a new car. J won, and a five-year-old Navigator was selected. The group stuck their hands out across the table and gave each other a team palms up agreement.

The next morning, all piled into Pat's car and drove to the Winnsboro Ford, Lincoln and Mercury dealer and selected a burgundy Lincoln Navigator, which was the closest to the University of South Carolina Garnet color that could be found. After the paperwork, Pat was left to drive home alone because the others wanted to ride in the Navigator during its maiden voyage.

On Sunday, J went to church and upon returning, found that Marie had prepared lunch and that Pat and Hab had some visiting to do and would not join them. During lunch, J said to Marie, "You know, Marie, I've been thinking that it would be appropriate to visit your parents again, and I think you are mentally prepared to do that. You might have a few extra pounds on your frame, but I don't see it as a problem. They'll be so glad to see you that they either won't notice or won't care and won't comment." J added, "Now that you have your own phone and we all have so many allotted minutes per month, I hope you are feeling free to call them whenever you want to. I've been in the habit of calling my son and daughter every Monday night at eight thirty for quite a while. I chose that time because I get a reduced long distance rate at night, but that doesn't matter now. I think I'll call them during the day, especially on the weekends when they aren't working, now that I have my Blackberry. As soon as I get a little more familiar with e-mailing and texting, I'm going to do that too every time I think of something to share with them. Going to be a modern man, and I'm about to enter, kicking and screaming, into the twenty-first century!"

Marie chuckled at J's admission and proposed metamorphosis and talked about calling her brother to see if they could both travel to New Jersey and make it a good family visit. Later in the afternoon, she reported that she had talked to Tom, that he would be able to take time off, and that he would come by on Friday and drive together.

J went for a Sunday afternoon walk with his dogs as the temperatures cooled in the evening and when he returned, Marie told him, "Dr. J, I took a mystery call shortly after you left. This woman called and said she knew you years ago and would like to come and visit. I tried to give her your cell phone number, but I haven't written it down yet. I told her that I was sure you would be delighted to see her, and she told me that she would arrive Wednesday. She told me she would be flying into the Charlotte Airport and I gave her directions from I-77. She said she didn't need anybody to pick her up. I asked for her name, but she just laughed and told me she preferred to surprise you."

"Lord, Lord! What am I going to do? Two women in the house, and one of them a page from past history! Guess I need to take extra vitamin B-12 starting tomorrow. Maybe I'd better call Doc Searcy and get some tranquilizers just in case I won't need the B-12. But I'm sure I'll manage to get through it. Reckon I'd better shine my shoes or something."

Wednesday came and in late morning a taxi drove slowly up the driveway. J went to meet the mystery guest and when the taxi door opened and the mystery lady stepped out, J exclaimed, "Louise."

Louise smiled and returned the recognition, "Thanks for remembering without being prompted. It's been forty-five years since we've seen each other."

J began to apologize, telling Louise that he would have met her at the airport and saved the obviously expensive taxi ride, much less the inconvenience.

Louise just smiled and said, "Well, we won't worry about that. Let me say it's so good to see you. Don't just stand there, give me a hug!"

Hug they did for a prolonged time before J recovered enough to grab her bag and invite her inside, entering the house as J usually did, through the kitchen. Marie met them at the door and introduced her as Marie Tradonio, with no other explanation, and J in turn introduced Louise. "Marie, I'd like for you to meet my old and long lost friend, Louise, and I'd tell you what her last name is if I knew it. I think I remember that when you were in college your name was Moore." Louise laughed and said, "J, you're right, it was Moore, but I've had three since then. It really doesn't matter what my name is now, and Marie, it's very good to meet you," extending her hand.

Marie finished preparing lunch while J escorted Louise to a guest bedroom. After lunch, Marie insisted that the cleanup was on her, and the two old friends moved to the den for their catching up conversations.

J began by asking, "Louise, I expect I should begin by asking what's happened in your life in the past forty-five years."

"It's a long story."

"We have plenty of time, and I'd like to hear it."

"The last time we knew each other was when I was a student at Carolina. I expect you didn't know this, but I moved to New York City to begin my career in something. My parents could afford it and paid for everything. I had a small apartment and met a young editor for Time magazine and married him six months later. The marriage lasted for twenty pretty wonderful years until he died of a heart attack. We were part of a pretty large social circle and through those friends I met another type A personality and married him after being single for a couple of years. He finally accomplished what he set out to do, that is to drink himself to death. Those two years were the most miserable of my life and I was, quite frankly, happy to be out of the marriage. I again stayed single, still in New York, for a couple more years and met a divorced fellow and married him about eight months later. That was the third and I swear it will be my last. Breaking in husbands is a hard task!"

J interrupted the story by saying, "I can't tell you how delightful it is to see you again! From time to time, and I don't know what triggers these memories, but I remember when I was home on leave from the army for a week or so. I remember distinctly the night that my mother told me that there was a young lady who had just called her on the telephone and told her to tell me to step outside to the sidewalk in front of our house, and she would be by shortly to pick me up. She had no idea who the person was and was laughing, asking me if I was going to go. I told her that of course I would, got up from the couch, went to the bathroom, slicked my hair, checked myself over, and walked outside. A few seconds later this little MG TD two-seater collector's dream came down the street and stopped right in front of me. This beautiful long-legged six-foot-tall blonde girl opened the door that was put on backward from other cars and unfolded, smiled, and stuck out her hand and said, 'Hi! I'm Louise Moore. Stand right there for just a sec while I tell your mother that I'm abducting you and don't wait up.' We got in the MG, and off we went. I asked where we were going, and you said, 'Do you have to ask?' and I told you yes, that I had a curiosity about such things. You finally told me that we were headed for Pawley's Island and wait for the pavilion to open. 'Okay with me,' I said, and you tore off down the highway, paying no attention to speed limits or whatever or whoever was in front of you. We found a place to park near the beach, took off our shoes, and walked on the sand. It was a beautiful afternoon and evening. At night along the beach were some creatures out of the sea that gave off a blue fluorescent light. Back then the pavilion was the place to go to shag. Remember how devastated all of us were when the place burned down to the marsh it was built over? That was the end of an era. I think all the shaggers moved up to either Harold's at Ocean Drive or to Myrtle Beach. By the time we got back home, it was nearly daylight. What a grand evening! I remember seeing a great deal of you in the next several days that we were in our hometown, and then you left. I don't remember why or where you were headed, and I didn't hear from you for a long time. But there is something that I need to apologize for because it has bothered me since then. You wrote me a letter and invited me to a dance, and I wrote back with a lie. I gave you a complicated, convoluted excuse as to why I couldn't make it. If I had been truthful with you, I would have pointed out that you gave me a list of things I would need to bring, such as a tuxedo, a cumber bund, shiny black shoes, a bowtie, and such and would have told you that I appreciated the invitation. But I just couldn't afford those things, rental or not. But you evidently accepted my awkward, unnecessary excuse because a year later, I received another invitation from you. Unfortunately, my financial situation hadn't changed. There was no way in God's creation that I could afford a weekend that I'm sure would have been absolutely magnificent. I didn't receive any more invitations from you, of course, and I don't blame you. I do remember that someone in town sent my mother a newspaper clipping of your wedding announcement. I seem to recall the part about him being an editor or associate editor at *Time*."

Louise said, with a note of sadness, "J, if you had told me that you couldn't afford those weekends, I would have sent you the money. I wish I had known."

"And I was afraid you might do that. That's the reason I gave you such bogus excuses."

Louise sighed and asked about J's parents.

"They are no longer with us. Mom and Dad died pretty close to one another about twenty years ago, and my brother James didn't return from Vietnam, so I'm the last of the family. But enough about me. I'm anxious to hear about you and your life. I know you married the editor. Do you have any children?"

"I have three brats. Their father was so busy climbing the corporate ladder that he didn't have time to get to know them. He knew he was neglecting them, and me for that matter, so he compensated by giving them everything they wanted. They had things they didn't need and sometimes didn't even really want. They went to places they didn't need to go. They all three went to the best of prep schools and the best of colleges, and they all married someone they met at the country club. I have more grandchildren than I can think of and have difficulty remembering their names. The grandchildren are following the same route, and it's disgusting. If they want it, they get it. I think a hard day's labor would do them in. When they finished college, there were openings for them—not at the bottom to work themselves up, but close to the top. You know how it is—money marries money. It's not what you know, it's who you know. They have extreme difficulty identifying with the working people of the world and can't relate to people who are struggling to make a living."

J nodded his head in agreement, and reluctantly added, "Well, Louise, I don't think you had to struggle very much either, did you? As I recall, your father was a successful vice president of a railroad company, and your grandfather was Dr. Hart, our local veterinarian. But hey! You turned out all right. Look at you. You look great and seem to be happy. Outside of your grandchildren who have lifestyles that you would prefer to be different, it appears to me you're doing well, physically and mentally. Changing the subject slightly, and maybe we ought not to be talking about this, but would you be shocked if I told you that you were the first person to give me a lesson in sex education? Don't look so shocked and think I'm out of mind. I remember it well, to quote Maurice Chevalier. I don't know how old we were, but we weren't even teenagers. I was very ignorant of the facts of life and let you know it, so you escorted me into your grandfather's study and pulled out a book and began to tell me, 'Now this is an egg and this is a sperm and this is what happens when they unite. This is what a fetus looks like in the first month then the second month and worked your way through the whole subject of pregnancy including birth itself. You were a precocious little girl, Louise, and I loved you then and still do. I think you would be surprised at how often I've thought about you and wondered how life was treating you. I've been asked, through the years, to speak to a lot of audiences in a lot of different places, and sometimes I have chosen as a subject *The Concept of Hell*. I am certain you don't remember making a little badge of balsam wood with a safety pin glued to the back. You gave it to me, and I was absolutely delighted. Chances are that was the first time I thought I was in love. The inscription on the balsam wood, written in ink, was *Louise Moore loves John Stewart*. That little balsam wood badge was the most precious thing I had ever received and when I left you that day, I went back to our house, went to my bedroom, the one I shared with my brother James, and I tried to find a place that I could hide this invaluable treasure. I remembered the old fashioned desk that my parents had in the hallway and that it had a secret compartment. I thought to myself that that was the secure place for this badge. I went out into the hallway and opened up the little trap door, but to my horror and disappointment there was a badge exactly like mine, except it said *Louise Moore loves James Stewart*. I was crushed, mad, furious, dejected. I tore my badge up with my teeth, chewed it up and spit it out. That afternoon, you were having your birthday party—I don't remember what birthday it was, and I had been invited. But after being rejected by the love of my life, I was not going to go. My mother kept encouraging me to go, telling me, "Now, J, you've been invited. Please go." That was probably the first time I told my mother 'No." I said I will not go, I shall not go, and nobody can make me go. Well, I did real well with that resolve until about the time your party started. I got on my bicycle and I rode to your grandfather's house, where you were staying for the summer. I rode around the block and around the block and around the block. I don't know what I was doing. Maybe I was hoping that somebody would come out and say, 'J, come on in.' After riding around the block four or five times, I decided that I had ridden enough. Do you remember those big oak trees that were located just to the north of your grandfather's house? Well, I pulled my bike over to one of those trees and leaned my bike against one of them and then, in the best of Indian fashion, I made my way, darting here and there until I got close to the house. I put my ear to the wall of the house, and I could hear something but wasn't quite sure what the sound was, so I moved to where there was a window. You might remember that the windows in that house ran from the ceiling to the floor. I slipped quietly to a window and peeped in to see everyone inside having a grand time, eating cake and ice cream and laughing, and some were playing games. What I tell groups that I speak to on the subject of hell is that hell has to be like the situation I found myself in. Having been invited to a grand party and due to my pride or stubbornness, I chose not to go. Hell is standing on the outside looking across the way and seeing people you know and love celebrating and having a good time. I imagine I have used that illustration hundreds of times and every time I do, I wonder what was happening in the life of Louise Moore. On a couple of occasions in the past few years that I have owned a computer and have learned to use the Internet, I've said to friends I'd like to learn to find people. What I didn't share with them is that person I wanted to find was you. I wanted to find out where this old friend is and what she is doing. Maybe I shouldn't use the word 'old,' maybe just say a friend from long ago whom I have lost. I've asked for help in how to find people, specifically you, and some of my computer literate friends told me that they would be happy to, but I guess they forgot to follow-up because none of them have come forth to show me."

J stands up, reaches down and takes Louise's hands and helps her up off the couch. When she's standing, he puts his arms around her and his cheek against hers and holds her close for a long time. Louise cries with genuine tears running down her cheeks at the story J just related. Thoughts of what might have been, and probably what should have been, raced through her mind. She privately cursed herself for being just like her children and grandchildren—chase the dollar and not the love. She also cursed herself for being such a flirt for giving out little wooden badges, declaring her love to several people, especially to brothers. Her mind was stabbed with remorse as she recalled that she had given such badges to all the boys she met that summer. She muttered the words, "O God! What my life has been! I've been arrogant, brazen, social climbing, greedy, possessive, proud—all those things and more—for what?"

J devilishly broke the silence, saying, "Speaking of old, that birthday party was in the summer, in August, when you were spending the summer with your grandparents. I expect your birthday is close. Is it?"

Louise regained her composure, loosened her hold on what she considered the best man in the world, reached for a Kleenex to dry her tears and said, "It's today, you old bastard!" Laughing as she reached her arms around J again, said, "Thanks for remembering, I think!"

After the classic hug, which would have done the hugs seen in the movie *Casablanca* proud, J changed the subject, saying, "I've been blessed with so many memories, both good and bad. These memories have molded me, or rather chiseled me, into a long life with jewel encrusted friends like you. I don't wish to live my life over, because I've had so many losses like losing you, but I'm happy for the ride. And speaking of ride, let's go for a ride."

J leads Louise outside to the golf cart and the four-legged girls jump on the backseat. As they rode through the woods to the fish pond, they would jump off to explore some movement or scent, run ahead then jump back on, like children having fun. They pass the ball park and J proudly tells her the stories of the neighborhood and the make-the-rules-up-as-you-go baseball games. J proudly pointed out his prize blueberry patch, noting that the fruit bearing season was over, peaking in the end of June. He mentioned that he did have several bags of the frozen fruit in his freezer. They ride to the edge of the pond and promise to go fishing if there is time. Louise suggests tomorrow for a fishing trip, but early in the morning when it's cool, admitting the heat of South Carolina Dog Days was getting to her. "I'm used to luxury, J, and this heat is killing me. I've lived in the lap of air conditioned opulence too long. Let's go back." J agreed and apologized for not recognizing gentility, and asked, "By going fishing in the morning, does this mean that you can stay?

Louise smiled a coquettish grin and said, "I guess you didn't notice that I had my overnight bag with me when I got out of the taxi, O Observant One. Yes, I can stay—that is, if you'll let me."

J admitted, "No. I didn't remember the overnight bag. I was so busy wondering what mystery woman might be visiting me in the middle of the summer and then seeing who you were and how strikingly beautiful you still are and that you were standing in front of me in my yard, I don't remember whether you had any clothes on or not. But then again, I guess I would have noticed if you didn't have anything on. Of course, you can stay."

Louise laughed, throwing her head back. "J, you're impossible, just like you always were! But I guess we should ask your young wife if I can stay before I unpack," looking at J with an inquisitive expression.

J looked like he had been hit with a well swung two by four. "You obviously mean Marie. I completely forgot to tell you about Marie. I know that appearances are everything. Let me tell you about Marie and as soon as I finish telling you about her, I'll tell you about Pat and Hab. God! What a lot to talk about that's happened over the past fifty years. Marie has only been a part of this household for eight months!"

J began, being careful to omit the part that he and Marie were technically, legally married, told Louise the stories of Marie and Pat and how they came into his life and his relationships with them, concluding with the news that Marie would be leaving to visit her parents with her brother later in the week. The story took so long that it was concluded at the thinking rock. J did think to provide a cushion from the golf cart for Louise and her gentility. The rock did provide a cool seat under the shade, rendering the humid air to be bearable.

When this long revelation was over, Louise told J, "J, can we go inside? This heat is really getting to me and this rock is nothing to compare with your sofa. Remember, I've been living an urban, comfortable life," adding the last sentence with laughter.

As they were heading back to the house, J asks, "And how would a sophisticated, urban lady used to comfort like to celebrate her birthday? We can dress up, although you're still very well dressed (Louise still had her tailored traveling suit on, complete with stockings and high-heeled shoes.) and go to Columbia for dinner, or—" when Louise interrupted.

"Absolutely not! I want to spend as much time as I can with you in this place, and I want to get out of my traveling clothes and into something soft and rumpled, if I can borrow something like that. Surely you have a candle somewhere that we can stick in a pancake or something for a birthday cake. And something else, you mentioned that you had blueberries in your freezer and I'll bet simply because you're Southern, you've got an ice cream churn. I'd like some blueberry ice cream for my birthday!"

J smiled, saying, "I'm sure I do have a churn sitting around some closet or storage space. I'm equally sure that the only thing I really need to get is some salt for the churn. Let me work on that while you change."

J and Louise go in the kitchen, find Marie at her computer, and tell her that a party is in the making. Louise asks about borrowing something comfortable, visually measuring Marie then requesting some old, soft jeans. She then turns to J and asks for the loan of one of his T-shirts, preferably one that was well-worn. Marie took Louise in tow while J began his search for the churn and used his new Blackberry to call Pat to invite the two of them to the party and to enlist her help in pulling it all together. After plundering around in several closets, J retrieved the well-worn, hand crank ice cream churn. The search for salt resulted in nothing but a pile of rock salt in the corner of the closet and a well-deteriorated indistinguishable paper bag around it.

When he returned to the kitchen, Marie and Louise were just entering from the other end of the house, chatting and laughing. Louise looked just as good in faded jeans and a stained T-shirt as she did in her Saks Fifth Avenue outfit but obviously more comfortable. Marie took one look at the churn and questioned, "What's that?" J explained that we were going to make blueberry ice cream for Louise's impromptu birthday party, to which Marie posed a second question, "We? And just who is 'we'?"

J said, "All of us. Ice cream design and manufacture requires a joint effort and your part is to turn the crank on the churn."

After a ride in the blue pickup to Jordan's store for ice cream salt, the process began. In the interim, Pat and Hab have arrived and a high-calorie, high-sugar content dinner was being prepared. Marie was given the first stint on the crank, followed by Hab, followed by Marie again, and then concluded by J, the self appointed decider of when the process was complete. Needless to record is that a good time was had by all.

Weather, or rather temperature, in the South Carolina Midlands in the month of August can be predicted with uncanny accuracy by the long time natives. Dog days begin on July third and end on August eleventh. (The brightest of the stars in the Canis Major constellation is Sirius, which is also the brightest star in the night sky. In the summer, Sirius rises and sets with the sun. During late July Sirius is in conjunction with the sun, this time period being from twenty days before the conjunction to twenty days after and is called dog days after Sirius, the Dog Star.) During this forty day period, temperatures can result in a stifling atmosphere. Visitors to the area rush to air conditioning comfort, with natives close behind. Amazingly, this all changes around August sixteenth, give a day or two. Cooler air comes in, welcomed of course but unexpected, and sometimes arrives in the middle of the afternoon. Such was the case on this day. The relative temperature was actually quite pleasant; so J and Louise returned to the rock, cushion in hand, after dinner. Marie and Pat volunteered to do the after-dinner cleaning as a birthday present, which was gratefully accepted.

When relatively comfortable, Louise told J, "J, I am pretty computer literate, and when I decided to come to see you, I knew I needed to know what was happening in your life. I was pleased to read about the honors you've received as a distinguished member of the university faculty and consistently being selected by students as their favorite faculty member. I then read about the tragedy of your wife and children's deaths. I wondered whether a visit to you would be appropriate or how you would respond, but I decided to come anyhow."

At the mention of his wife's accident, J pursed his lips and bent his head.

"I shouldn't have brought that up, should I?" said Louise.

"No, it's okay. It's just amazing how long grief lasts and how easily it's triggered. Sometimes I do all right, but most of the time, I don't when the subject comes up."

They talked for a long time about the accident, ending with J pointing out the tombstones in the cemetery, now fading from sight in the gathering twilight.

Louise hesitated, but asked anyhow, "Let me ask a prying, unnecessary, crass question. Have you ever thought of remarrying?"

J quickly replied, "No. We had such a grand, grand relationship that I sort of felt that any association after that couldn't measure up to the standard we had."

"Tell me about your two older children."

J took a long time talking about his children and their lives and their many accomplishments. As he wound up the discussion of the children, J turned the conversation to Louise by saying, "You've told me something about husbands number one and two, but you haven't said much about number three."

"He's handsome, successful, very wealthy, very generous with the family, which includes my children and our grandchildren," and went on to describe his work, his education, and his interests.

"Are you happy?"

"It's an on-and-off-again situation. Sometimes I am, or maybe I rationalize that I am. There are certain kinds of happiness that money can bring, but there are other kinds that can't be bought, as you know. When I return to the airport and remember that I'm not going to the main terminal but to the private jet section, I realize how special I am and that he wants me to be. If money could buy happiness, I would be one of the happiest people in the world. From what I've said, you can conclude, I suppose, that he wears a very wide Republican stripe. The only time he gets angry with me is when I start talking and acting like a Democrat. He has so much, but he wants more and more. He's been talking lately about buying a plantation somewhere in South Carolina or Georgia. When I ask him why, all he can say is that it would be nice to have one and so and so has one. But you asked me whether I'm happy or not, I would have to give you the vague answer of yes and no. I read something the other day by a person who has been long dead. It was a quote, something like, 'A faith to live by, a self to live with, a work to live for, someone to love and to be loved by, these things make life. So if we learn to give ourselves, forgive others, and live with thanksgiving, we need not seek happiness—it will seek us.' I've found that to be true. I know I have a great deal of the world's possessions. I consider myself, as well as my husband, as a very rich person. I have been blessed with family, a multitude of friends, great memories, a successful vocation, and financially accomplished. I've got more than I ever expected or deserved. I've got more than I need. I find great pleasure in giving parts of it away to those charities I feel are deserving."

J nodded in understanding, and honed in on the last sentence. "If your husband is in a generous mood someday and wants to help out some deserving groups, rush to your computer and look up information on Heifer International, OXFAM, Feed the Children, Save the Children, the Emergency Relief Fund, and the Jimmy Carter Foundation. You might tread lightly on the Jimmy Carter Foundation or, on second thought, forget it altogether because it would represent a Democratic view. The Emergency Relief Fund is one that Paul Newman was so involved with. He's a person I had a great admiration for. He's made millions and he's given millions away. He represented the thought that we really don't need a great deal in life and we're not going to need it for very long, considering the big picture."

"You're beginning to sound like a preacher, J. No, on second thought, you sound like the J Stewart I knew years ago with maturity."

The conversation returned to Marie, Pat and Hab, with Louise asking more questions. She summarized at the end of the conversation by saying, "So you're still picking up strays, I see."

"What do you mean by that, Louise?"

"I remember the three legged dog that you adopted when you were twelve or thirteen, so I'm not surprised that you still take in animals and people who find themselves in difficult situations. That's what I mean."

"As you can see, when my wife and I built this house, we have four bedrooms downstairs. The reason we built the house as we did was that we decided when our children were grown and gone, we would become foster parents. We even talked about having as many as eight children at any one time. It goes to show you what brave plans we had at that point. I guess my desire to take in strays goes back a long time. By the way, when you mentioned by three-legged dog, Roscoe, that I had completely forgotten about, it reminded me of a story of a handwritten sign nailed to a telephone pole that read, 'Lost. One three-legged dog, mixed breed, right ear torn, blind in left eye, recently neutered, answers to the name of Lucky. Please call this number. No reward. Just want my dog back.'

They chuckle over the unlikely name on the sign, and J continued, "Do you have any pets?"

Louise replied, "Yes, I have a French poodle."

"Figures," J said with a smile.

"What does your husband enjoy doing?" J continued.

"Mostly making money, as I told you. He goes on exquisite and expensive hunting trips, such as going to South America to shoot ducks. He's been on big game safaris in Africa, but I really don't know if he enjoys those trips or not. I think he goes just because his friends are doing the same thing. But enough of our families. I'd like to go in now and get away from the bugs and split a bottle of wine with you, if you have some."

"I think I do have some wine that was given to me several years ago. I saw them just today when I was looking for the ice cream salt. I hope it's still good. I rarely drink, but I do enjoy a glass of wine occasionally. If I get a little silly, cut me off. I don't know whether you knew this or not, but my father had a problem with alcohol and I expect that's the reason that James and I both stayed clear of drinking. On a hot summer's day I do enjoy an occasional cold beer, especially when people are around doing the same. But on a special night like this, wine sipping would be a crowning event. Let's do it!" arising from his rocky throne and offering his hand to Louise.

The closet was reshuffled and J emerged holding four bottles of wine, covered with a thin layer of dust. He handed them to Louise and told her to select because she knew more about what she was looking at than he would. Louise looked them over and selected the second one handed to her. Fortunately, the person who stored the bottles long ago did know enough to tilt the bottles so that the corks remained wet and swollen, preventing the contents from turning into vinegar. The aroma of the contents, when uncorked, filled the room.

Glasses were filled, wine sniffed, sampled, and refilled. Louise and J found comfortable positions on the couch and began to talk about old times.

The next morning, well after daybreak, Marie exited from her room and was heading for the kitchen when she looked in the den, finding the couple on the couch, locked in each other's arms, sound asleep, with two empty wine bottles and glasses sitting on the coffee table. She must have made a sound with her giggle at the sight, because both opened one eye each and stared at her. "Well, well. Looks like we might have a couple of winos that sneaked in last night!" Louise looked at J and whispered, "Caught!" J replied, "Right." Marie laughed and kept walking to the kitchen. When Marie was out of earshot, Louise asked, "Did we have sex? It looks like our clothes are intact, but I have that glorious rosy glow like a morning after, tinged with a headache and a stiff neck." J answered, "You know, I feel the same way, except my headache is more than a tinge and my back's seriously sore. I don't know if we had sex or not, but out of respect for the elderly and half-dead, let's say we did and keep our smiles and rosy glow. But I have more pressing problems right now," as he unwound his arms from hers, preceded by a peck on her cheek. "I must brush my teeth among other things." Louise told J, "And shave while you're in there, because you've got little black and red and white things growing out of your face!"

J hastened away, but called out to Marie in the kitchen to add another scoop of coffee to the coffee machine.

After tooth brushing, shaving and the other necessities, the two adults entered the kitchen to find that Marie had made a true country breakfast, proudly presenting the pot of grits that she made.

After breakfast, J and Louise returned to the den to straighten up the debris from the night before, laughing as they picked up the wine bottles, the glasses and the empty package of Bugles. J said, "Remind me not to drink this label anymore. I want to remember what I've done. What did we talk about, anyhow? Louise replied with typical Lewis Carroll clarity, "We spoke of cabbages and kings, and oh so many things. Remember, I don't talk about my nights out with a handsome man that isn't my husband." J retorted, "Yeah, you don't remember either, do you?" While replying to Louise, he thought to himself, "Yes, I guess it's better not remembering. This way, we can imagine and let our individual dreams be fulfilled." His mind's eye flashed on the image of Dr. Phil on television as he would counsel a client, saying, "There is no reality, only perception," with J silently adding, "and hope and imagination."

Louise broke the short silence by saying, "Remember, you were going to take me fishing. How do we go about it? J admitted he had forgotten about it, adding that his brain cells had been destroyed during the night but would collect the tackle and return shortly.

In a few minutes, J reappeared, motioning to the door and offering a crumpled hat, adding that all successful fisher people have comfortable but ugly hats. Louise found he had loaded the fishing gear into the golf cart, and the dog girls were prancing, ready to go. Just before stepping into the golf cart, Louise said, "Excuse me. I forgot something. I'll be right back," and scooted back to the house. She found Marie setting up her laptop for her day's work, and said, "Marie, I, uh, need to ask you something—"

But Marie interrupted. "Louise, I think I know what you're going to say and please don't worry. I keep things very privately. Consider me as the original Sphinx when it comes to being silent. God knows, I don't want anybody speculating on my actions. Go and have a good fishing trip with J." Marie then added, "But before you become exposed to anyone else, you might want to use some of my cover up makeup to hide the beard rash on the side of your cheek!"

"Thanks," Louise replied. Marie stood up from the desk, walked over to Louise and raised her arms, saying, "And give me a hug while you're standing there." After the long hug, Marie said, "I'm so glad you're here. Now go! Don't keep your prince and your chariot waiting!"

Louise did as she was told, went outside, and climbed into the golf cart chariot with Ben Hur; and when they started, off she said, "J, while I think of it, let me tell you that I really like Marie. You did the right thing by helping her." J only nodded in agreement and wondered silently, "What brought that up?"

As they traveled through the woods on their way to the pond, Louise put her hand on his shoulder and motioned for him to stop. She pointed to the left at a large owl perched overhead, giving them the once over. J said, "What? What are you pointing at? I don't see anything." Louise leaned over and whispered, "Owl!" Only then did J realize that he was not able to see anything out of his left eye. Several thoughts raced through his head. "What's going on? When did this happen? Is this going to spread to the other eye? What'll I tell Louise? I haven't told her about my tumor, but I might have to." After those few seconds of panic, J compensated by turning his head hard to the left, and sure enough, there was a large barn owl staring at them. Louise whispered, "I thought they only came out at night so is there something wrong with it?" J told her that owls do in fact come out during the day and search for small prey, like field mice, during the day. The dogs running ahead and beside and in back returned and barked, causing the bird to fly away. Louise said, "So beautiful! What a treat to be in the middle of the woods like this and see all sorts of life! What a paradise, you lucky scoundrel!" J agreed and continued on their way.

It was a great day for fishing. In fact, the first time Louse cast her artificial minnow into the pond she found herself in battle with a large bass. After squeals and cries of "What do I do now?" and J coaching, the bass was landed and placed on a stringer in the water. Excited now, Louise made four or five casts with no strikes, but on about the sixth, she was repeating the process of landing another bass. Louise asked J if he planned to fish, but J confided that he was having too much fun watching her, and besides, he was too busy taking fish off the hook for her. He said, "No, I can do this any day. This is your special day, fooling around in the South Carolina woods with an old fool with a hangover (he thought.). He tallied the count and recommended that she try some more so they would have five, one for each member of tonight's dinner group. "And by the way, there's a house rule around here that every person cleans what they catch, you know." Louise retorted, "If that's the case, I guess I'd better walk home and cut these creatures loose. I've never cleaned a fish in my life and it's too late to start!" J relented by promising to clean the creatures if she would do the honors of catching one more, hopefully of the same size. Louise quickly accommodated by landing another bass, this one just slightly larger than the others.

The rest of the morning was taken up with the fish cleaning, putting the gear away and preparing the fish for the frying pan. After an early lunch, J excused himself to take a much-needed nap and more aspirin, giving Louise and Marie time for a long conversation.

The rest and the aspirin must have reduced some brain swelling caused by the unaccustomed alcohol intake because after his nap, J's eyesight returned. He reminded himself that the tumor was still there, lurking in the recesses of the brain cavity, and even though its progression was inevitable and quicker than he might have suspected, brain swelling alcohol might not be the thing to do.

Pat arrived early and volunteered to do the fish frying and offered to teach Marie to make hushpuppies. Louise was delighted. She said, "Hush puppies! I haven't heard that word in I don't remember how many years. I am truly in the South!" and gave a little Pawley's Island twist.

After dinner and the cleanup, Pat reminded Hab that it was a school night and they had to go home. Marie stayed and talked for a short while and excused herself for the night.

"Well, here we are without chaperones," Louise said, adding, "and there's the third and last bottle of wine that's been aging too long. Care to join me?"

J poured himself a very small portion and spent a lot of time sniffing the aroma and swirling the contents in the glass. Louise asked, "J, I have a question. What do you think might have happened if you had been a rich boy?"

I would have packed my tuxedo that I already had and jumped on a plane and flew to Vassar to be the date of a beautiful, long-legged young woman and fell in love all over again as I did when I was twelve and again when I was twenty. That's what I think would have happened, but it didn't."

"I wish you had been a rich boy or that I had been a poor girl with her head screwed on right, looking for value and not for money."

"But I wasn't and you had your sights high, and that's all right. What's the old quote, 'It's better to have loved and lost than never to have loved at all'? Providence didn't smile on us that way. It wasn't meant to be. There's nothing that went wrong with either of us. You had your upbringing, which was rooted in success, measured by money. I had mine, rooted in spending more time doing things for other people than for myself. I was used to making do, for being thankful for small successes, looking for approval, trying to overcome the forces of economics. I've lived a good life, one that I wouldn't want to live over but glad for what I've experienced. You've lived a good life too, Louise. I'm just so happy that you looked me up and that you're here. So put that glass down and stand up and let me hold you like I've held you before."

They woke earlier than they did the day before and tiptoed to their separate rooms before Marie arose.

After showers, Louise and J met in the kitchen. Louise looked around and said to J, "I hope you're not expecting me to cook. Are you? I haven't done that for years . . ." She hesitated and not saying the word "either."

J laughed and told her, "No, I'm not ready for the house to be set on fire, and I'm a little queasy from the spirits we've had, and I'm running low on antacids. Let's just make some coffee. Marie is expecting her brother any minute now to pick her up in a rental car and drive to New Jersey to see their parents. He was supposed to fly into Columbia, arriving at six this morning, and will rent a car at the airport. When we see them off, we're going to the truck stop restaurant at the Great Falls exit, which is on our way to the Charlotte Airport. They make the best pancakes served with real

Jimmy Dean sausage, and besides, you need to know how the other half of the world lives!"

As soon as the Joe DiMaggio coffeemaker had finished its final gurgle, Marie's brother drove up as predicted.

After the truck stop breakfast, served by Irma Baker, the whirlwind waitress, obviously living off of black beauties and coffee (who calls everybody "honey," "sugar," or "sweet thang"), J and Louise began their trip to the private plane terminal, just off Billy Graham Parkway in Charlotte.

The trip was made without much conversation, with hands held until the traffic became too treacherous, requiring J to keep both hands on the wheel.

They turned in to the edge of the parking apron, where Louise's pilot was waiting. J took her overnight bag and gave it to the pilot, who began to stow it. Louise walked to the lowered staircase and lingered for a moment, then said, "Can I kiss you again?"

J nodded in agreement, adding with a hoarse whisper, "Yes, of course. Chances are we will never see each other again. But, Louise, I want you to know that at age twelve or thirteen or whatever age it was, and again when I was home on leave and you were spending time with your grandparents, I thought you were a beautiful person, and I loved you. You're still a beautiful, elegant lady, and I still love you in a special kind of way. Our lives have been spent apart, as providence would have it, and we can't put that back together again. Enjoy the rest of your life, as I intend to enjoy mine, especially with these memories. And may God bless you richly."

Louise hugs him, kisses him tenderly, and walks up the waiting stairs. She stops at the entrance to the plane, turns, smiles, and gives a gentle wave. J brings his hand to his mouth, kisses it, and blows it in her direction. She eases past the pilot, who raises the stairs. J waits as the pilot coaxes the plane forward and onto the edge of the runway. There is a wait until the control tower gives permission to enter the runway; then she is gone. He remains on the ground in front of the hangar until the takeoff, knowing that she is looking out of the window and waving. Suddenly, a great truth comes to him. He doesn't even know her name! In all of the conversations, all of the walks, all of the hours on the sofa, he has neglected to ask Louise for her address, phone number, or even her married name.

The ride home is devastating. J keeps repeating to his self, "How stupid can you be? Why didn't you ask? Where can I find it? How stupid can you get?"

When he reached Shalom, now without any guests, J parks his Navigator and walks slowly to the door. He makes his way through the kitchen and down the hall into the living room where the large antique secretary he inherited from his mother stands. He lied to Louise about chewing up and spitting out the balsawood medallion she gave him when he was twelve. It was still in the secret compartment, and he had to see those words again, "Louise Moore loves John Stewart." J opens the secretary, pulls down the writing shelf, and reaches back to release the secret catch that exposed the small compartment. The small drawer slides open, not only revealing the balsawood medallion, now stained with age, but also a personal card from Louise that includes her name, address, phone number, cell phone number, e-mail address, and fax number. J picks the card up with trembling hands, lifts it to his nose to smell the faint lingering scent, and realizes that there is some writing on the reverse. The back of the card reads, "Louise Moore loves John Stewart, and I always have."

DR. J'S SEPTEMBER 2008

ALL J WANTED to do was to go to his recliner and go to sleep. He had made the trip from the Charlotte Airport without incident but couldn't recall any of the turns he made. After wiping the tears from the card in his hand, he returned it to the secret "hidey-hole" and slowly closed the secretary. He then went outside, greeted the dogs, fed them, and went inside to his faithful recliner, stretched out, and went to sleep.

And then it was suddenly September. When the calendar page was turned, J thought of the words to the 1950s "September Song." The words, as he recalled them, were these:

> Oh, it's a long, long while from May to December, but the days grow shorter when you reach September. When the autumn weather turns leaves to flame, one hasn't got time for the waiting game. Oh, the days dwindle down to a precious few. I'll spend with you these precious days. I'll spend with you. Oh, the days dwindle down to a precious few—September, November, and these few precious days I'll spend with you, these precious days I'll spend with you.

Oh god! Where did the time do? What did I do with it? What do I do now?
Those thoughts were shattered by the presence of Hab coming through the kitchen door. It was the first day of September, coming in like a bang with Labor Day, and what a beautiful day it was not to have to labor. The sun was shining hot, the sky is blue, and there's been a slight cooling since the last part of August. Just right for relaxation, contemplation, and fun—like fishing.

'Well, Hab, are you all ready for a day of fishing and lazing and that kind of stuff?"

"You folks got it made, you people of leisure. I've got to work. It's a big day at the ball park, and I was hoping you would take me to the IGA (grocery) to get some hot dogs and stuff to sell."

"How many games are going on today?"

"Two or three, I think. There's one at ten o'clock this morning, another one at noon or as soon as they get through with the first one, and I think there's another one about dark."

"Well, come on. Let's get Blue Baby fired up and go to the store and get your dogs on the fire before ten. Do you know when the Black Beauties Team's going to play? I want to watch them, especially. They've got some awesome players on their team and I hear that some of the boys are home from Iraq and have been invited to fill in. Maybe we ought to call a scout from the Atlanta Braves and tell him to come over and take a look at some of these fellows who really know how to play baseball."

"Dr. J, don't waste your breath and don't pull my leg. They ain't a one of those fellows who could sit on the Braves bench. Most of dem is over the hill and don't know the rules either."

"Young man, there *isn't* one, I agree, who would be big league quality, and most of *them*, not dem, are probably too old for starting out in professional ball. One of the things you need to concentrate on this year is the speaking of the English language. Continuing to speak the local language might be acceptable in strictly social circles, but it will label you as being unable to communicate with the rest of the world when you do step out in the commercial world. Now come on and let's go to the store and get your stuff. I assume that you saved enough of your profits to pay for these supplies?"

By the time the grocery run had been made and Hab's stand was operational, the first game was beginning. Rather than returning to Shalom for lunch, J decided to stay, watch the game and give Hab some business. The pitcher for the Black Beauties, the local group, used all sorts of motions. It was a show in itself. In fact, his pitching styles, if you could call them that, were comical. He would wind up and sometimes pitch over-handed, sometimes side-arm, and sometimes under-handed. He kept the batters and his own catcher wondering what he was going to do next. Signals from the catcher meant nothing. His antics worked, however, and there were a number of strike-outs. There were also a number of hits into the sunflowers bordering the field, and some hits bounced into the flowers. There was great cheering when a home run was batted.

Between the seventh and eighth innings, umpire Jones came to J and told him he needed a break, and would he please finish the umpire duties for the last two innings. J, of course, accepted and took his position behind home plate.

The crowd applauded when the switch was made. On practically every call J made, the crowd booed. The coaches from the teams didn't approach J in protest, though, realizing that it was all in fun.

At the end of the game J retired from his newly appointed job. The regular umpire had returned from the business he had to take care of. James Jones rented several houses in the neighborhood and it was collection time. Jones's rule was simply to pay on time, every time, at the same time, or face eviction. If the time and date of collection was deviated from, all bets were off and excuses could be expected.

When he returned home, dusty and full of hot dogs, he found that Marie had returned from her visit to her parents. Tom was in the process of leaving.

That afternoon, J received a telephone call. Marie was nearby and heard J say, "That will be fine. I was expecting your call. I'll look forward to seeing both of you on Wednesday. I don't know what it'll be just now, but I'll have something for lunch. Good to hear from you."

J turned to Marie and told her that the call just received was from Elizabeth's sister-in-law, asking if she and her husband could visit on Wednesday. He explained that this was a sort of annual pilgrimage for them, to travel the relatively short distance from their home in Chester to bring flowers to Elizabeth's grave. Elizabeth's birthday was September third, Wednesday's date. He added, "And Marie, this is unusual and somewhat out of character for me, but I'm going to ask you to find something to do that day away from here. I have described our relationship to all of my friends who have visited since you came here, but this is a couple that seem to go out of their way to criticize and I'm just not in the mood to give them an explanation. I hope you understand."

Marie immediately replied that she indeed did understand and told J she was most appreciative of the explanations he had given to his visitors, followed by saying she needed to run some errands and see some people in Columbia anyhow, then asked for permission to use the Navigator. J agreed, saying that he didn't need to have to explain the Navigator to this couple either.

The next day, Tuesday, brought a call from J's local insurance agent, who needed to tell him an adjustor would be coming out to discuss the settlement of his claims associated with the wreck.

The adjustor was very professional in his questions, explaining that the Toyota was a total loss, and described the handling of the roasted deer in the front seat. He marveled at how the two of them weren't killed by the collision, the rolling of the truck, or by the deer coming through the windshield. He continued by telling J that he was still trying to determine if the collision killed Marie's child or if the child was dead before the wreck, explaining that in made a considerable difference in the amount of the settlement. J decided that it would be in his best interest to turn the settlement over to his lawyer and friend, Jack Westerfield, to handle the case. The adjustor agreed that such representation would be appropriate, advised that he would communicate with Westerfield, and ended the conversation. Before the adjustor left, J called Westerfield and asked him to represent his and Marie's interests in the case, and gave him the name of the adjustor. Westerfield agreed, and told J to bring Marie to his office in the next few days to sign the appropriate papers and to discuss the details.

The next morning, Marie was dressed and ready to go to spend the day away from Shalom. She asked what time the visitors would be leaving so she might plan her return. J replied that Jonathan and Gaynell's visit times could be predicted with extreme accuracy. They arrive at ten thirty and leave at four thirty, regular as clockwork, he said.

Jonathan was Elizabeth's older brother. He and Gaynell had been married for fifty years and are the parents of two children. Jonathan was a retired Methodist minister, having served a number of small churches throughout South Carolina during his active ministerial work time. Jonathan was one of those people that are highly critical of anyone's behavior that seems to be only a little out of the mainstream. Gaynell was more critical, if possible, than Jonathan. They had chosen to retire to the Christian family home, his grandparents, in Chester, only fifty miles from Shalom or less, but the two families were not close. Because of their puritanical outlook, always expressing faux Christian shock at just about everything they were not involved in, J had not reached out a hand to them, and they, in turn, had not sought out J. The couple lived by rote and by schedule with nauseating dependability. One of the things they had done since Elizabeth's death was to visit her grave on her birthday, from ten thirty to four thirty on each occasion. The visit was pointedly to visit the graveyard, and not necessarily to visit J. Such was the situation on this day.

J looked out of the kitchen window at ten thirty and saw the black compact car (color and unnecessary size was considered to be ostentatious) draw up to the graveyard, and two elderly people emerge with a bundle of cheap plastic flowers, and stand by Elizabeth's grave, ignoring the courtesy of going to the house first to greet J. J waited a few minutes to give them their privacy then walked out and greeted them. Both had pained expressions on their faces and feigned tears. "She was a beautiful and bright girl," said Jonathan, stepping over and shaking J's hand. "Beautiful and bright, to be sure," J responded, stepping over to give Gaynell an awkward, stiff hug, trying to get away from the scent of the lilac dusting powder that pervaded Gaynell's space. J invited them in, walking to the front of the house and entering the living room instead of his usual kitchen route that he used welcome everyone else.

After the usual inquiries of the pleasantness of the trip and the weather, J inquired about the couple's children, which brought a burst of tears from Gaynell. J apologized, with words similar to, "I hope I didn't say something wrong." Jonathan replied for Gaynell, saying that it had been a difficult time for them in the year since they last talked, explaining that their daughter was in the process of divorcing her husband of over twenty years, and their son was currently separated from his family. Even after looks that meant, "Jonathan, you talk too much" from Gaynell, Jonathan continued. The son, according to their daughter-in-law, has a problem with alcohol and as a result can't keep a job. That couple has college age children and the financial disaster was jeopardizing the children's education. The daughter, Lucy, forty-eight years old, has three children and has never really grown up. She says she needs to 'find herself' and her continual absences from home have caused her husband to file for divorce. "We've tried talking to them and praying with them, but they just won't listen. We've done everything we know how to do."

Gaynell's tears had dried, leaving tracks down her heavily powdered face, and broke her silence by saying, "I can understand why some people don't want to have children. They can be a blessing or they can be a heart-breaking curse, like ours have been. I love both of them and I've told them so and told them to pray for one another and to change their ways, but they don't respond to our love and guidance in any kind of constructive way."

Jonathan turned to J and told him, "Thanks for loving our Elizabeth and for making her time here on earth so joyful. I know that she wishes she could be with you and with her older children."

J nodded his head momentarily and then said, "I want to tell you something, and I hope you don't think I'm crazy. But just about every night I go out to that rock in the front yard, Elizabeth and I talk. She assures me that all is well with her and the children. In a way I can't explain, she also communicates with me on current issues that I'm dealing with and gives me assurances and encouragements and offers suggestions. There is a great deal of love between us still. I miss her physical presence, but I enjoy our visits."

There was a long period of silence as Gaynell looked at Jonathan, Jonathan at J, and back to each other. The sound of the dogs playing outside could be heard. Jonathan broke the silence by saying, "I think those dogs enjoy life."

"They most certainly do. They are great companions and give me great joy."

There was another painful pause in the conversation, broken by Jonathan announcing that it was time for them to go, adding the usual, "It was good to see you and that you're doing well." There were no questions on the health and welfare of J's children, and J didn't offer any mention of them. He did suggest that they follow him over to Winnsboro to the Country Kitchen and have lunch before they left town, which was accepted.

J returned to Shalom a little after one o'clock and decided to return to the recliner for a nap because of some partial vision in both eyes. The vision was obscured by an expanding area of jagged lines, visible in both eyes, expanding until his entire sight pattern was affected.

After the nap, the vision was restored; and J felt refreshed, reminding himself that he might just have had the last annual visit from his sanctimonious in-laws and that he was just as happy that it might be the case.

As expected, Marie returned to Shalom about five thirty, bringing a person with her in the Navigator, followed by another car with two more people. J met them at the kitchen door and saw that each was bringing a couple of paper bags. Marie explained that she had spent the day with three of her friends and suggested they come and see the labor camp she was working in (with a smile, followed by giggles from the visitors). "We stopped by Number One China, and we each bought our favorite Chinese food and another entrée so everyone could have a taste. I think we have a little of everything the restaurant had to offer. I hope it's all right with you. And may I borrow the golf cart and take them on a ride through the woods and to the pond? All of these are city girls, and it would be like taking them on a safari!"

J gave her his assurance that it was all right with him and told her that he had been encouraging her to bring friends. He promised to call Pat and Hab to come and join them with their chopsticks, if they had any, noting that the quantity of Chinese food was enough to feed a small army.

After the woods tour, Pat and Hab had arrived, and the table was set for seven. The young ladies were all atwitter at the beauty of the woods and the sights they saw. One mentioned how beautiful the place was.

J picked up on that manner of speech and said, "I'm glad you said 'place.' That's a distinctly Southern description. A Southerner doesn't say, 'Come to my house.' He or she says, 'Come to my place.' It's an expression of ties with the land and the love of the place of our roots." In exaggerated Southern speech, he continued, "So I'm delighted that y'all have enjoyed the place, and I hope you'll come again." There was a unanimous positive response, in unison, all accepting the invitation.

J followed up by suggesting that they return on Thanksgiving for dinner, unless they were going to their respective homes. None of the girls were planning to go home. One was from New York, another from New Jersey, and the third was from Ohio. J told them the invitation included a guest also, telling them that he had a custom of inviting a lot of people in the community that would otherwise be at home alone. All promised to mark their calendars for the event.

The month of September proceeded without incident or visitors. The temperature took a turn from the stifling heat of August, with a very welcome cool morning appearing on the twentieth. *The days dwindle down to a precious few in September*, thought J as he began his role as moderator of the current events discussion at dinner. Hab started off by saying that Piko of the Florida Gators was the best quarterback he had seen in college football. Marie offered that the biggest news event of the month was John McCain selecting Sarah Palin to be his running mate. Pat reported on the news of an impending recession, with Marie agreeing, noting that Starbucks was closing several stores. J talked about one hundred college presidents recommending lowering the drinking age to eighteen and that the MADD organization was indeed mad, as well as the Association of Police Chiefs expressing their disapproval of the idea. Someone mentioned that September was the month of hurricanes, pointing out that there had already been close calls with Gustav, Hannah, and Ike. Financial bailouts were discussed, along with the large annual salaries of Wall Street executives, and the sale of Merrill Lynch to the Bank of America. J mentioned the news of Ted Kennedy being diagnosed with a brain tumor and Paul Newman dying at age eighty-three. The Newman news evolved into a listing of the movies he had played in, including Cool Hand Luke and Butch Cassidy and the Sundance Kid. As usual, the discussion returned to political news, with

Mitt Romney's religion being frequently mentioned, and Jesse Jackson's overheard desire to have Barack Obama castrated.

J found a point for closure and offered to pray for all they had talked about, which included prayers for the future of the country, for the candidates, for truth in debates, for those losing homes due to foreclosures, for military servicemen and women, and gave thanks for all they had been so graciously given.

With that, September continued to dwindle away.

THE TENTH MONTH of the year crept in as if borne by tiny cat feet. There was no dramatic change in the weather, but there was an inexplicable sense of urgency, of change, of anticipation. It was football month at the university. The Carolina band drums could be heard stirring the blood of even the least competitive. Flags stuck on vehicle windows gave the impression of traveling at great speed. Wal-Mart, Lowe's, and Home Depot received large shipments of mums of all colors. Leaves began to change color, and some began to wither and fall to the ground. The grass was still growing, but the pace dramatically slowed. Squirrels began their harvest of pecans even though the nuts had not shed their bitter green outside layers. Deer began to move in the forests. The State Farmer's Market vendors began to display large, plump sweet potatoes, and watermelons began to disappear. The rhythm of the earth was saying it is time for a rest, but the earth's people, especially in the northern hemisphere, were saying it's time to move, to shake it!

J thought of another song that described the month, this one being *Autumn Leaves*. He even used Marie's laptop and the Internet to Google the title, not quite remembering the lyrics. He found that *Autumn Leaves* was originally written in France in 1945 and was entitled "Les Feuslles Mortes," which, if interpreted literally was "The Dead Leaves." The music was written by Joseph Kosma and the lyrics written by French Poet Jaques Pervert. In the United States, Savannah, Georgia's native songwriter Johnny Mercer wrote the English lyrics in 1947, to be sung by Jo Stafford and others. The film *Autumn Leaves* (1956) starred Joan Crawford and featured the song sung by the silky throated Nat King Cole. The lyrics are as follows:

The fallen leaves drift by the window,
The autumn leaves of red and gold.
I see your lips, the summer kisses.

Since you went away the days grow long
And soon I'll hear old winter's song
But I miss you most of all my darling
When autumn leaves start to fall.

While J sat at Marie's desk looking up the song's story as told by Wikipedia, he noticed that two of Louise's cards were on the desk. When he mentioned it, Marie said that Louise left them with her, offering to find her a job in New York if she was interested. Marie told her that her work here at Shalom was not complete yet, but was very appreciative and was really entertaining the idea of working in the city.

Her work was, indeed, coming to an end until J gave her a folder filled with poems written by Elizabeth to compile and edit.

A day or so later, Marie was surprised to receive a phone call from a young man named Samuel Pipen, who was a friend of Lee's. After talking for some time, Marie learned that her name had come up in a conversation Samuel had had with one of her friends that visited her at Shalom, and had given him the Shalom phone number. The purpose of his call was to ask her to go out with him. Marie at first rejected the idea outright then told him she would have to think about it, that it had been a long time since she had dated and she needed to be sure she was ready to resume a social life. She told Samuel to call her again in a day or two if the offer was still good and discussed the call with J. In a fatherly manner, J helped her sort out her feelings. "It has been a while since the loss of your child, the termination of your pregnancy, and the hurt of rejection, and if you like this person, it's probably appropriate to insert a little fun into your life. I think you should agree to go out with him, if you know him and trust him." Marie explained that she knew him from double dating with Lee at the beginning of their relationship and found him to be the best of the crew that ran around together.

Samuel did call the next day, sounded excited that she had accepted, and received directions to Shalom.

When Sam arrived, he was introduced to J, who recognized him as a student he had seen around the campus but had not met before. After exchanging pleasantries, the young couple left for Marie's first night out in ten months.

J felt somewhat at odds with himself after Marie left. Pat was now teaching pretty much full-time and had gone to a PTA meeting, and Hab was working on homework. Sunset in the first part of October in the

Midlands comes around seven in the evening, and the temperatures drop pretty dramatically after the sun goes down. J sat on the rock and smoked until the chill ran him inside. While sitting and smoking, he reflected on his returning to pipe smoking upon learning of his brain tumor and how much he really enjoyed his pipe. When it became too cool to stay outside, he rummaged through the refrigerator and decided on creating one of his favorite, simple meals, a bologna, and American cheese sandwich. He even decided to polish off the remaining can of Budweiser, left over from a recent shrimp boil that Pat had concocted. The coolness of the day, the relaxation enhanced by the Bud, and the senseless political speeches on television contributed to J's sleep in his recliner.

Around midnight, he was awakened to the sound of the front doorbell ringing. When he investigated, being puzzled because the door was never locked and there should be no need to ring the bell, he found Sam pushing Marie against the door, with Marie resisting. When asked what was going on, Sam answered belligerently with slurred speech, "She's not being cooperative. She cooperated with Lee any time he asked, and she's trying to put me off! I want what she was giving Lee and I want it now!" staggering and almost falling.

"Are you drunk?"

"Hell, no, I'm not drunk. I only had two to three (holding up four fingers) drinks, and I can handle it. Now get out the way, old man, and let me get on with getting what I want. Lee told me how much she liked it and was quick to give it away and I want some. She ought to be more cooperative," laughing as he tried to get the long word out. "Everybody knows that she's a damn nympho. She does it with everybody else, and I want some," he said, adding with emphasis, "Now! Right cher!" He laughed again.

J told Marie to go inside, which she did, and J grabbed Sam by his shirt collar and slammed him into the side of his car, saying, "Young man, you're drunk and because you're drunk I'm assuming that you're not responsible for what you're saying. It's time for you to leave. No, let me change that. You're in no condition to drive so I'll give you a choice. Give me the keys to your car and get in it and sleep it off and come get the keys in the morning or come inside with me and spend the night on the sofa with the bathroom nearby. I could give you the choice of getting in your car and leaving, and I'll call the highway patrol and tell them where you are, if you haven't killed yourself before they spot you, but I'm not. Now let me walk you to the house."

Sam smiled and said, "Anythin' yo say, Big Daddy! Roll on! Go Gamecocks! Go Cocks! An' speaking of . . ." J pulled his shirt collar tighter and Sam finally shut up, turned, and threw up on the ground just outside the car.

J helped the dizzy, stumbling Sam into the house, took him to the bathroom and made him rinse his mouth out, and then enlisted Marie's help in tucking him in with a blanket on the sofa and a solid trash can beside him.

"I'm sorry I encouraged you to go out. Maybe the time isn't right yet."

Marie related that everything started out fine. After dinner in Five Points, they ran into some of his friends and walked over to Goat Feathers where he had two beers in quick succession. She explained that he really didn't have that much to drink, but it went straight to his head. She thought that he was going to pass out so she coaxed him to get in his car, which she drove back to Shalom. Sam slept some on the way, but when he got out of the car to see her into the house, he began his demands and ended up trying to force her to have sex on the front stoop. "I was very glad when you came to the door, Dr. J. Thanks for coming to my rescue. You handled him a whole lot better than I ever could have."

"He said some very bad things to you and about you and I regret that. Maybe you should talk to him about that in the morning. I wouldn't let it lie."

"I most probably deserved what he said, Dr. J."

By this time J and Marie had moved from the den where the sleeping Sam lay, into the kitchen, and was sitting there.

"Let me tell you about my relationship with Lee. I met him at a party and he was by far the most handsome young man there. He came and talked with me and we danced and had one good conversation after another. The next day when I got back to my room, there were a dozen red roses there for me. We started dating regularly, and we had a good time. He had a great car, was a good dresser, was handsome, and took me to places I would never have been able to go with anybody else. He seemed to have access to all of the private clubs through his parents. I was totally swept off my feet. After dating several weeks, we spent a lot of time hugging and kissing, and he started going a little bit further and I really didn't want to say no. I had had sex with some fumbly boys in high school and on a couple of occasions at Carolina after football games with alcohol involvement. So when we began our sexual relationship, I must confess that it was the most thrilling and exhilarating thing I had ever done. I didn't know I could enjoy anything as much. From that point on, we really didn't go out, we just simply went to his apartment and we spent all of our time in bed. However, the more I got to know Lee, the less I was impressed with him as a person, but the sex overpowered my thinking. It got to the place that sex was the most important thing, and my relationship with him was secondary. The night I got pregnant, I threw all precautions to the wind and didn't insist on his using any protection. I was willing to take the risk and I paid for it. I don't think I'm a nymphomaniac, but I will have to say that it was something that was most thoroughly enjoyable and I looked forward to it. Sam said something about being a mink, but since I'm a city girl, I don't know what that means."

"Well, we can talk about the sex life of minks and rabbits some other time, maybe include it in one of our supper discussions, but suffice it to say, it is frequent and vigorous. Right now, though, let me tell you that sexuality is one of God's great gifts to mankind. It is enjoyed, but great gifts can also be easily misused. Let me assure you that even though it might be wonderful in the relationship you had, just wait until you're in a marriage relationship and you and your partner respect each other—it moves to a much higher level. I suggest you go to bed and unwind the best you can, but first let's check on Sam. One common cause of death in drunks is suffocation from throwing up and not being conscious enough to move."

The next morning, Sam was gone but left a long note, rather a letter, on the den coffee table. It was addressed to Marie asking for his apology for his behavior to be accepted and to extend the same apology to Dr. J. He described his behavior as being totally unacceptable. He expressed his regret and admitted that he is not a person that should drink at all, citing an inherited gene from his father, that he realized he had made some very embarrassing statements and made a fool of himself. He asked for forgiveness and wished her well. His last statement showed compassion and remorse for his actions by writing, "You deserve better in life than you've had so far." It was signed simply "Sam."

The next day was a very quiet one. J and Marie met for a long while discussing the work that she was doing and the things she should work on next, this lasting until dinner and resuming after.

J went to bed but before daylight woke with a start, having had a dream that seemed to have lasted all night. J dreamed that he was awakened during the night by Marie getting in the bed with him, dressed only with large dangly earrings. He dreamed that she curled her nude body next to his; and when he protested, telling her that he didn't think that was the thing to do, she only made him hold out his hands to caress her breasts. In his dream, he protested loudly, telling her, "Young lady, there are so many things you don't know. You're young, and I'm not. This isn't going to work. It's not right. With that, in his dream, she took her index finger and pressed it to his lips just as Elizabeth did when it was time for a conversation to end. With that, he awoke with a start and got up. He looked at the clock and found it was only a little after four in the morning. He walked to the bathroom, then to the den and turned on the television. After listening to the inanity of rehashed political speeches and expert opinions that supposedly interpreted the outcomes, he returned to bed around five. Around seven, J awoke again, remembering another dream he just had.

This time, he was sleeping, and Elizabeth walked in and sat on the side of his bed and told him, "John Witherspoon Stewart, you've been a bad boy, haven't you?"

In his dream, J answered, "Yes, I guess I have been."

"But the whole time you were thinking about me, weren't you, bad boy?"

"As a matter of fact, truthfully, I was. When she put her finger on my lips and told me to stop protesting, she became you. I could see you and not her."

J recalled that Elizabeth continued, "You know, I can understand that, and I'm not going to give you a hard time. You and I both know there is nothing to prevent such from happening. Nobody alive would be the wiser unless one of you told someone else, and I love you too much to hold it against you. After all, both of you are single in God's eyes, and you are legally married, remember?"

J recalled that the dream continued, but in a different venue. Elizabeth talked about the children and then that she had a great surprise coming for him, a surprise she couldn't tell him about, but he would discover it, and he would be all the wiser for it. She told him the surprise would be somewhat of a mixed blessing, that it would bring him tremendous joy and at the same time raise questions about what to do with that knowledge. The dream ended, as he recalled, with Elizabeth reaching over to him, placing her forefinger on his lips and telling him, "That's enough. No more talk. Good night, my husband."

The next day and for several days, J and Marie sensed a need to keep a distance from each other, not knowing exactly what had happened or what to do about it.

On Columbus Day, J received a call from a young man he identified as one of his graduate students who wanted to come to Shalom and spend several days with him, to review the thoughts he had for his graduate paper. He explained to the supper table crew that his name was Walter Johnson and he was one of the brightest students he had. "He's in the process of writing his dissertation and I hope he will eventually land a job on the faculty. He has those characteristics I admire. He's bright and loves to teach and loves the interaction of people. He'll be here a few days so we can talk without interruption. I hope you'll think as much of him as I do. He's not pretty, but he's handsome in a rugged sort of way. He's really a farm boy at heart and is extremely bright, and the kind of person that doesn't need to be entertained. He's coming on the seventeenth."

Hab spoke up and reminded J that he was supposed to take him to the State Fair that day. J said he had forgotten that, but since Walt is a very adjustable fellow; maybe he would join them.

Just as J finished making that comment, he saw, or actually thought he saw, a movement out of the corner of his left eye. He exclaimed, "Why, Henry! I haven't seen you for years! Where have you been? Where did you come from?" He stopped and became silent for several reasons. What he thought he saw was a gray-and-white tabby cat, holding his tail at a peculiar angle and twist. He recognized the cat as his old pet, Henry. But Henry was gone. His image disappeared just as quickly as it appeared and simply wasn't there. The other reason for stopping his conversation in mid sentence was the fact that Henry was dead. Henry died at age twenty-two in 1986, twenty-two years ago.

J looked up to see all of the round table members staring at him. Marie had her mouth open in disbelief. Pat was giving him that "What the hell's going on here" look with her head cocked, so that a lot of the whites of eyes showed. Hab said with youthful innocence, "Who's Henry? And where is he? I don't see anything."

J was at a loss for words momentarily then laughed and told them he thought he saw a gray-and-white tabby cat walk across the room and disappear, and that it looked just like Henry, a pet cat they had for years. He tried to pass it off quickly, changing the subject to the weather. The group laughed and said things like they would like to meet Henry and quickly decided it was time to clear the table and take care of the dishes, suggesting that they would take care of everything and sent J to the den to watch the evening news.

Before going home that night Pat approached J and asked if he was doing all right, suggesting that maybe she should spend the night at Shalom. J quickly dismissed the idea and assured her that he was fine.

Days passed, and on the seventeenth, Walt arrived, as punctual as ever. Since this was a Saturday, Hab and Pat were not in school, and all were talking about the planned trip to the State Fair. True to the usual change in weather during Fair week, the morning was nippy and seemed to be getting colder. All decided to leave about two in the afternoon and return after dark.

Just after lunch, around one in the afternoon, J told the fairgoers that he wasn't sure he could describe how he felt, but it was unusual. He didn't have a headache as such, but his mind didn't seem to be functioning as it should, and felt he should stay home, delegating the escort duties to Walt. Pat, Hab, and Marie began to search for warm clothing, but Walt approached J by saying, "Dr. J, this is embarrassing, but I don't have but about twenty dollars in my pocket, and wonder if . . ." J saw the dilemma and provided three fifty dollar bills from his emergency money drawer. Walt expressed his appreciation and his embarrassment, but J cut the conversation short, "Don't let it worry you at all, Walt. I've been a graduate student myself and I know what your financial situation must be. Go and have a good time and take of that bunch."

Attend the Fair they did. The first thing to look at, just inside the gate, are the livestock exhibits, followed by the quilting and canning competitions, the South Carolina Wildlife exhibits and the new technology fascinations. The rides and the hot dogs and the cotton candy came after that, along with the smells of popcorn, candy apples, and bear claws. It was almost nine o'clock when Pat called time out, and the rest agreed they were ready for the trip home.

When arriving at Shalom, the group found one of the dogs, Princess, running back and forth near the kitchen door, and barking. A quick check of the house revealed that J was not there, and apparently had not been there for some time, there being no evidence of dinner. Princess was allowed in the house, but she kept barking and running to the back door. Pat organized her thoughts quickly. The dog would lead them to J, but they needed to find flashlights and the small first aid kit. She also thought of trying to call him on his cell phone, only to discover that it was ringing in the den where he left it. The group, armed with flashlights, headed out the door and followed Princess as she led them into the woods. Hab said, "Do you think he's lost?" Pat surmised that he could be, that he wasn't feeling well when they left, but rationalized that he knew the property like the back of his hand, all 215 acres of it. Princess urged them on, running ahead and impatiently returning for them and running off again.

After a considerable distance, through the walnut grove and into the deep woods, Hab announced that he smelled smoke. Hurrying through the next hundred yards or so, they could see a flickering fire, with J sitting beside it, being guarded by Victoria. By this time Princess had arrived and took her place close to J as he sat and smoked his pipe.

After the many questions, J admitted that he really didn't know what had happened. He did remember that he decided to go for a walk through the woods with the dogs and suddenly realized he didn't know where he was. He remembered being cold and the sun was setting so he gathered some dry branches and built a fire and decided to stay there until someone found him. Other than that, he didn't remember how he had gotten there. The fire was contained and mounded, and J was coaxed up, declaring he was able to walk. There was a discussion among the rescuers as to which direction they should head out in, with each having a different thought. Finally, Hab suggested that they let the dogs lead them, seeing that Princess had been able to find J and Victoria in the dark. J agreed and told the girls, "Okay girls, show us the way!" They obliged, running in front of the group and then waiting for them to catch up. All expressed relief when the lights of the Shalom house came into view.

After assurances that she didn't have to spend the night, Pat and Hab went home, but returned early the next morning. J seemed normal, except for being a little unsteady on his feet. Pat lectured J on the necessity of staying home until he could see Dr. Woods, and if he ventured out again anywhere, to do anything, he must take his cell phone with him.

Pat called Dr. Woods on his private number as he had instructed her to do as soon as she could get to the phone. The good doctor surmised the tumor had begun a growth spurt and he needed to see J the next day. Pat refused to leave, staying at Shalom, grading papers, and lining up a substitute for the next day. Marie and Walt urged her to let them do the transporting and waiting, but Pat would have none of it. She would be with J as long as he needed her.

The visit to Dr. Woods was followed by a CT scan, followed by another visit to Woods. Dr. Woods called them both in and said, "J, this thing is growing faster than I thought it would. We talked about radiation and those kinds of things and you told me that you weren't interested, and there isn't a way to stop the growth or even slow it down. I have to tell you that in my professional opinion, you may not have more than a month or two left. With that in mind, I urge you to get all of your personal affairs in order to make it easier on Pat and your children. You don't have much time left, old friend." Pat struggled to keep tears back but managed in silence.

They left the medical plaza in silence, until reaching the Navigator. "I guess we want to go home?" J asked that she ride through the university on the way to let him look at the buildings then head home.

The silent ride was over, and when Pat made sure J could get out of the SUV and into the house, she followed him to the den and closed the door. She walks over and hugs J and begins to sob. "Dear Lord, my heart is breaking. Dr. J, what are we going to do?"

J replied with all simplicity, "I reckon my appointed duty is to die, Pat."

Pat released her hug and sank to the floor on her knees and lifted up her folded hands, "Oh Lord God, take this cup away from him. O Lord God, be with us!" She stops speaking and resumes her hug and said, "I don't know how I can bear this."

J replied in his best fatherly manner, "Pat, You're much stronger than you think you are. You'll get through it. I hope you'll miss me. You will go on with your life. When my time does come, and I leave this land for a far better place, I hope you'll take time and go sit on the rock and Elizabeth and I will both talk with you. You might not hear the words but your mind will pick up on what we're saying."

"You promise?"

"I promise. In the words of the Christ, I will not forsake you or leave you. God willing, my spirit will come along with Elizabeth's and we'll communicate in our own special way."

Pat reaches for the box of tissues, dries her tears, but can't remove the red from her eyes.

J sits in his recliner and thinks about the Pat that has been his caretaker and companion for the past ten years, and most of all, friend.

In the days that followed, J found frequent opportunities to talk with Walt, the things going on in his life, but mostly about his dissertation and the progress he was making on it. Walt was supposed to leave on Tuesday, but asked if he could remain a few more days, declaring that he was ahead of schedule on the dissertation and would like to just hang around.

A week later, after his departure, Walt called again asking if he could spend the weekend and would J mind.

J agreed and smiled as he put the phone down, knowing that Walt was not really coming to spend the weekend with him or because of his love of the place, but that he had taken a fancy to Marie. Much of the time that weekend was spent walking in the woods with Marie. When the weekend was over and time came for Walt to leave, Marie walked him out to his car and took a long time to say good-bye. When he left and Marie returned to the house, she told J, "He's beautiful." J nodded his head in agreement.

"He asked me how our arrangement came about and I told him the whole story, including my affair with Lee and the baby."

"How did he take it?"

"He just reached over, put his arms around me, and told me, 'I'm sorry you've been hurt so badly. I hope your hurt heals and I hope it heals soon.'

"And I said to him, 'Walt, you're a good doctor. I think my healing has begun. Thanks for coming back this weekend.'"

J gave Marie a hug and said, "May God bless you, and God bless Walt as he goes about his business."

J and Marie sat at the kitchen table and began to plan for Halloween decorations. The month was just about over. They couldn't hear the wind pick up or the whisper of the dead leaves being picked up and spread in disarray over the lawn and accumulate in the edges of the house. Some of the leaves still have some of their color and a little bit of moisture, but many of them have lost their shapes, have become wrinkled and dry and, well, dead.

DR. J'S NOVEMBER 2008

THE FIRST TUESDAY of November 2008 was of course election day. Not just any old election day, but a presidential election day. After a vote around the kitchen table, Hab was allowed to stay up and watch the returns. After all, this was a historic occasion, one that would have far-reaching results and would perhaps forever affect the economic lives of all that would live long enough. J made a point to comment on John McCain's generous concession speech. He pointed out, mostly for Hab's benefit, that nowhere else in the world would a rival such as McCain concede with such civility. He told Hab that the United States of America had the duty to teach the world to be civil, and by citizens all over the globe watching this election, there might be hope for the governments of their countries and find new avenues of peacemaking. There was change for the sake of change.

The next evening, J received a telephone call from a person who said he would not identify himself, but had something that he felt he must share with J, something that was bothering him greatly; and he felt that J would know what to do with the information.

It seems as if the caller was a friend of Frank Lee Howell Jr.'s and had been invited to watch election returns at Frank's apartment the night before. After most of the returns were in and the winners at least projected, Frank asked his guests if they would like to see a little adult entertainment. After having consumed a case and a half of beer, all agreed that some cheer would be welcome. It turned out that Frank had set up an elaborate video camera system in his bedroom, with an equally elaborate DVD recording system. He could activate the system without his partner's knowledge, which would allow their sexual activity to be videoed from the ceiling, the head of the bed, and the foot of the bed—timing the sequence to allow all angles to be shown. The first video Frank selected was scenes involving Marie. The caller said that Frank had meticulously cataloged the DVDs by partner and by date and kept the DVDs in a special cabinet in his room, securely locked. The caller went on to say that he observed where Frank kept the key, that being under a gamecock figurine on his fireplace mantle. The caller related that he became disgusted and left the room and found that he not only had videos of Marie, but often other women, whose names he wrote down on an envelope he found in his pants pocket. The caller waited while J searched for pen and paper and recorded the names of the women. Another bit of information Frank offered was that he and his fiancée were planning to announce their engagement and that the lucky lady was to arrive in Columbia on Saturday morning prior to the announcement that night. J thanked the anonymous caller, promising that he would see to it that justice prevailed.

J called Marie in to the study and related that content of the call and shared with her the list of women that he had written down. He asked if she had consented to being videoed, which she vehemently denied. When Marie recovered from fits of crying from humility and rage, she told J she had a good idea of who the caller might be, speculating that it might be the young man whom she dated a month or so ago. Her reasoning included the fact that he was about the only one of Frank's friends who drank with reserve, and she expected he still was ashamed of his behavior at the Shalom front door.

The discussion of what to do continued into the wee hours of the night. J reminded Marie that it would be in her best interest not to be personally involved with any face-to-face confrontation with Frank. J reasoned that he knew of her intense feelings toward the young man and was afraid she might be carried away in a moment of revenge and do something she would regret. After some time, Marie agreed. What J didn't tell her was that a settlement between her and Frank's father had been worked out by an attorney friend of J's; and in the settlement agreement, she would be legally bound to avoid any contact with Frank after her last contact with him, which was last winter. She would have to ensure that her name would not be associated with any action taken. J, because of his association with Marie, had to be sure that his presence in any action would not be known.

Around three in the morning, the two formulated a plan. Marie would attempt to find the telephone numbers of the women whose names were listed, call them, tell them of the existence of the videos, and let them handle the rest, with the request that if they were successful in obtaining the videos that she would be called and given a chance to get them to be destroyed. Marie knew several of the victims and selected one she knew had had a stormy breakup with Frank.

The next day, Marie made her call to her selected leader and provided the information, which was received with shock and anger. Promises of retribution were made, and a plan was hatched.

As Marie found later, this is what the plan entailed: The leader of the group met as many of the former lovers on Saturday morning as she could locate. Two members of the group were now married. They agreed to watch Frank's apartment and wait until his fiancée arrived and give them time to get in bed, which they were confident would happen. One of the group participants would knock on the door until it was opened and insist on coming in to see, one more time, the place she had had so much love and pleasure, forcing her way in if she had to and making sure the rest of the group would be right behind her. This worked, and sure enough, the current fiancée was found in bed, covered with only sheets and an engagement ring. The group confronted Frank, while one found the key under the gamecock figurine and unlocked the cabinet. Another found and ripped the wires out of their concealment to the wide-eyed disbelief of the fiancée, who began to scramble for her clothes. Frank was attempting to call for help when another jerked the phone cord from the wall, and another found and smashed his cell phone, then flushed it down the toilet. One of the more-imaginative victims pulled a hammer and a nail from her purse and asked for help to turn Frank on his head and stand him against the wall, announcing that she was going to nail his scrotum to the wall and leave him there. She speculated that sooner or later, he would become unable to maintain his upside-down stand, which would allow the nail to do its work. Frank began to yell and then scream with horror at the thought of this end result. The fiancée, now fully clothed, grabbed her suitcase and exited with haste—but after removing the two-carat diamond and throwing it in the toilet that had just digested the cell phone. The larger of the group rescued Frank from the upside-down crucifixion but slammed his face so hard against the wall the sheetrock broke through after breaking the nose, blood spurting all over.

The whole scene lasted only six minutes; but that was long enough for the cabinet to be cleared out, the video equipment to be wrecked, the fiancée to leave with the group, and Frank to bleed.

When the operation was complete, the leader reported back to Marie, who gladly borrowed J's Navigator and met to receive her DVDs. The leader thanked Marie profusely for providing the information, agreeing that the content of the videos, had they not been destroyed, would haunt them the rest of their lives. She told Marie that some of the women talked briefly about legal action against Frank but decided that the publicity they would necessarily receive outweighed the possible outcome of a lawsuit.

Marie returned to Shalom with the discs, mentally arguing with herself over whether to look at the content or not. It was as if the cartoon depicting an angel on one shoulder pleading for the discs to be destroyed without viewing and the devil on the other shoulder urging Marie to take "just one peek" was real. Each of the little characters would alternately win a point, only to be destroyed by the next reasoning. When Marie returned to Shalom, she found that J had built a large wood fire in the den fireplace, to cut the chill of the November evening, so she made an instant decision to listen to the angel and threw them, one by one, into the inferno.

J and Hab spent their Saturday afternoon watching the Carolina Clemson football game on television. It was a disaster for Carolina because the team seemed to have their minds in some far away land, compared to the Clemson team, who came to play.

On Sunday evening, after polishing off the leftovers from the noon meal, J reminded the roundtable group that, due to his episode of becoming lost in the woods, the election predictions and campaign promises they had neglected their little current event talks. Much of the discussion dealt with recall of the presidential campaign talks. The Joe Biden and Sarah Palin debate had a prominent place in the discussions. Someone read where a sheriff somewhere announced that he was not going to execute any more foreclosure evictions. Tampa Bay beat the Red Sox three to one. The Iraqi Cabinet wants the United States forces out or at least a deadline set for troop withdrawal. The peace plan has been extended by the Saudis. USC (University of South Carolina in this household, always) almost beat LSU, but it didn't quite happen. Wake Forest beat Clemson. OJ Simpson's luck ran out. Some astute (?) bureaucrat made the statement that the reason the banking industry hasn't been more closely supervised was because he felt the industry would regulate itself. Sarah Palin received criticism for a shopping spree. The Supreme Court addressed profanity, declaring that the "F" word is one of the most vulgar, graphic, and explicit descriptions of sexual activity in the English language. (Really? Another astute observation.)

Military personnel are still being killed in Iraq and Afghanistan. The Florida Gators showed no mercy on Georgia, or South Carolina, for that matter. Michael Bloomberg wrangled a waiver allowing him to run for a third term as Mayor of New York City. The Bush's extended an invitation to meet with the Obama's, resulting in a magnificent display of graciousness. Phillip Fulmer was fired from his job as coaching job at Kentucky but walked away with a four million-dollar settlement. Tommy Bowden lost out at Clemson and his severance package is only three and a half million.

This type of discussion continued for some time until J tried to stifle a yawn, which triggered talk of cleaning the kitchen and preparing for next week.

Monday morning was back to work for Pat and for Marie. J felt pressure to get things wrapped up, and he spent a lot of time in his study sorting various papers and writing notes to be discussed with Marie. This sorting, discarding, note-making, and turning things over to Marie continued for the whole week.

On Thursday the twentieth of November, as J and Marie continued their work, the phone rang, and the caller identified himself as a deputy sheriff with the Fairfield County Sheriff's office. "Dr. Stewart, I've been asked to call you by a young man in our custody by the name of Hank Aaron Brown. He says that you know him and he needs some help from you. He says that his mother is a school teacher who substitutes in various schools and he doesn't know what school she might be in today. Is this right and do you want to give him some help?" J replied that of course he would help Hab, and asked, "And you have him in jail? What's he been charged with?" The deputy answered, "Well, we do have him in custody, having been brought her by the highway patrol, but we've had a little trouble in the jail and he's at the hospital right now. I expect him to be brought back here shortly." "I'll be there in just a few minutes," J told the deputy, and after a cursory explanation to Marie, he ran out the door to Blue Boy and drove out of the driveway. He mentally reviewed the situation and Hab was correct, Pat was working at a different school and he either didn't remember which one or Pat had just mentioned in passing where she would be. She did mention to him that she was riding with a fellow teacher and this recollection was reinforced by seeing Pat's Toyota parked on the side of the road, just before the Shalom entrance.

Risking a speeding ticket, J hurried on to the Fairfield county jail. The usual modern security systems were in place, including passing through a metal detector. After the third attempt, with the scanning device detecting a belt buckle, two errant coins, and a key, J was allowed access to the chief deputy on duty. J's question of what happened was answered by the deputy, relating this sequence of events. It seems as if a highway patrolman observed Hab driving his mother's car on the shoulder of the road. When the patrolman investigated he found that Hab had no driver's license and no registration and assumed that Hab had stolen the car and brought him to the jail. J asked if he could see him, and the deputy said, "Well, not just yet. You see, we put the young man in the holding cell with several others, and one of the fellows in there roughed him up, actually tried to sexually assault him but was stopped by two of the other men in the cell. In order to check him out, we took him to the Fairfield Memorial Hospital." J exploded in anger, and turned to head out of the door. "Where are you going, Dr. Stewart?" asked the deputy. "I'm going to the hospital!" blurted J.

"Sir, please wait right here. He should be returning very shortly. I understand that Deputy Hale is transporting him back here as we speak."

"Then let me go back to the cell and tell that son of a bitch that he better hope he spends a long time in jail because I plan to be waiting for him if I'm alive and I'll take care of his sexual problems once and for all."

"Sir, I can't let you do that. I know you're upset but nothing would be gained by your going back there except subject you to some legal action. Please sit and tell me what your relationship to Hank Brown is."

J calmed down enough to recognize the appropriateness of the deputy's actions and words and began to assist in the ever present paperwork. When this was almost finished, Sheriff Culclasure, well known to J, arrived, and beckoned for him to come into his office. The sheriff's words of apology fell on deaf ears as J began to berate the actions of the highway patrolman and began demanding that he talk to him, right now, in the sheriff's office.

Sheriff Culclasure, known to J by his nickname "Slick," defused the anger, or at least tried to, by saying that the patrolman was not available right then, and besides, he was doing his job. He said that he had talked to the patrolman and was told that Hab asked him to drive to your house where you would identify him and give the patrolman assurances that he hadn't stolen the car. Hab explained that what he was attempting to do was to drive on the shoulder of the road for the short distance from his driveway to yours and then take the car to your house and wash it for his mother, to surprise her when she returned home from school. The patrolman, of course, refused. Sheriff Culclasure commented that he frequently disagreed with the "piss and vinegar" approach that young highway patrolmen frequently took, but that was a different agency and there was little he could do about it. Slick did tell J that his jailer should not have placed Hab in the holding cell with the men and promised to fully investigate and would probably issue some disciplinary action. One of the deputies knocked at the door then handed the Sheriff the report from the hospital emergency room doctor. Slick looked at it and passed it along to J. While J was reading it, the sheriff summarized by saying, "No penetration. Just scared to death," and instructed the deputy to bring Hab in to his office. By this time, J was beginning to return to being rational and asked the sheriff to please convey his thanks to the men in the cell that pulled Hab away from the offender, which the sheriff promised to do.

The deputy brought Hab to the Sheriff's office, entering with tears streaming down his face as he ran to hug J. They hugged for a long time, with J giving him words of comfort and assuring him that he wasn't angry with him and questioning him about his encounter in the cell. Sheriff Slick told the two of them that he was taking the responsibility of releasing Hab to J's custody, to go home, and that he would deal with the highway patrolman and the pending charges of driving without a license and without proper registration. He instructed the two of them to go to the jailer's desk and retrieve Hab's possessions, which included the keys to his mother's car.

J and Hab rode home, mostly in silence, with J giving him comfort, telling him that he will get over it even though it was a bad experience.

They had not returned to Shalom very long before Pat walked up from the driveway and asked, "Does anybody want to tell me why my car is parked on the side of the road?"

"It's a long story, and I think your son is the person to tell you," leaving the kitchen table to them.

After the tears, explanations, assurances, and promises, J drove the two down the driveway to retrieve the car on the side of the road.

On Monday of the week before Thanksgiving, Marie related to J with sparkling eyes that Walt had called and asked if he could spend Thanksgiving with them and asked if his visit would be okay with him. J replied that he has no problem with Walt's visit but reminded her that they were also obligated to a visit from three of her girlfriends for Thanksgiving dinner. Marie insisted on an answer, saying, "So that means 'yes'?"

J smiled and said, "Yes, that's a yes. Tell him to come on."

The Thanksgiving dinner guest list seemed to be growing every day. Counting the usual four, plus Walt, plus the three girls and their guests, when added to the ten that J invited, brought the total to twenty-one. Pat and Marie prepared the grocery list, gave it to J and Hab, and sent them on their way. J added several things, and by the time they returned, there was a Navigator full of food.

J began the day early with his barbecue duties. He and Hab spent the previous weekend dusting off the barbecue grills that had been resting for a long time; but now they were all in use, with chicken, ribs, pork shoulders, and tenderloins—all at one time. J and Hab were running back and forth between the grills, sprinkling water to put out grease fires and mopping barbecue sauce where needed. The aroma permeated the entire Shalom yard.

Shortly after noon, the guests began to arrive. Marie's girlfriends and their male friends, six in total, all arrived in one vehicle, surely illegally due to the lack of seat belts. J wondered how they all fit in the car and how they would fit on the return trip after a large dinner. Walt had arrived earlier in the day and had been enlisted into barbecue duty. The neighborhood guests, those who would have otherwise spent the day alone, came in by twos and threes.

The group gathered in the living room, where J asked if anyone cared to offer thanks and was pleasantly surprised when Walt volunteered and delivered an excellent blessing. The food was served buffet style, with each person finding a place to sit. Ten found places at the large dining room table, some scattered to the den, some to the kitchen table, and some in the living room. After dinner, no one was in any hurry to leave, some choosing to watch football, some just engaging in conversation.

In the middle of the afternoon, J retired to the rock with his pipe and engaged in a conversation with his wife, only to be interrupted by Marie and Walt.

Marie spoke, saying to J, "Dr. J, Walt has invited me to ride with him to his parents' home. He would like for them to meet me. Is it all right with you if I do?"

Instead of the answer she expected, J told Marie, "Let me think about it for a while. Why don't you two go for a walk in the woods and come back, and then we'll talk." Puzzled by his response, Marie and Walt agreed and walked away.

After about thirty minutes, Marie returned alone and asked J, "Dr. J, I wasn't expecting the answer you gave me. What's wrong?"

J replied, "Actually, nothing's wrong, Marie. I think it would be great for you to go to meet Walt's parents. I've noticed over the past weeks that things are developing between you and Walt rather quickly, and I wanted to warn you to go slowly. There's a time and a place for good things to happen, so don't rush. There's plenty of time. I'm afraid that you might let your emotions carry you away. You've been treated badly by men that you've trusted, and Walt presents a whole different type of person. I think you need to get to know Walt well, something you haven't taken the time to do with your other male friends, and that's led to disasters, at least the two that I'm familiar with. Please take your time and do your homework, speaking as a professor. I can see why Walt is carried away with you. You're a beautiful woman, but you know that. You are smart, intelligent, and have great conversational abilities. Walt is a gentle person who would love to take care of you, particularly after you've told him of your relationship with Frank and the child. You need to be sure he is interested in you as a person and not someone he needs to care for. Both of you are extremely intelligent and capable in most aspects, but I'm not sure of the depth of your wisdom. All I am saying is to take time, to be sure. I know of some of the hurt you've had in your relationships, and my wish is that these hurts would not be repeated. By all means go and meet Walt's parents. I know them, not well, but well enough to know they are good people and have raised a fine son. Just be careful, go slow, and take your time. I hope you understand."

Marie told him she understood and expressed her appreciation for his concern about her well-being and returned to Walt.

The guests left in the order they arrived, all expressing their appreciation, with many of them taking leftovers for the rest of the week. When all left and the kitchen was finally cleaned and the leftovers put away, J asked Pat to join him in his study.

"I want to tell you some things, Pat, and I want you to write them down and type them up for me when you get a chance."

Pat agreed and retrieved a paper and pencil.

"The first is a letter to the Fairfield county coroner."

"My god, Dr. J! What are you doing? Are you suddenly feeling bad? What brought this on?"

J laughed and replied, "No, Pat, nothing's changed. I'm feeling as good as I did earlier. You know, after being around me for as long as you have, that when I decide to do something, I like to do it right away. This is something that I need to do. You and I know that we have no guarantees for our future, even for the next few minutes, and this is something that I want to take care of. Please bear with me. I hate to lean on you in this way, but you're the person I feel the most comfortable with in matters like this. Let's go on.

"As I said, this is a letter to the coroner. When he comes to examine my body, should I die here—and by the way, I hope I do instead of in some hospital or somewhere else—please see that he gets this letter. I'll sign the letter when you type it, and I'll get it notarized so there should be no question as to its authenticity. My wish is to say to the coroner or the appropriate person that I want any parts of my body that might be useable to be harvested. Maybe parts of my skin or some of the internal organs might be salvageable.

"While we're at it, let's go a step further and write an obituary. I would like for this obituary to go to the newspapers in Columbia, Greenville, Charleston and Greenwood. It should say, 'John Witherspoon Stewart, my age, died at home, list the date. He was the husband of one, father of four, and friend of many. He served three tours of active duty with the U.S. Army, served as a faculty member at the University of South Carolina in the Department of Philosophy. Funeral services will be announced later. I think that'll do it."

Pat said, "Is that all?"

"Yes, that's all I need to say."

"That's going to be a very short obituary."

"Well, now that you mention it, there is something else to add to it. So if you will, put this in as a postscript. 'To friends of John Witherspoon Stewart: If you have read the above death notice, you will know that I am dead. A couple of things I would ask of you—first, don't go to any trouble to attend my burial but rather spend a little bit of time visiting some other old person who is still alive. Secondly, don't send flowers but make a contribution to some cause that aids children in the third world. Thirdly, get yourself ready to join me in the great hereafter. I hope, for your sake, that it will be no time soon. Thanks for your friendship you have given me through the years we have known each other. By the way, I have recently given up smoking again.'

"Another thing, Pat, this is to be given to the person who makes the arrangements for my funeral. I would like to ask Dr. Tommy Smith, my friend of many years, to be in charge of the services. I leave it to him to select the appropriate scriptures to read. Also, I would like for Reverend James McCarley to be present and to bring with him the choir or members from the First African Baptist Church and call on them to sing two spirituals. I am also requesting that the Black Beauty Baseball Team select six of their players to serve as pallbearers. In addition, I would like to engage Jack Branson to prepare a buffet for one hundred people, to be done here at Shalom after the burial. I'm trying to think of a local band that I've heard but can't think of the name. When I remember it, I'll tell you and add it to the list and ask them to play during the buffet. I think that's all I have right now. When you get that put together, I'll get the notary to put the finishing touches on it. Thanks, Pat.

"And, Pat, you know that I do things impulsively. But also, Elizabeth and I have been having a lot of conversations lately, and she reminds me that my time is running short, and I should get all of the things I need to do out of the way before I join her and the children. She tells me that I am in for a great surprise soon, that she couldn't tell me what it was, but I would be shocked and pleased. I asked what I should do to prepare for it, and she told me there was nothing I needed to do, that it would all work out. Please try not to be upset, Pat. But my time is drawing near, and I'm ready for it."

Pat said nothing, folded her work notes, and left the room. When J followed a few minutes later, Marie looked at J and said, "Pat seemed to be very upset when she left, crying and sobbing and wouldn't talk to me. Can I do anything?"

"We were dealing with some very personal things, but she's a strong person and will be all right eventually. She's tough and has had lots of ups and downs, but that proves to be helpful as we go along in life that's full of disappointments or things that happen that we wish wouldn't. I would give you the same advice. Be tough, young lady."

DR. J'S DECEMBER 2008

DECEMBER 1, 2008, emerges as a beautiful, sunny, cool day. Temperature begins at fifty-five and peaks at sixty-eight. Leaves have, for the greater part, all withered and fallen, leaving the white oak trees around the Shalom house looking naked. Hab has earned his money in the past few weeks raking and disposing of leaves. J is working in his study, sorting papers, thinking to himself that the stack is finally getting manageable. Marie has been hard at work in another room.

Marie suddenly knocks at the door and says, "Dr. J, I have a question that needs an answer. Are we married? I know we went to the notary and that poor creature filled out some papers and said some words about marriage, but I have never been sure. My thought is that it really never happened, but I'm not sure."

J countered with a question of his own, "Would you like to be?"

"Under the current situation, no."

"Very good. Why aren't we married is the question. Well, there's a simple legal reason. In South Carolina a couple has ten days to file a marriage license after the wedding, and we didn't do that. In fact, the marriage license is still collecting dust in the sun visor of the Toyota, as far as I know, but I suspect it was burned to a crisp and blew away after the wreck, so there is no record of our marriage, whatsoever. I don't even see how we could be considered married in the sight of God, either, and so the answer is a simple no, we are not. How do you feel about that?"

"Good" was the simple, one-word answer. They smiled at each other and returned to their respective tasks, Marie continuing her editing and J sorting and shredding. As the trash can filled, he recalled some of his thoughts of several months ago when he thought his children would curse him after his death about the dearth of papers he had left behind, them trying to determine whether or not something was worth keeping or even worth going through. He was now coming to the end of that task and would be relieving them of such a dilemma.

As the first Saturday of the month approached, J asked Pat if she would be able to help him for a couple of hours. She agreed so he located his Blackberry and called a number he had found in the *State Newspaper* a day or so before. "Do you still have the 2002 Nissan for sale that you advertised a few days ago?" The answer was a yes, and J began to give the person some information, including his name. The lady with the car recognized J's name and voice, having been one of his students a few years back. She introduced herself as being the former Sally Gravel and identified the classes she had taken from J. J listened and suddenly exclaimed, "Sally Gravel. Honey blonde hair, sat on the front row, right-hand side?" They chatted on for several minutes about the small world they lived in, how nice it was to be remembered, and recalled minutia before getting around to talking about the car. It seems as if Sally was now Sally Michaelson, a wife and mother of three children. The car belonged to her grandmother and the twenty thousand miles showing was in fact actual mileage. Grandmother only drove it to the grocery store and church and to visit relatives during the last years preceding her death. J told Sally that she should consider it sold, and he would be going to her house within a couple of hours to pick it up and asked her to prepare a bill of sale, but leave the name of the purchaser blank.

His next call was to Pat, asking him to pick him up to carry him to Columbia. Pat drove, with J giving general directions until they reached the edge of town. He consulted the city map he brought with him, commenting that he used to be familiar with the north end of Columbia, but things were beginning to look the same to him. The address was found, and Pat asked what he was planning. J confided that he saw an ad in the paper by an individual advertising a 2002 Nissan for sale and he thought it would be a good car for Marie, and that it was time for her to have one of her own. Pat agreed that the idea was a good one, but shook her head at J's lack of consideration to involve Marie in the decision. "Same old J," she muttered, half under her breath, "always doing something for somebody without their knowing what's going on. Nothing ever changes." J looked at her with surprise, never considering that maybe, just maybe, he should have consulted Marie first. Too late for that now, though. He had already committed to buy the car, and he planned to drive it home and present it to her. He had not thought far enough ahead to decide whether he should hide it somewhere and present it to her at Christmas or if he should give it to her when he took it home. Oh well, he decided he would decide on his way home.

The car was spotless, just as described. Sally Michaelson was waiting with the bill of sale and J made out a check. Pat told J that she would leave him then take care of some errands in Columbia while she was there and let him drive the new purchase home.

Sally asked if he could spare some time and come in and talk, which J agreed to do. The two visited longer than anticipated, the total time approaching an hour instead of the fifteen minutes he mentioned to Pat.

J left with his new purchase, taking some time to become familiar with mirror adjustments, brakes, signals, etc. He headed out in the direction of Blythewood, but as he drove, he suddenly realized there was nothing familiar. He found an interstate and drove onto it, but still nothing seemed to look right. He drove for an hour and finally turned in to a rest stop. He consulted his map, to no avail. Suddenly, his cell phone rang; and to his relief, it was Pat asking where he was and if he was all right. She asked where he was, and he told her he really didn't know, that he was stopped at a rest stop on an interstate. In desperation, he asked the occupants of the car next to him what the location of the rest stop was and was told that he was on Interstate 20 near Camden, which was on the wrong interstate leading north from Columbia. He told Pat, and after a lengthy conversation, Pat reluctantly agreed for him to attempt to drive himself home. She knew the rest stop area and gave him explicit directions as to how to get off at the next intersection, turn under the underpass, and get on the road on the other side of the interstate. She made him promise to answer the phone when she called, which was going to be every ten minutes or less. J thought that he had a recollection of the area now and promised to follow her directions. The process worked. Pat called J every ten minutes or less, reviewed with him the route, verified the scenery he was seeing, and gave him prompts on where to turn. In an hour and fifteen minutes, J entered the Shalom driveway to find Pat standing in the driveway waiting for him. When asked how he was, he told her that he felt very confused, frightened, and helpless and that the experience concerned him greatly. Pat made a mental note that J must not drive again.

At dinner that night, J presented Marie with the keys to her car, along with the bill of sale, describing it as an early Christmas present. This was a total shock for Marie. She accepted the gift graciously and thanked him profusely.

After dinner, J declared that he was going to church the following morning and asked if any wanted to join him. Pat quickly agreed, with a silent vow that she wasn't going to allow him to drive, but didn't want to tell him.

Sunday night, after dinner, the four Shalomites watched a television special entitled *Scream Bloody Murder*. This program made it very clear that the United States, through its history, has been more concerned about political successes or endeavors and the power controlled by the political party in office than concerns about human rights. When the program ended, J postulated that the lack of concerns about the human rights of others says a great deal about them as a nation today. J turned to Hab and told him he hoped things would change during Hab's lifetime but doubted if it would. He told Hab that if he ever found himself in a position of power and influence, please use it for good purposes.

After J's short civics lesson, the subject quickly turned to the football game they watched the day before, the rivals being Florida and Alabama. They agreed that it was quite a good game. J commented that one might understand why a coach would run up the score if his team could, but he had never agreed with the principle of beating the opponent into the ground. He went on to say that it would seem to him that if the coach knew the game was won, he would let those fellows on the second and third string play to gain experience in a real conflict. J said that he had no respect for coaches who run up scores, and it is apparent that there are some who do that, even in this day and age.

The next several nights of television news were filled with the scandal of Illinois Governor Rob Blogdonovich attempting to fill the senate seat vacated by President Elect Obama. J's comments, after listening to the content of some of the tapes, dealt with the foul language used by the governor. He went on to wish that somehow ten politicians could be put in a blender and out of the mix would come one statesman. He pointed to the account of the Mayor of Birmingham being brought up on 101 charges of impropriety, and now being investigated for possible federal charges. Also in the news was Charles Rangel's alleged ethics violations, making it seem as if one politician after another was being found corrupt. The good news, as the group saw it, was President Elect Obama's decision to retain gates as the Secretary of Defense and Hillary Clinton as Secretary of State. Bringing Hab into the conversation, J asked him of his opinion of O.J Simpson's conviction and sentencing to thirty-three years in prison. Hab thought the sentence was heavy for the apparent crime committed and thought that Simpson's being acquitted of the murder charges in a case that seemed open and shut had a lot to do with the length of the sentence. He went on to say that he didn't understand why Simpson didn't just go to the authorities and say there are some people who have stolen stuff from me and are selling it and I want it back."

Pat wanted to talk about the bailout of the big three auto manufacturers, pointing out that the Japanese manufacturers have been diligent in building gas efficient autos and hybrids while Detroit build things like Hummers, stating that in her opinion the big three had lost touch with the common man and economics.

Pat also attacked the Pope's statement that anyone who voted for Obama should go to church and offer a full confession of their sins. She heatedly commented on his statement that no woman will have a role of responsibility in the Catholic Church as long as he is the Pope, and if someone is going to be a good Catholic, they must follow the faith but really mean to say as interpreted by him.

J wrapped up the current events discussion by announcing that his two children would be coming home for Christmas and he was looking forward to their visit. He then began to enumerate the things he was thankful for, which included the group around the table and the good grades that Hab was bringing home. He interrupted his list and turned to Hab to tell about the things he was thankful for. After a short hesitation, Hab said he was thankful for a nice warm house to live in and a mother who he knows loves him and for the newly elected president of the United States. Pat listed her thanks for Hab, for the direction the country was headed, for the opportunity to teach, for friends and family, and for the fellowship she enjoyed around the table. Marie, without hesitation, listed her thanks for Walt, who has made her feel clean and whole again, for the three around the table who have accepted her into this family, for second chances, and for hope that comes out of despair. J concluded the comments that he had started by saying he was thankful for faith, for providence, or providential happenings, for memories and joy. At the conclusion, all stood and hugged.

December fifteenth signaled the middle of the month that was rapidly moving to conclusion. When J was sure Pat would be home from her teaching duties, he called her on her cell phone and asked her to come over because he needed to have a serious talk with her and asked that she not bring Hab. When she arrived they went into the J's study and sat facing each other, after closing the door, something J rarely did. "Pat, I have done something that I intended for good, and I'm afraid it is going to have the opposite effect. I see now that I should have let sleeping dogs lie, so to speak. I'm afraid that what I have done will cause you a great deal of pain, and I apologize profusely before I tell you. I have a folder here with a lot of correspondence in it. You can read it; study it, when and if you want to. It was about two months ago that I ran across a friend of your husband, Joe Frazier Brown, and asked where Joe was now. He had Joe's address with him and gave it to me. I wrote Joe and told him about Hab and his growth, both physically and intellectually, and what a promising future he has. I also told him that I knew of a laboratory in Cincinnati that does DNA paternity tests. I told him that I had a piece of cloth with Hab's blood on it, from when he fell off his bicycle a few months back and I would pay for the test if he would agree to sending a sample of his blood to the lab. I didn't hear from Joe for some time and thought that he would not want to go through with it. But one day out of the blue, Joe called me on my cell phone and told me that the question of Hab's paternity had been on his mind for many years and that he appreciated my suggestion and would like to take me up on my offer. I thanked him, and told him that I thought that was the thing to do to settle his mind forever, and he agreed. I sent him all the information about the laboratory, sent a check to pay for it, and sent the snip of the washcloth with Hab's blood on it, and asked him to send it on. The laboratory form had a place to send copies of this information, and I listed my name and address and asked Joe to give permission for a copy to be sent to me."

J continued, "I received the report from the lab in this morning's mail and I almost fell over when I read it. The report reported that there was a 00.0 percent chance that Joe Frazier Brown was the father of Hank Aaron Brown."

Pat began to sob and shake and placed her head in her hands and began saying, "O God, O God, O God!"

J said, "Pat, can we talk about this? Maybe not now, but sometime?"

Pat replied, "No, not later. We need to talk about this now."

"Are you up to it?"

Pat dried her tears, composed herself, and began. She related that on the night of the Senior Prom for the high school that she and Joe Frazier and J's son Jack attended, she went with Joe. This was planned by their mutual parents, who were friends. Jack was supposed to take Shirley Migliari, but she came down with mono a few days before, so Jack went alone. After a couple of hours at the dance, about six couples, Joe and Pat included, went outside. Joe didn't drink but some of his friends offered him some alcohol, which he began drinking like lemonade, which resulting in Joe becoming drunk in short order. He was so drunk that all of sudden he turns to me and tells me to take my clothes off, that we were going to do it right then and there. When I refused, he wrestled me to the ground and started tearing my clothes off. He managed to get me on the ground, got on top of me and penetrated me while I was calling out for help. A couple of Joe's friends ran over and pulled him off me, but as he was being pulled off, he discharged all over me. About that time Jack was walking in the direction of his car and one of the fellows stopped him and asked him to help. They explained that Joe had gotten drunk and had raped me, and since he didn't have a date, could he take me home. Jack agreed without hesitation. He and I were friends, having been in several school clubs. Jack asked me if I needed to go to the hospital and I didn't want to, but I would like to go somewhere and take a shower. He decided to bring me to your house. We got in the house through the basement and he showed me where the shower is down there. I must have stayed in there for twenty minutes or more. You and your wife had already gone to bed, and didn't know we were there. Jack gave me a large beach towel before I got in the shower, and I was wrapped in it when he came back to check on me. He hugged me and told me he was sorry for what had happened, and I don't really know what happened after that, but it ended up with us on the bed in that room. I guess the excitement was too much, because he tried to penetrate but it went all over me again. I wasn't sure that the act was ever completed. I got up and showered again, and he took me home, after he borrowed some clothes that belonged to Rebecca. He took me home and I tried to go inside with no lights on, but when I went in I found my parents and Joe's parents waiting for me. My father went out and thanked Jack for bringing me home, and he left. There was a long, heated discussion, as you can imagine. Three days later Joe and I were married. Joe wasn't happy about this marriage, and I, of course, wasn't either. It was one of those marriages that both of our parents thought was the honorable thing to do. For the next nine months I felt like I was being raped every night. You know the rest of the story. When Joe saw Hab, he knew it wasn't his child. Hab doesn't have anything near his coloring or his features. Thank God for your wife and how she saved me. Joe would surely have killed me if it hadn't been for her."

J rose from his chair, went over to Pat, who stood, and put his arms around her. "Are you saying that Hab is Jack's son? And my grandson?"

"That's the only thing that makes sense, Dr. J."

"Do you think Jack has any idea of any of this?"

"I don't think he has a clue. I have known Hab must be his child, but now I know."

"What should we do about this, Pat? Do you want me to talk to Jack? Or do you want to? I don't know what to do . . . just don't know. I do know that I have caused you great trouble because I expect Joe has received his copy of this report by now and has called his parents for vindication. I don't know how Joe's parents will handle this, but I don't think they'll be quiet about it, and I don't know how to protect you. But I know from experience that this isn't the end of the world. We'll find a way out of this. My greatest regret is that I won't be here to go through this with you."

"Dr. J, I know you'll be with me in person or in spirit. You always have. Now let me go to my house now and see if I can absorb all of this."

After Pat left, J put on a coat and went to his rock. As he sat there in silence, he thought, "Is this what Elizabeth's been telling me about a great surprise, and that I was in for a great shock?" J sat there until dark in silence, with no word whatsoever from Elizabeth.

Three days later, on December 18, Marie approached and asked a favor. "May I ask Walt to come and spend some of the Christmas holidays with us? He's going to be out of school from now until the first week in January." J gave his consent, mentioning that they would have a house full of people, and as soon as we figure out how many will be spending the night, you might want to get a motel room for Walt. "As a matter of fact, Marie, you might want to invite your brother and he and Walt could share a motel room. Think about that." Marie said she had thought about inviting her brother, but was reluctant to ask because she knew J's children would be there. Now that he mentioned it, she said she would like to invite him.

The next day Walt arrived, and after visiting a few minutes, asked J if he could talk to him, which J, of course, granted. They retired to the rock and Walt asked, "Dr. J, I have always respected you and your opinions and I know that your answers are always honest and frank. What would you say if I want to ask Marie to be my wife?"

"Walt, there are a few things I need to tell you. If you are looking for answers, I would tell you that Marie is indeed a beautiful young woman, intelligent and industrious, and she possesses many skills that will take her and her partner into a very happy life. Like most of us, she has a history and, as she has told you, not all of it's been pleasant. She told me that she has told you of her experience that led to her pregnancy and the loss of her child. My question to you is, can you live with it? Do you think you love her, or can love her enough to forget that chapter in her life? Do you think you can put that information behind you enough to never bring it up again? It is absolutely essential that you don't. You can never become angry with her over some other issue and bring that past up as an example of repeat behavior. That will destroy trust and your ultimate happiness and your marriage itself. The both of you must enter into marriage with a clean slate, with your past experiences used to enrich your marriage and not tear it down. Can you do all of that?"

Walt said, "Marie is the greatest thing that has happened to me, and I love her like I have never loved before. When I introduced her to my parents, they took me aside and told me not to let her get away. I don't want to think about losing her. She's made my life meaningful and complete. I plan to ask her to marry me soon, but not right now. I hope she'll say yes."

J said, "I don't think you should have any worries about that, Walt."

J continued, "Walt, do you believe in providence?"

"I think I do, but what do you mean?"

J advised, "Look up the definition on Wikipedia or somewhere and I think you'll agree that Marie came into our lives here at Shalom, and by providence that caused you to come into her life and her into yours. I know I believe in providential happenings, and I think you will too."

At that time, a car was entering the Shalom driveway bearing J's daughter Rebecca and her husband. J saw them and turned to Walt and told him, "Go to your lady. Spend some quality time with her. I'm glad you're here and wish you the greatest of happiness in your lives."

The next day J's son Jack arrives and this is a time of hugs and questions and laughter and joy. Before long, Hab is there, and he and Jack are in the edge of the yard, shooting baskets.

In the early afternoon of the twentieth, an unexpected auto enters the Shalom driveway. It is a new Cadillac that exudes new car smell when the doors are open. The surprise visitors are Dr. Jason McIntosh, III and Millicent, known as Millie, Mrs. John M. L. Banks, IV. Both are smiling ear to ear. As soon as all of the introductions and hugs were over, Jason announced that they had something to announce, that being that the two of them were planning to be married, and asked J to be the best man, which J did not answer immediately. When he did answer it was a noncommittal one, something like if I'm around I'll be happy to. J jokingly asked, "Well, let me ask you one question, Millie. How do your children feel about that old man riding on a tired old worn out charger coming into your life, sweeping you off your feet and ready to change your life drastically?"

Millie giggled like a young school girl and said, "Actually, two of the three are all for it. The youngest is the holdout, but I'm sure she'll come around."

"And how about your children, Jason? Are they all on board?"

"As a matter of fact, they are celebrating. They are as happy for me as they could possibly be. I've been lonely too long and they recognize it. They see this as the providence of God at work, just as I do." After that happy announcement and a cordial visit, the couple left, allowing J to enjoy his visit with his children.

When all of the hoopla died down, Jack and Rebecca found Pat, busy in the kitchen, and asked her to join them at the rock. When they had settled as comfortably as possible on their rock seat, Jack began. "Pat, Rebecca, and I compared notes and we both received letters from you about Dad. Your message was somewhat cryptic, telling us that you wished we could come as soon as we could for the Christmas visit and plan to stay as long as we could. The way it was written it seemed as if you were trying to tell us that something important was going to happen during that time. What's going on?"

Pat took a deep breath and said, "I don't really know if anything will happen during the time you're here or not. I have no way of knowing for sure, but I know that what I have to tell you is very hard for me to do. Your father is a very, very sick man. He doesn't look it today, and may not. I've been trying to get him to write you or call you and talk to you for several months now and tell you what his condition is. He keeps putting it off, saying that he doesn't want to burden you. That's the way he is, as you know. He also likes to do things on the spur of the moment and likes to surprise people, which I find extremely frustrating. Anyhow, your father has a brain tumor, which was diagnosed last December. His oncologist and friend, Dr. Stanley Woods, told him and me that he had ten, twelve, or at most, fourteen months to live. The symptoms come and go, and are not consistent. Sometimes it affects him by a disturbance in his balance, sometimes by him not knowing where he is, sometimes with various pains in different parts of his body. Dr. Woods warned about mood changes, but he seems to have a sense of the mood swings coming on because he'll get up and stay by himself until it passes. For the greater part, he hasn't been in pain and, from what Dr. Woods told me, will not have great pain."

Rebecca broke into tears, saying, "I wish he would have told us sooner. Sometimes I get angry with him for being so damned self sufficient and not wanting to involve others."

Jack asked, "What's the name of the type of tumor? I know there are many different types and I'd like to look it up."

Pat replied, "I think the name of the tumor formation is Glioblastoma, but I'm not sure of the spelling unless it's in front of me."

Jack thanked Pat profusely. Pat said, "You are his children. You do what you think is best with the information I have given you. Whether you choose to say nothing to him or go in and talk to him frankly, will be all right with me. I'm sure he won't say anything to me about telling you, but if he does, so be it. I think you have a right to know and I'm glad I told you."

Pat left the two siblings sitting on the rock, holding each other, giving each other words of consolation as best they could.

When she entered the house she found that Marie and Walt had a change of plans. It seemed that Marie's brother could not join them during these holidays, and Walt wanted to spend time with his parents, with Marie at his side. They were all packed and ready to go, saying that their plans were to return on the thirtieth.

During the next mornings' conversations with his children, J receives a phone call, says the usual "How are you's," "Glad to hear from you's," "That sounds good to me's" and ended with a "Eleven o'clock is good. See you then." Jack and Rebecca looked at each other, before Jack asked, "And what's that all about?' after noting that J hadn't planned to say more and they were about to be in for another of his surprises. Jack never liked surprises and that was one characteristic of his father's that he disliked.

J recognized there was a need for his children to know so he began to explain. "Dr. Owens, the Dean of the School of Arts and Science wants to come out. He wanted to know if you and Rebecca would be here because he wants to speak to you. He also wants to see if I have finished the two manuscripts that I'm supposed to be finishing before the end of my sabbatical." They chatted on until eleven when Owens arrived.

Dr. Owens introduced himself, exchanged pleasantries, and asked J how the manuscripts were coming along.

"They're finished. Marie Tradino has been helping me put all the material together. She's not here at the present, but they have all been put together and edited."

Dean Owens then turned to Rebecca and asked if the two of them might have a private conversation, which, of course, was granted.

When they were settled in J's study, Owens said, "Let me get right to the point. I called an old friend this past week, the dean of your school, Dean Simpson. We were classmates for several years and in our conversation, we wished each other a joyous Christmas. He then wanted to know how we let you get away from us. He went on to say that you were a bright and shining star in their history department and he thought surely that I would have gotten in contact with you and would have you teaching at the University of South Carolina. He gave me a great deal of information about what you were teaching and especially dwelt on your promising future. He tells me you are going to be an outstanding historian. Evidently you've already written some things that have been published and what I want to ask you is if you would be willing to consider a position with the history department at the university?'

Rebecca thought for a few seconds and replied, "Well, things get complicated. I am married and my husband is a PhD in Philosophy."

Dean Owens said, "Yes, I know that. I've been raising questions about him as well. In the next four to twelve months, we are going to have at least two historians retiring, and two persons in the philosophy department retiring, and it might be possible for us to work out something that would give both of you opportunities."

Rebecca said, "I'm flattered but this is something that I would have to talk with my husband about and give a good deal of consideration to because things are going extremely well where we are right now."

"Will you at least think about it?"

"Oh yes, definitely. I consider this an honor to be considered, and we'll both give it a lot of thought."

The dean continued, "That's great. I didn't expect to get an instant answer, but I'll be in touch. If you would like to talk further before I get back to you, here's my card with all the contact information on it. Let me share one other piece of information with you which is not public knowledge yet but there are a number of persons who have initiated a campaign to raise enough money to endow a chair in the School of Philosophy in honor of your father."

"That's great news. That's wonderful. I'm excited about such an honor for my father. He will be so pleased. Thanks."

"Well, it's not going as well as we had anticipated. We did not anticipate the financial collapse of some of the banks and the auto industry, but money has been coming in and when the economy changes for the better, I'm certain the necessary amount will be raised."

Dean Owens continued, "J has every right to be proud of this honor and it is well deserved. I don't know of any other faculty member in the School of Philosophy who is so appreciated. We'll miss him. I was somewhat surprised last December when he told me he was ready to retire."

Rebecca said, "Concerning the history department at USC, I have been most impressed with the writings and the lectures by Dr. Walter Edgar."

"We all are. He's bringing very positive attention to the university due to his scholarship and his warm personality that shines in his lectures. I think the two of you will get along fine.'

"Let me talk with my husband, and I'll be in touch with you. The offer sounds very attractive."

Dean Owens stood and took her hand and asked, "His name is not really Socrates, is it?"

Rebecca burst out laughing and said, "I didn't think I heard you call him that! It's a funny story. When he was about nine or ten years old, he was spending the summer with his grandparents, and his grandmother decided that he needed to take a dose of castor oil. And he fought it, but it was forced down him. He accused his grandparents of trying to poison him, and they simply said to him, 'You ought to be a good Socrates and take your poison graciously.' So the name Socrates hung around, and he says that's when he began to have an interest in philosophy. He wanted to read about Socrates, and it branched out to other philosophers. So when his friends were saying they wanted to be pilots or firemen or policemen when they grew up, he would say he wanted to be a philosopher. And he is a good one, and he's going to be a better one."

"I'll remember that," said Owens.

They walked back to the den where the dean picked up the manuscripts and said, "It's been nice visiting with you, and I hope to see you again soon." After he departed, Jack asked again what that was all about, and Rebecca said, "Well, he didn't say anything about the conversation being confidential, so I'll be glad to share it with you." She gave the group a detailed summary of her conversation with Dean Owens.

J said when Rebecca finished, "Well, it seems like you have an inside track. They'll have to advertise, and when they do, they'll receive a couple of hundred resumes. So, young lady, you should feel honored."

"I am, but Socrates and I still have to talk about it."

J asked Rebecca and Socrates to walk with him, and after selecting coats, they walked in the direction of the woods. J turned to Rebecca and told her, "Rebecca, I've been talking with your mother a lot lately, and she wants me to give you a message."

Rebecca was shocked. She asked, "Daddy, are you all right?'

"Yes, I'm fine."

"And you've been talking to Mama?"

"Oh yes. I've talked with her almost every day for the last ten years, but our conversations have been more frequent lately. She wants me to say something to you. You're thirty years old now and evidently very successful in your work. You're married, but you've never talked about having children. The message from your mother is it is true that there are certain risks in having children. The biggest risk is the heartaches they give you, but the rewards in having them outweigh all of these possibilities. She says she knows how devastated you were when we lost James and Margaret and thinks that you think the pain you feel could be spared somewhat if you had no children, and the sure way is to have none. She hasn't said to tell you to have children but only to give it consideration."

"Daddy, are you sure you're okay?'

"I'm fine. I'm not delusional, although I might sound like it. I haven't completely lost my mind. I'm forgetting more and more things, but most of the time, I do fine. I'm acting on your mother's behalf and simply saying that you should think about having children. The two of you talk about it, as you do everything. And whatever decision you make, that will be fine with us. Know that your mother and I will look down on you and will pray God's blessings on you in whatever you do"

Rebecca and Socrates said nothing. They just looked at each other and nodded in agreement.

Rebecca asked what the plans were for Christmas dinner, saying she would like to go shopping for the meal. J announced that he had other plans for Christmas dinner, and as usual, it would be a surprise.

On Christmas Eve, J loaded everyone in the Navigator, allowing Jack to drive, much to Pat's relief; and all attended the Christmas Eve services at the Mt. Zion Presbyterian Church. J proudly introduced his children to practically everybody in the church. When they returned home for a modest dinner, J assembled all of them in the dining room. He turned to Jack and Rebecca and said, "Especially for you, Rebecca, I don't really know what kind of tradition you've established for the two of you, but I like to open presents on Christmas Eve. So let's do it now, but I've got a few things that aren't wrapped. I'll be right back."

The first item was a small chest that he gave to Rebecca. J said, "I should have given you these things years ago but never could bring myself to do it." The contents of the chest were Rebecca's mother's jewelry, the sight of which brought a flood of tears and much mopping with Kleenex. The bottom of the chest was a note, handwritten by her father, which was a narrative of when each piece of jewelry had been given and for what occasion.

J turned to Jack and said, "Jack, your gift is a little bit more controversial. And to be honest with you, I really don't know whether you would even want them." He left the room and returned shortly with several guns. J continued, "I gave up hunting years ago, but these are several shotguns and rifles. The shotguns are Browning, made before the Browning Company was sold to Japanese interests. I've not ever shot but one of them, and I doubt if a box of shells has been shot with it. They are collectors' items. And you, of course, can do with them what you would like to do."

He turned to Rebecca's husband and said, "Socrates, I'm going to give you a gift that has a long story behind it, and I really don't know whether the story is true or not because I have no documentation." J walked over to the buffet counter and pulled out a beautiful mahogany box and handed it over. "These are dueling pistols that were allegedly owned by the Rutledge family of South Carolina. You may recall that Archibald Rutledge was the poet laureate of South Carolina. His home, located near McClellanville, can be toured. I think it belongs to the State now. I don't think they were ever used in a duel, but they do have historic value. I hope you never have the occasion to remove them from the case."

J next handed Pat a jewelry box which contained a string of beautiful pearls. He explained that he had purchased them to give to Elizabeth, but the accident occurred before he could give them to her.

Hab was looking disappointed, as if to say, "Have you forgotten me?" But at that time, J said, reading his looks, "No, I haven't forgotten you, Hab. Go outside to the wood pile, and you'll find a piece of canvas covering the wood and something else. Pull the canvas back, and you'll find your present."

Hab ran out of the house, and it was only a few minutes before all around the table heard the sound of a moped revving up. They walked to the door and saw him disappear in the darkness of the driveway, with the lights on, and then make a turn and repeat the trip.

The remaining group returned to the dining room table to present J with his gifts. Pat had alerted Jack and Rebecca to the fact that J had returned to his pipe-smoking, and the main gift was an expensive Meerschaum pipe. Other gifts complimented the pipe, such as a tin of tobacco with the brand name "Presbyterian Elder," another was butane lighter, and a fourth, a pipe-cleaning tool.

J continued with his gift-giving. He disappeared and then returned shortly with chest of silverware. He gave it to Rebecca and explained that it was a set that he and her mother had collected over the years, and he was able to finish out the pieces after her death. He told Rebecca that he was giving it to her because she might be in the position to do more entertaining in her later years when things were not so busy.

J left the table again and returned with a large box, this time presenting it to Jack. The box contained twenty-four silver goblets. It seems as if their friends knew they were collecting them and would receive one or two a year from them.

After the gift-giving, J began to tell his children and Pat about the house they were now celebrating in. He explained, "I should have kept a diary or put all of this down on tape but never got around to it. This is a sort of a history of this place and this house that I don't think we ever shared with you. The year before we were married, I bought these 220 acres for a hundred dollars an acre. We didn't do anything with it for a time, and we lived in Wales Garden Apartments, on the next hill over from the university. Your mother decided it was time to build a house, with me pointing out that we couldn't afford it. She insisted and began drawing up plans, plans for a house that would accommodate ten children. After that, we contracted with Sam England, who lives down the road, to dig the basement, but to do it when he was between jobs so we could get a cheaper rate. Over a period of a month, he did dig the basement, a hole thirty feet by seventy-two feet. While digging the hole, he uncovered a huge boulder with an unusual shape, twenty-six feet around and relatively flat on top. That was removed and placed in the front yard and has become my thinking rock. He also found fourteen smaller hunks of granite, some of them becoming tombstones. The smaller rocks he removed became the retaining wall, with the dirt removed piled behind it, which we called the terrace. Things remained as they were for several months until Elizabeth came home all excited one day, announcing that she heard that the A & P Store in Winnsboro was going to be demolished, and a bigger and better one was to be built. The excitement came from her being given the concrete blocks for the price of removing

JERRY HAMMET & HAROLD GUERRY

them. I only shook my head, but she persisted. I don't know how many concrete blocks she got or how she managed to pay the trucker to load and unload them, but there were literally hundreds of them. We spent the next several months coming up here and cleaning and stacking those blocks. Before long, we had saved up enough money to pour a concrete foundation. We had a curious neighbor, old Mr. Tindal, who was a retired builder bored out of his mind. Mr. Tindal volunteered to help us lay concrete blocks. I was never that good at it, but your mother was. It didn't make a whole lot of difference anyhow because the inside of the blocks were to be covered with plaster or stucco and the outside would be a veneer of granite. We had great fun laying those blocks and laughed and nursed our blisters during the weekends. Another friend was one of the professors at the USC Engineering Department, and he wanted to find a place to experiment with heating and cooling, using ground water. I think it's called geothermal systems now. With his and his students' help and us providing the material, copper pipes were laid out through the floors. When it was all over, we had a grand party. When we recuperated from that undertaking, we decided to go ahead and begin the framework of the house and use it for weekend camping until we could finish it. About that time, we discovered that ten acres of our land had a lot of huge long leaf pines growing on it that had been spared from an earlier harvest due to bad weather. We decided that we could use that timber. And the result is that all of the two-by-fours, two-by-sixes, and two-by-eights, the flooring came from those trees. About that time, your mother discovered that an old hotel in Columbia was being torn down, so she rushed down and bought light fixtures and chandeliers galore. Another stroke of luck was the finding of a boxcar load of plywood that was being unloaded, and a flaw was discovered. A friend of a friend told us about it, and we were able to buy ninety-six sheets of three-fourth-inch plywood for less than half the price. Actually, this person called your mother who didn't consult me but went ahead and bought the whole carload. We were blessed again by Mr. Tindal, who rounded up a crew of unemployed carpenters and helped us finish the house, just in time for Jack to be born. We furnished the place with late Salvation Army and early Good Will and a lot of auction house bargains, especially the artwork. That's basically the story of the house. If either of you ever want to build on this property, there's a grove of walnut trees a couple of hundred yards away that would make some awesome paneling. But I don't think anybody would ever have as much fun as your mother and I had in building his house. It was built by a couple in love and who remained in love."

There was a long awkward silence, broken by J getting up, putting on his coat, and walking out of the door into the darkness to sit on his rock.

After a few minutes of looking at each other, Rebecca got up, put on a warm coat, and sat beside J. She put her arms around him and asked, "Daddy, are you talking to Mama?

"Yes," was the simple answer.

"Daddy, tell her I love her, and I miss her, and I'm glad she's here and looking out for you."

J began, "We've been most blessed, Rebecca. Your mother and I have been most blessed with family, faith, and friends."

Rebecca was unable to say anything. She just hugged her father a little tighter. A few seconds later, they were joined by the two girls, Victoria and Princess, let out of the house by Pat. Victoria put her head in Rebecca's lab, and Princess put her head in J's. J turned to Rebecca and said, "These dogs have been a blessing too."

"I know, I know. I can see what a comfort they've been."

The solemn moment was broken by Hab's flying up on his moped, jumping off and hugging J around the neck, exclaiming, "Thank you. Thank you. Thank you!"

The next morning, Christmas morning, was one when no alarm clocks were needed. Hab was out on his moped, going around and around every road and driveway he could find and remain on the property. Pat came over, bringing Hab, and began cooking a breakfast fit for kings and queens. After breakfast, Rebecca said, "I don't feel like I will need anything to eat for the next two days, but you said you had something special in mind for lunch on Christmas Day. When will we find out what your surprise is?"

J replied, "Well, be dressed in comfortable casual clothes and be ready to go around ten o'clock. We're going to Columbia and be prepared to be surprised. It's going to be something you'll feel good about."

Pat said, "Dr. J, I think I'm going to need your assistance in something. Hab doesn't want to go anywhere, including his grandparents, but wants to stay here and burn up all the gasoline you have riding his new moped. I'm going to need help convincing him otherwise."

J said, "I'll speak to him. He needs to go to his grandparents. He can ride his new machine another day. Let me go out and talk to him."

J managed to flag Hab down and convinced him that he had obligations to his grandparents, and besides, he was about to run out of gas and tomorrow was another day. It was now ten o'clock so the Navigator was loaded with J,

Pat, Rebecca, Socrates, Jack and Hab, with Pat making sure Jack drove, and directed him to drop Hab off at his grandparents. J directed Jack to head to Columbia, and it soon became evident from the side of town they were entering that they were not going to the Governor's Mansion for lunch. J directed Jack to the Salvation Army and told the group that they would have Christmas dinner here, but after they had served people who had no other place to go on Christmas. Rebecca asked if they were homeless people and J replied that she was right, but the politically correct term was "temporarily dislocated." He admitted that he didn't think he could ever get used to the present day politically correct term.

After their duties of serving seemingly hundreds of people, it was time for them to get in line to serve themselves for their Christmas dinner. They sat at a rough makeshift table and gave thanks for their many blessings.

They returned to Shalom, tired but filled with gratitude for the experience. As they turned into the pave road, off the main highway, there was Bubba standing by the road, waving. J had Jack to stop, and introduced Bubba to his children, then found a paper bag he had stashed with Snickers in it, gave each person one and Bubba two, and resumed their travels.

Upon returning to Shalom, the question became how many different bowl games would be on television that afternoon and night. One speculation was that there must be thirty or more and one suggested that if they ran out of titles, a Flea and Tick Bowl could be established, sponsored by a company that sold dog and cat medications. All agreed that it would be a catchy title.

The day after Christmas, J came out of his room and gathered all together at the dining room table. He posed the question, "Why is it that we burden ourselves with things that we don't need and never get rid of anything that somebody else could use?" He produced a cardboard box, set it down on the dining room table, opened it, and said, "In this box, I have six pocket knives, seven pairs of fingernail clippers, two pair of toe nail clippers, three gloves, all of which I will never use. I also have tie clips, tie tacks, and a half bottle of Vitalis Hair Tonic and a tube of Brylcream. I don't even know if they make this stuff anymore. Rebecca even asked what Vitalis and Brylcream were used for.

"I have a dozen watches, some that run and some that don't. When was the last time anybody ever bought a bottle of ink? I have two. I must have ten or 15 fountain pens, and some of them may be collectors' items with some value. I looked in my closet and found four pair of hunting trousers there. I haven't been hunting in twelve years. There are three or four pair of hunting boots, two pair of combat boots and I really don't plan to go to war again. In the corner of the wardrobe I have at least six or seven snake sticks and I don't think there are that many snakes left on the property. I must have, I don't know how many, ties, all of them out of fashion, but I still have them. I also think a shoelace salesman must have been here, because I've got twenty or more packs of them. Shoe horns. I counted them. Fourteen. I think I must have a shoe horn for every pair of shoes I've owned in the last ten years. There are six packages of handkerchiefs. Nobody uses handkerchiefs anymore. And they're still in the packages. I tell you, for the next few days, I'm going to be busy getting rid of stuff. I think I'm going to have to go to the liquor store for some empty cardboard boxes to pack everything in.

Jack asked, "Dad, are you getting ready to move out?'"

J replied, "That's the situation, son. That's the situation. Who wants to make an old man a cup of coffee?"

Being provided with coffee, J takes a sip and continues, talking rapidly, almost frantically. "You know, I have had enough football to last me for the rest of my life. I have rejoiced with the Panthers beating the Saints, I have grieved with the Detroit Lions. Losing sixteen games in a row is depressing. I was glad to see the Falcons come forth. I'm not sure how I feel about the Eagles beating the Cowboys, but they sure did beat up on them. It was good to see Matt Ryan come forth as an outstanding quarterback."

Hab, who had joined the group, was listening and interrupted the rant, saying, "Michael Vick was better."

"He might be. He just might be. I've been thinking about suggesting something to you, Hab. Why don't you write a letter to Michael Vick and tell him how much you appreciate him as a quarterback. I'm not sure that he's getting much mail these days. I think he would be delighted that a young man would write him, wish him well and express the hope he would once again be seen on television playing on a professional team."

J continued after the aside remark to Hab, "Let's join in a celebration for Vanderbilt and congratulate them for winning the first bowl game since 1955. That was a long, dry spell. I think we should design some sort of an award and send it to Chip Saltsman for the DVD he set out entitled *The Rock, the Magic Negro*. He ought to receive an award for stupidity. And I'm getting real tired of hearing about the illustrious Governor of Illinois, Mr. Blago. I watched a few minutes of the USC game and it looks like Iowa will show no mercy. Doesn't look good at this point. I wish I could see things clearly like some politicians see them, such as this Hamas-Israel thing. There's Hamas shooting—what is it?—160 rockets into Israel, and Israel more than three hundred air strikes into Gaza. Israel moves tanks in, and Palestinian kids throw rocks at them. I wonder if this situation will ever resolve itself. I wish both sides would stop this foolishness, but I guess they'll continue at each other's throats until the love for their children becomes greater than the hate for their enemies. I don't remember who said that, but I thought it was profound and worth remembering. But enough of my pontificating. I've got to get back to my packing," and got up and headed down the hall with a box. About half way down the hall, he dropped the box, turned around, came back and said, "And another thing." He paused for a second or so, as if he were searching for what he wanted to say, then said, "We need to pray for our President elect, for his safety, and for him to get an extra measure of wisdom because he's going to need both" then turned and walked back down the hall, but turned around and headed back.

"Dad, you're on a real roller coaster of emotions this morning," Rebecca said.

"Well, yes. I've been thinking about the shortness of time and the vastness of eternity and that's a serious sort of thing, but I also realize that I have been extremely blessed by your presence (looking around the room to all there) and have been encouraged by thinking about the hope that's ours."

At that time, Marie and Walt return from their trip. Pat, Hab and Jack hug her and shake hands with Walt, and Marie is introduced to Rebecca and Socrates.

Marie turns to J and said, "Dr J, are you preaching again?"

"Yes, I have, and I hope you heard enough of what I said to learn something. I'm glad you're back with us. Did they run you off or did you decide you had stayed a fair amount of time?"

"Actually, I could have stayed longer and Walt's parents wanted us to stay, but for some strange reason, I had a feeling it was time for me to come back and that's what we did."

J appeared to ignore what Marie said, and went to the door and whistled for Victoria and Princess, who came running. "Girls, it's too cold for you to be out there. Come in and watch the fire."

J then turned to Marie and said, "You got here just in time. We're getting ready to start opening our Christmas presents." Everyone except Marie recoiled in shock. Jack blurted out, "Dad, we did that a week two days ago, remember?"

"We did?"

"Yes."

"Are you sure?"

There was a nervous laugh around the room, and someone said, "We're sure."

"Had I been drinking?"

Jack said, "You might have been, but we didn't know it."

J responded, "I know the problem. Deduction is a marvelous thing. The fire in the fireplace has been burning and its consuming too much of the oxygen in the room. Open up those windows over there, Jack, and I'll open the door and we'll get some fresh air in here. That's all we need, just a little more oxygen. As soon as your Mother gets here, I'm going to give her her Christmas present and she will be delighted. We're going to go on a cruise around the Greek island, something we've always wanted to do. After we get back from Greece, we're going to Ireland. I think we're going to stay at least a month. Now after I've told you that, don't give the secret away when she walks in. Let me be the one who tells her. I don't know why she hasn't gotten here yet. This is a terrible time for her to go look at property. She said it was somewhere near Beulah Land, but I can't even find it on the map, but she says that's the place to be and you know I never argue with your mother. Hopefully when she walks through that door, which should be any minute now, she'll have a map and I can see where she wants us all to move to."

Everyone in the room stood in stunned silence, except for Pat. She walked into the next room with her cell phone and called Dr. Stanley Woods on the private number he had given her. She related what was happening and asked if he should be taken to his office or to the hospital, but Woods told her that it wasn't necessary. He only said, "Pat, I'm sorry. Just watch him and don't let him drive or get out of sight. I suspect this is approaching his time. Call me when you want to."

J was still talking rapidly. "I think I'll go outside and wait for her. She should be here any time, and she might have something she wants brought in," walked to the coat rack, selected a heavy coat and walked outside. Pat assembled all around her and related what Dr. Woods said and warned that the end might come at any time. Rebecca began to cry and clung to Socrates. Tears welled in Marie's eyes, and Hab was wide-eyed in disbelief, and clung to his mother. Jack went to the coat rack and walked out of the door to be with his father, who was headed for the rock, with Victoria and Princess at his side. J had walked ahead of Jack and when he reached the rock, J was sitting with the dogs' heads in his lap. Rebecca and Socrates followed as soon as they could get coats on.

When Jack, Rebecca, and Socrates reached the rock, J was sitting in his usual spot, motionless. His eyes seemed fixed, looking down the driveway, with a half smile on his face. Jack tried to talk to him but got no response. After several attempts, Jack told the others to help him get J back to the house. They were able to get him to his feet, but had to support him all the way. Pat met them at the door and directed them to J's bedroom, where they stretched him out on his bed, with all of his clothes on. Pat told all, "Dr. Woods said his time was very near, and the end might come this way. I asked him if we should call for medical help when this time comes, and he said that it would not be necessary. Just make him as comfortable as possible and be with him."

Rebecca sobbed and left the room long enough to compose herself. Marie and Walt sat in the den together, holding hands, with Hab sitting next to Marie.

In just a few minutes, Jack entered the den and announced that J's death had come, that he wasn't breathing and his heart had stopped. Pat wiped away tears and picked up her cell phone and called the sheriff's office and asked him to notify the coroner. Sheriff Culclasure arrived in less than a half hour, escorting the coroner. After a short examination, the coroner came out of J's room and extended condolences to all, then asked which funeral home should be called and if there was any living will or advanced directives. Pat produced them, holding back tears as best she could. She and the coroner, with Rebecca and Jack and Socrates sitting next to her, went through the arrangements as J had outlined them. The coroner stayed until the funeral director arrived, and all of them went over J's wishes once more. The funeral director said he would make contact with the newspapers J had listed to make sure the obituary would be printed in all of them.

As the funeral director and the sheriff left, a stream of visitors began to enter the Shalom doors. The pastor of the Mt. Zion Presbyterian Church came, followed by several members of the Black Beauties Baseball Team, Bubba, neighbors, and friends. The details of the service as J had planned them were shared with the pastor and the funeral director. J included some last-minute thoughts beyond those he had Pat type up, those being such things as dressing his body in a costume he had made several years before when he played the part of the Bethlehem innkeeper at a church play. He suggested that it looked like a travelling gown, and that's what he wanted to travel in. Always the unusual, always the off-the-wall surprises—those were J's trademarks, even to his funeral.

Pat excused herself and made several phone calls to Millie and Jason, Louise, and several more. Pat had the foresight to call Jack Branson, the caterer from Camden, a couple of days before to give him a heads-up that the funeral might be soon. Arrangements with Jack had been made several weeks before, and advance payment had been made. Pat called Jack and made the final food arrangements. The house phone rang incessantly with people extending their sympathies and offering to do anything that might be needed.

The obituaries appeared in the Friday morning papers, just as J had written them. The *State Newspaper*, however, carried a two-column article on J's life, his position, his reputation, his eccentricities, and his contributions to the university and to the community.

The Shalom occupants rose early on Saturday morning and made the last few actions needed, such as making sure the cemetery was clean and orderly, selected appropriate parking, parked vehicles, and picked up some late falling leaves.

At ten o'clock, Branson and his crew arrived and began to set up tables, the pallbearers came and stood by, and the funeral director and his staff arrived. Although flowers were discouraged in the obituary, tons of them were being constantly delivered anyhow. A crowd of friends parked reverently in the proper spaces and began to gather at the funeral tent. As the eleven o'clock hour struck, the pastor to the Mt. Zion Church began his service. At the conclusion, gospel singers sang the usual songs of "Amazing Grace" and "Ode to Joy," but also provided such songs of praise as "I Done What You Asked Me to Do." At the conclusion of the service, the funeral director provided shovels to Rebecca and Jack, who ceremoniously placed small shovels full of earth onto the casket. They passed their shovels to the Black Beauty pallbearers and to Bubba, who took turns with the ceremony. The funeral director announced that the crowd should step away while the burial site work could be completed, then invited them all to return and extend condolences to the family, Pat, and Hab. After that, the funeral director introduced Jack, who announced, "My father gave specific instructions on how this funeral should be conducted, and that has been done. He also asked that all present should join us under the catering tent that has been set up by Mr. Jack Branson. His wish was that all of us should try not to make this sad occasion, but one of joy and celebration of life and the fulfillment of his long wishes to join my mother and sister and brother that are buried here. Let me offer these words of thanksgiving, and we can proceed to the tent in the yard."

After all of the visitors and the caterer left, the group retired to the house. Pat called them into the dining room and told them she had been instructed to give the envelopes she had in her hand to each of them. She suggested that they might be very private, and if they wanted to retire to another room to read the contents, that would be all right. She handed the envelopes out, and each did as she suggested, finding a private place.

Pat found her spot at the kitchen table. She opened the envelope with trembling hands and found a note, handwritten by J, and another envelope that had been opened. The note began with an apology from J. He said that he apologized for opening the letter in the envelope, not looking close enough to realize it was addressed to Pat, only discovering his mistake when he saw a check inside made out to Hab for $1,000. He continued, saying it was from his old friend of long ago, Louise, thanking Pat for writing her and telling her of J's ailment and predicted demise. He wrote that he only then realized that Pat had written his old friends, and they had responded by visiting him in the last months of his life. He wrote, "After thinking about what you did, I thank you. The visits from those people from my past gave me great joy, and you are responsible for that. Thanks, those visits did indeed brighten my days. J."

The day after the funeral, the local tombstone dealer, Buddy Hirschfeld, was called; and he came out with his portable sandblasting machine and made the inscriptions on the tombstone.

DR. J'S WILL

ATTORNEY JACK WESTERFIELD presided over the reading of J's will on short notice to accommodate Rebecca and Jack. Westerfield began by saying, "Let me say at the beginning that Jack or Rebecca might question some of the provisions of Dr. Stewart's will. And if they, or either of them, want to break it, there is a good possibility it can be done. Dr. Stewart gave me specific provisions to be included, and I suggested and he consented to make a video so he could speak to you personally after his death and possibly explain the rationale for some of the provisions."

West started the video, which presented J smiling and sitting on a stool. J began, "Let's take care of the most important thing, and that is that I leave you my love and respect. All other matters are secondary. Now let me begin with the rest of what I have to say. Most of you, if not all, know that I started a tax-free fund in 1998, with the proceeds from life insurance policies that had been taken out on Elizabeth's, James's, and Margaret's lives. And now the proceeds from my life insurance policy should be added to that total.

"From this total, I would like for $18,000 to be given to the Mt. Zion Presbyterian Church, which is the amount of my annual pledge. I would like for $1,000 to be given to each of the following persons. They are Robert Bubba Plowden; Sally Smith, who works at Burger King in Winnsboro; April Johnson, who is a cashier at Food Lion in Ridgeway; Mary Green, a cleaning lady at the university; Susan Phillips, who works at Krispy Kreme Donuts in Winnsboro; Jack Williams, who comes around from time to time looking for part-time work; Reverend James McClarey, pastor of the First African Baptist Church; the congregation of the same church to purchase bells for the church steeple. I would like for $2,000 to be given to the Black Beauties Baseball team for new uniforms, $5,000 to be given to Marion Johnson whose husband didn't return from service in Iraq and has three small children, $1,000 to Luther Jones who spends a great deal of time picking up trash along the highway in appreciation for his efforts. One of the greatest gifts I would like to give is for $100,000 to be put into a 629 educational trust for Hank Aaron Brown. I would like to give $5,000 to Marie Tradino, in addition to the amount of back wages I haven't paid her, plus the title to the 2002 Nissan vehicle that I have already presented to her. I would like to give to Patricia Brown—who I consider my adopted daughter, the person that I have relied on for the past ten years almost constantly, who has been my supporter, my caretaker, and my confidant—the cottage she lives in along with the acre of land it is situated on and the cancelled promissory note for the payment of the house, plus the amount of salary that I have not paid her to date, plus a total of $80,000. I leave the ten acres of land across the road, which is the ball field, to the Fairfield County Recreation Department, with the stipulation that it be renamed the Bubba Plowden Field, with a sign that reads that it is dedicated to a man filled with sweetness, gentleness, and love. I need to mention that I entered into a contract with Joe Black, investing $20,000 to build a kennel on property owned by me. I would like for the acre of land that the kennel is situated on to be given to Joe and an agreement drawn up for Joe to pay back the $20,000 at $2,000 per year to be given to Helper International. Whatever is left from that fund is to be divided equally between my son and daughter, Jack and Rebecca.

"There is another large sum of money that has been placed in a fund, which is the settlement from the trucking company responsible for the death of my wife and children in 1998. I would like for my children to distribute funds to these agencies as memorials to their mother and siblings. Those agencies are Heifer International, Doctors without Borders, the Emergency Fund, Feed the Children, Save the Children, the Carter Foundation, the Salvation Army, the Presbyterian Villages of South Carolina, Columbia Theological Seminary, and the Thornwell Home for Orphans."

Westerfield stopped the video at this point and said, "We are talking about a large sum of money. If either of you, Jack or Rebecca, have any differences of opinions about your father's generosity, let me know. And I'm sure we can alter this list." Westerfield resumed the video.

"The remaining things left in my estate I give equally to my son and daughter. Included is a portfolio of stocks held by the Edwards Company. There is an IRA account through the university, the 220 acres of land, minus the acreage given to the ball field and to Joe Black that the house sits on goes to my son and daughter. I regret that I have not resolved whether or not to put the property in trust so that it cannot be developed, but that's going to be left up to the two of you. As to the upkeep of the property, since neither of you are currently living here, I suggest that you continue the sharecropping arrangement I have had with Jack Hill, who has been caring for the blueberry patch, the pomegranate trees, the pecan trees, and the fish pond. He's an honest man, and I trust him to keep the property as it should be.

"Also, I would like to ensure that the two dogs, Princess and Victoria, are cared for. They should be kept together, wherever they are. Please find someone who will love and care for them."

Pat asked Westerfield to pause the video and said to the two children, "If it's all right with you, please let me have them. They are comfortable with us, and I will take good care of them." Both nodded in total agreement, and the video was resumed.

"The other items are the Lincoln Navigator that I resisted buying but now admit that I have enjoyed it, and the blue pickup. I leave that to my children to dispose of as they see fit. Use scientific methods to determine ownership, such as flipping a coin.

"The last item I would like to say in this gathering is to Hab. I am asking that you consider this a personal favor. I know that you are proud of your name, Hank Aaron Brown, and you should be. But I would ask that you consider changing your name to John Witherspoon Stewart III."

This shocker caused everyone in the room to sit up and look at each other. No one said a word as J's voice continued, "Hab, I have always felt that you were my kin, and I would be honored if you would take my name. With that, I'm sure I'm leaving many things out, but Jack Westerfield can fill in the blanks with his competence and my trust. My children, your mother and I have been blessed in so many ways. But the greatest blessing is you, our children. On matters that have been left unsettled, I trust you will resolve them as loving brother and sister. I leave you with my love. May God be with you and guide you through the rest of your lives."

Westerfield concluded the reading but asked Rebecca and Jack to remain. He told them that J had covered almost everything nicely. He gave them copies of the will and told them to read it and give him a call if there were questions. He told them that he had ideas about how to protect the property as J spoke of, and he would share them with the two when appropriate. He asked, "Now how about the houseguest, Marie?" Rebecca answered, saying that she was planning to return to the university to complete her master's and would be leaving in the morning.

Rebecca added, "We need to talk about the house. At the funeral, the executive director of the Providence Presbyterian Presbytery mentioned to me that the Presbytery had made arrangements for a missionary to be assigned to the Presbytery for a year, and arrangements had been made for the couple to move into a small apartment, but they became ill and will be unable to serve. At the last minute, a substitution was made with an agricultural missionary who has a wife and four teenage children, and they are desperately looking for a larger place. I would like to propose that we allow the Presbytery to use the house, giving them a lease from month to month. They would move in pretty quickly."

Jack agreed.

"I think that Dad would like that, and I certainly have no need for it, at least for the foreseeable future. Let's do it. Jack, would you draw up an appropriate lease? I would suggest rent of just a minimal amount, just to make it legal. We can move all of the personal stuff we won't have time to remove into the basement and lock it up so they can have the rest of the house."

That evening, everyone pitched in, sorting clothing and personal items, those that were to be given to the Salvation Army and those to be placed in the basement to be dealt with later.

The next morning, Marie packed her car and said her good-byes to all. As she prepared to drive off, she noticed a note placed on the inside of the visor. When she pulled it out, she read, "Young Lady, don't forget to take out insurance and transfer the title!" The note brought tears and a lump in her throat. Marie looked at the note again and saw a postscript. It read, "One more thing. Please call Jack Westerfield and make an appointment. He has something to review with you." She recovered and was doing well until she passed Bubba Plowden standing by the side of the road, waving. Her emotions welled, and she waved back at the gentle giant.

The following morning, Rebecca and her husband took things to the UPS Store to be shipped back home before Jack took them to the airport for their return to Oregon. Hugs and tears and promises to keep in touch were exchanged. They flipped a coin, and Jack won the toss, winning the Lincoln Navigator. They decided at the last minute to have Jack Westerfield turn the title of Blue Boy over to the sharecropper for his use.

It was a lonesome ride back to Shalom for Jack. He felt as if his father was sitting in the other seat, still talking to him. When he arrived at Shalom, he walked out to the rock and sat in silence. For the first time, he felt the presence of his mother and his father next to him and the chatter of his brother and sister playing at his feet.

That night, all of the visitors and family were gone except for Pat, Hab, and Jack. Pat prepared the evening meal as Jack watched and made small talk. After dinner, Hab went to the den to watch television, leaving Pat and Jack to clean the kitchen. Jack said, "Pat, we need to talk."

Pat answered with a simple, "Yes, we do."

"Is Hab my son?"

"Yes, he is. I expect your father told you so in his letter and probably gave you a copy of the DNA report."

"Yes, he did. I didn't know. I knew we had a close encounter, but I didn't once think that I was the father. I don't know what to do. I wish things had been different. We had no courtship, only a few seconds of passion. I'll have to leave in the morning, and I just got a call from my commander that I am being ordered to take part in an exercise in Afghanistan, leaving just as soon as I arrive tomorrow afternoon. I'll be back here whenever I can, holidays, weekends—whenever I can. I'll do a lot of thinking in the days to come. Hopefully, God will speak to me because I don't know what to do."

Pat responded, "I don't know what to do, either. Because of the DNA report, I can't stay here. My family is already very upset, and even though it isn't supposed to happen, the school board surely will not give me a contract to teach in this county. I talked to your dad's old friend, Louise, to tell her of his death. And she mentioned to me that her husband and others had a substantial interest in a chemical manufacturing company in Virginia and if I was interested, she would see if there was a place for me in that company. I do have a degree in chemistry, you know. But for now, I'm going to take care of this place for the next few weeks until the missionaries move in. I have a lot of address changes to make, correspondence galore and a lots of other things. We'll have to see how it goes. I understand perfectly how you feel, and I'll have to admit that I love you, but I don't know you, and our worlds are very far apart. We'll see, and we'll find out what we should do. God bless you, Jack, and thank you for my son. I think it would be appropriate for Hab to change his name, but I think the final permission should come from you because you are his father, and he would be carrying your name into the future. When are you leaving? I'll see you in the morning, and I will be here to make breakfast for you, if you want."

Jack hesitated and said, "No, Pat. Don't come for that. I have to leave early, four or not later than five. I have to travel to Sumter and

JERRY HAMMET & HAROLD GUERRY

catch a flight about noon, and I have some military packing to do, but thanks."

Jack and Pat just stood there for a moment, looking at each other. Finally, Jack opened his arms, and Pat rushed into them. They held each other a long time, with tears flowing from both. Jack broke the silence by saying, "Pat, I would like to go in to the den and have a talk with Hab. I want to tell him that I acknowledge that I am his father and explain what happened and emphasize how easily things like that happen. I'll tell him that I encourage him to change his name as Dad suggested because I am in fact his father. I'll tell him that I have to go where I am ordered, but as soon as I get back, I'll come to see him and you. And by that time, maybe I'll have some sort of plan to share with you. Let me do this."

Pat tearfully agreed but insisted that she join them in this discussion. The two of them walked into the den where Hab was watching television. Hab looked up, first at his mother and then at Jack, and said, "What's happening? Both of you look like you've got something on your mind. Is this another Santa Claus story you're going to tell me?"

Pat began by taking the TV controls and pressing the power button. Hab's eyes got wider, and he sat up straighter.

"This is serious, right?"

"Yes. It's going to pretty heavy. It's a sort of a long story, so let me begin" And Pat began, "This happened before you were born. What I'm going to tell you is extremely personal, and I might have difficulty telling you this. Please bear with me. I am glad that we have had talks about the birds and the bees and how easy human reproduction can happen and how the results sometime last a lifetime. This is the story of how you happened to be born." Pat related the story of the prom, how her date and her subsequent husband tried to take advantage of her, how Jack rescued her and took her to the Shalom house to shower and dress, and the brief sexual encounter she and Jack had.

She continued, saying, "And, Hab, that is how you were conceived. That's how your coloring and features are so different from mine and from your grandparents on both sides. Jack is your father, Hab, and not the person you thought he was."

Hab's lips began to quiver, and his eyes welled up with tears. Pat let him cry through this news as Jack stood near Hab's chair and put his hand on his shoulder. Jack's eyes were filled with tears also, and he was unable to speak.

Pat continued, "We just found out. Dr. J sent a DNA sample of yours and had it compared to your father's, and it did not match at all. I expect that we'll be hearing from him pretty soon, and the meeting won't be a pleasant one. Because of your coloring and features, he suspected all along that he wasn't the father, but I don't think he ever suspected it might be Jack. Because of the DNA report, combined with Dr. J's love for you, is why he asked in his will that you change your name. I hope you will, and it would be very appropriate."

Jack recovered sufficiently to begin to speak slowly. "Hab, I didn't know this until I opened a letter from Dad. I have always loved you as a person and have watched you grow into a handsome young man who has been brought up well by your mother."

Hab interrupted and said, "And Dr. J, I suppose I should call him Grandpa."

Jack nodded his head in agreement and said, "And Dad to me, of course."

Jack continued, "Hab, your mother and I don't know exactly what to do from here. I'm still in the Air Force, and I will have to leave very early in the morning and will have to leave the country on a mission. I don't know how long it will be before I can return. I do know that whenever I can, I want to be a part of your life and see you often. I want to do those things with you that a father and a son should do. I am proud to find out that you're my son and proud of you as a person. Will you allow me to do that?"

Hab sobbed for a few seconds and nodded his head in agreement. He finally said, "I knew that I couldn't be my father's son and often wondered who my father was. I really thought it was Dr. J, but I didn't think I should ask. I often thought it would be nice to have you as a father but never, never thought you were my father. I'm glad you are, Jack . . . I mean, Dad."

That last ending brought smiles and tears. After a few minutes, Pat announced that it was time to go home, explaining that Jack had to leave early the next morning.

After a group hug, Jack watched as Pat and Hab walked arm in arm to her car, got in, and drove down the Shalom driveway.

Three days later, Pat was tidying the last few items at Shalom when an Air Force sedan drove into the driveway. Two men got out and knocked on the door, asking for Dr. John Stewart. When Pat asked for a reason for their visit, one of the men said, "It is to regretfully tell Dr. Stewart that his son, Lt. Col. John Witherspoon Stewart Jr., was travelling on official orders in Afghanistan and has been reported as missing. The Air Force is taking all possible actions to find him and return him as soon as possible. Is Dr. Stewart here, and may we speak to him?'

EPILOGUE

JACK'S LAPTOP HAD been left in his quarters before proceeding with his mission, which, of course, has not been divulged. The laptop was turned over to Rebecca as the next of kin once it had been thoroughly examined by air force personnel. One of the files was entitled CODICIL. In this codicil, dated the day he left for his mission, Jack acknowledged that Hab was his son and that his estate would ultimately belong to Hab, with the estate to be managed by Pat. Hab would only benefit financially from his estate at age thirty.

Pat corresponded with Louise and eventually became a chemist in a fragrance manufacturing plant in Virginia. As soon as she was settled, she enrolled in a master's program and later earned her PhD in chemistry.

Marie, after settling into her graduate work, made an appointment with Jack Westerfield, as J's note instructed her to. To her absolute surprise, she learned that, with J's guidance and Jack Westerfield's firm's expertise, she was awarded a settlement from Frank's father. The $1 million-plus demand had been negotiated, and after attorney's fees, the settlement amounted to a little over $325,000. After recovering from this shock, she and Walt called Louise and, through her efforts and guidance, moved to New York where she completed her graduate work and became employed by a major publishing house.

Rebecca, after many hours of discussion with her husband (who, by the way, was not officially named Socrates but was Dr. Aloyisus Pendarvis), decided they would apply for the University of South Carolina positions. After a lengthy selection procedure, both were accepted, offered positions, and began their teaching duties at the university. Rebecca decided to move into the Shalom house; but one of the first things she did was to remove the Shalom identification and replace it with PROVIDENCE.

Edwards Brothers, Inc.
Thorofare, NJ USA
August 23, 2011